JEKYLL ISLAND

TARYN'S CAMERA BOOK 5

Rebecca Patrick-Howard

"Death, thou art but another birth,
freeing the spirit from the
clogs of earth"

"there shall be no night there; and they need no
candle, neither light of the sun; for the Lord God
giveth them light: and they shall reign for ever
and ever"

PREFACE

The darkness closed in around her, thick and alive. There were *things* in the dark, no matter what Nanny and Papa said. She could hear them and feel them, just as plainly as she could hear her raspy breath and feel the coarse cotton of her nightgown against her skin, tender from her bath.

With tears sliding down her cheeks one big drop at a time she drew herself into a tight little ball, her arms wrapped securely around her knees, hugging them to her chest. Her damp hair fell in long curls that almost touched the floor. Why had she put up such a fuss when Nanny tried to comb her hair? Why hadn't she just cried and let it be over?

She was a big girl, nine years old, but she yearned for her doll like a little baby. Her daddy had brought it back with him on a trip and since her mommy died it was her closest friend. But now Esmerelda was waiting for her on her bed, just as alone as she was.

She hoped she wasn't scared.

Rocking back and forth now, she tried not to whimper, to let Nanny know that she was upset. *I'll be good, I'll be good,* she sang silently to herself, trying to block out the noises she was sure she could hear around her.

When something soft brushed against her cheek, she shrieked and a tiny amount of water flowed out of her. Ashamed at soiling herself, she mopped it up with the edge of her nightgown and then clutched her bony knees so hard her arms hurt.

She'd tried opening the door but it was locked, of course. Nanny had the key and she could see clear through the little hole to her bedroom on the other side. It was aglow from the lamp by her bedside, but the oil was burning out. If Nanny didn't return soon, it would burn out and then it would be dark. The thought terrified her and she shook harder, willing herself not to pass water again.

To make the bad things go away she closed her eyes and imagined a beautiful, soft-spoken woman at her side. Maybe it was her mommy but it was hard to see her face. She had a hard time remembering her mommy's face these days. The woman pulled her close, stroked her hair, and dried her cheeks. "I'm so sorry my darling," she murmured, the warmness of her chasing away the cold of the tiny room. "There, there."

She snuggled into the imaginary woman and sighed, tears of another kind gathering in her eyes. But then the small glow of light filtering through the keyhole vanished as the wick burnt out in her bedroom. Left in total blackness, she stood and thrashed against the heavy door, her small body barely making a sound. "Let me out," she cried. "Please! Let me out!"

The darkness offered no mercy.

ONE

RPH 2015

Jekyll Island shimmered before her—a sparkling diamond in the afternoon sun.

Although she didn't know it yet, Taryn was driving towards something that had been calling to her and waiting for most of her life.

Thirty-one-year-old Taryn had not been on a real vacation in years. Technically, she thought as she turned onto the causeway that would take her to the entrance gates, she wasn't on one *now* either. It was a "working vacation."

But she was willing to overlook the "working" part and try to focus on the "vacation" aspect as much as she could.

Now, as she cruised over the tallest bridge she'd ever seen, she clutched the steering wheel until her knuckles were white (bridges scared her for no rational reason). At last, she allowed herself to feel the faintest dashes of excitement.

This is going to be good, she thought to herself, *and just what I need.*

Her heart pounded wildly in her chest and the flurry of nerves that led to self-doubt and always accompanied her at the start of every of job threatened to take over. She ignored these things and tried to focus on the view before her.

The sky had poured buckets down on her earlier and now the marshes spread out below her, a patchwork of brilliant greens and dazzling browns still fresh from the early summer rainstorm. The canals of water that snaked between the grassy patches of land flashed in the sunlight and Taryn felt herself softening.

"Someday I'm going to come to a place like this and paint for fun," she promised herself aloud, "and not just to paint for work."

Taryn hadn't expected the level plains to be flourishing with such vibrant displays of color. After spending most of the past year amongst the rolling hills and dense forests of northern Georgia and central Kentucky, she'd thought she'd find the low country geography boring and uninspiring. However, with the shrimp boats dotting the river, the enormity of the lush vegetation, and the bright blue expanse of sky above her, she had to admit the scenery was anything *but* dreary.

She wasn't one who normally enjoyed driving with the windows rolled down. She didn't like her long red hair whipping her in the face, the sound of the other cars whizzing by, and the reek of exhaust fumes. But now she felt the occasion called for it.

Rolling them down as far as they would go, Taryn reveled in the warm salt air and sunshine that poured through the car. With nervous butterflies still coursing through her stomach, but with new excited anticipation, she flipped through the radio channels and found a classic country station. Turning Steve Earle's "Copperhead Road" up as much as her ancient speakers would allow, she sailed onwards across the Sidney Lanier Bridge in total contentment.

With the sun in her eyes, the soft breeze drifting in around her, and the steady thump of the music Taryn was oblivious to the long, dark shadows that followed behind, reaching.

*　　*　　*

ELLEN RUSSO WAS, BY FAR, one of the most formidable women Taryn had ever met.

Taryn's new boss (at least for the time being) stood on the steps of the Jekyll Island Club Hotel, clipboard in hand, with something akin to impatience flashing in her eyes. Her steel-gray hair was tucked into a prim bun and her Merle Norman makeup was almost professional looking, making her sixty-three years youthful.

Taryn was impressed by the hotel manager at once, *not* because of her no-nonsense appearance and attitude but because she wore a tailored business suit, complete with jacket, and seemed to be as fresh as a daisy. Taryn, on the other hand, wore a sleeveless top and cotton shorts and was sweating through both. She cursed herself for not stopping and changing at the gas station she'd passed and just hoped the sweat wasn't showing through her bottoms.

"Glad you arrived in one piece," Ellen declared, although Taryn didn't miss the fact that she made a subtle point of glancing at her wristwatch.

"The drive took longer than I expected," Taryn apologized, shifting her weight from one foot to the other in nervousness. "I ran into some heavy traffic around Atlanta."

"Everyone does," Ellen agreed. "Amy, my assistant, isn't here today and I just don't have time to give you a tour of the hotel and historic sites. She'll be here tomorrow in any case and will be available then. In the meantime, I'm sure you're exhausted and want to freshen up."

"Freshen up" was one way of putting it, Taryn cringed with an embarrassed smile. She knew she reeked. She didn't travel well. No matter how well she started out on the journey, she always arrived with limp hair, bloated from road food, wrinkled, and smelly.

With a slight wave of her hand Ellen gestured to the valet stand at the top of the stairs. A young, eager-looking young man jogged over and offered a mega-watt grin.

"This is Steve. He's going to help us travel to your lodgings. Unfortunately, we don't have room for you at the hotel. Since this is our busiest season all our rooms are *fully* booked. We do own quite a few houses here on the island, though, and rent them out. I have you staying in a small one, but I still think you'll be more comfortable there. It will give you room to spread out with all of your...supplies."

Taryn nodded. She *did* have a lot of "supplies"–a plastic tub with her paints and brushes, her laptop, a portfolio case for her canvases, and her collapsible stool and easel. And, of course, her camera.

She didn't mind the house, though. Although she was curious about staying in the gorgeous historic hotel that smacked of southern gentility in a moonlight and magnolias kind of way, she also enjoyed having her own space. Her apartment back in Nashville was cramped and dark, and the elevator and hallways always smelled like burnt cheese.

"Steve will drive your vehicle over and I'll transport you with mine. That way I'll be able to give you a mini tour on the way," Ellen said in a flat, accentless voice.

Taryn winced, remembering the candy wrappers and fast food cartons littering her floorboards and passenger seat. Steve smiled at her and winked, though, and she relaxed. He was, after all, a valet. He'd probably seen worse.

Taryn soon found herself speeding down the sidewalk in a quiet golf cart with Ellen at the wheel. While Ellen rattled off a condensed version of the island's history, Taryn was able to take in the tourists. They ranged from senior vacationers with huge cameras slung around their necks to bored teenagers poking on iPhones and frazzled parents chasing laughing toddlers.

The historic hotel's grounds looked like a small village, with the multiple "cottages" (bigger than most modern McMansions) boasting names like "Chicota" and "Hollybourne." There were thirty-three historic buildings in all. The hotel itself was on the National Register of Historic

9

Places. Once upon a time, some of the richest men in the country had built those houses and vacationed on the island, using it as a hunting club and resort where they could be tucked away from the prying eyes of the public. Original members of the Jekyll Island Club included famous men such as J.P. Morgan, William Rockefeller, Joseph Pulitzer, Marshall Field, William Vanderbilt, and dozens more that Taryn didn't recognize but were surely important and wealthy men of their time.

"The grounds are lovely, as you can see," Ellen lectured as she turned onto a road and picked up speed. "We take great pride in them. I'm sure, given your line of work, you'll appreciate all the history we have and can enjoy your time here when you're not working."

"Yes, I'm very excited about being here," Taryn agreed.

As a landscape artist, Taryn's clients hired her when they had houses or other structures that were in poor condition and were either going to be demolished or renovated. Taryn was not only skilled with a paintbrush in an artistic sense–her degrees in Historic Preservation and Art allowed her to reconstruct the often derelict buildings so that her clients could view them in their former glory. Taryn's paintings were often the only representation they had of what their beloved structures had looked like when they were first erected, especially since the majority of them were built before the rise of the camera.

Delicate, gray Spanish moss balanced with ease above them as it stretched across the spindly tree branches, dangling down to gently brush the top of the golf cart as they hurried on their way. Taryn decided that *everything* looked better swathed in the ghostly tendrils.

She itched to bring out her camera, Miss Dixie, and start taking photos right away.

Everything looked like a post card.

They zipped by a slow-moving horse and wagon carrying an Asian family who appeared as enthralled as she felt. She saw people of all ages, shapes, and sizes leisurely riding bikes down leafy sidewalks, small children wearing colorful helmets and struggling with cumbersome training wheels while parents cheered encouragement from their own bikes.

It was an amazingly peaceful setting and Taryn's blood ran warm with pleasure.

When she and Ellen pulled up in front of a small, but well-maintained, brick ranch house she saw that Steve was already there with her car. He stood by the edge of the road, lighting up a cigarette and looking up at the sky, her keys jingling in his hand.

Taryn bounced out and took stock of her temporary home for the summer. The yard, though shadowed by a live oak and a couple of pine trees, was lush and full of color from the soft green of the grass to the pastels of the flowers that spilled from ceramic pots on the front porch. There were houses on either side, but neither were very close and both had fenced in backyards for added privacy. Although the house was only a few yards from the road, a thicket of trees in the back gave it the appearance of being nestled in a forest. Another golf cart drove by but the road was otherwise empty.

Taryn, worn out from apartment living, was thrilled at the idea of having a house again, even if it wasn't really hers and it was just for a little while.

"You'll have enough in here to get you through the first few nights, supply-wise," Ellen intoned, handing Taryn the house key. "There should be enough dishwashing liquid, detergent, bathroom tissue, and the like."

"Where's the nearest supermarket?" Taryn asked. The island wasn't very big and she hadn't passed a store coming in.

"Well, there's not one *on* the island. The gas station has a few odds and ends you might be able to use but most people travel to Brunswick. You'll find your chain groceries there."

Taryn was taken aback. Brunswick was a bit of a drive and it wasn't like the island wasn't developed. People lived there as well as visited. Surely it could've supported a supermarket?

Ellen must have read Taryn's mind because she let loose her first peal of laughter. "I *know* it seems a little archaic, but we try to keep the island as unspoiled as we can. Don't let some of the condos and new developments fool you. Only a small percentage of the island can be developed; the rest must be maintained as wilderness. So you won't find many restaurants or shops here."

"Well, that's okay," Taryn shrugged. "I've worked in all kinds of different places and I don't mind the drive." Actually, now that she thought about it, she thought it sounded kind of nice. Not quite roughing it but not as commercial as some of the vacation spots she'd seen.

"I'm going to send a golf cart for your disposal tomorrow but you also have a bicycle in the garage. Many people here prefer bike as a method of transport and our bike paths cover most of the island. They're working on expanding the paths on the southern part now."

Taryn groaned inwardly. It had been years since she'd last ridden a bike. She was *sure* she'd make a fool of herself trying to get on one now. But, as a kid she'd loved it and she could certainly use the exercise after all the fast food she'd consumed on the ride down. She'd give it a go.

"When you're not working you'll have plenty of spare time and you might want to check out our beaches. Our beaches are some of the best on the Atlantic," Ellen boasted. "South Dunes is centrally located and has shower and restroom facilities. It has a dune ridge that's more than twenty feet. *Very* impressive. Driftwood Beach is, by far, one of the most beautiful places in Georgia. And then there's Glory Beach."

"Where the movie was filmed?" Taryn offered.

Ellen nodded.

"Just *please* be careful of the turtles. It's against the law to disturb their nests. You'll also want to be wary of the fire ants. They're faster than they look–step in a nest and they'll be crawling up your legs in a matter of seconds. You'll never forget their stings."

"Fire ants and sea turtles," Taryn echoed. "Got it."

"And as long as you're not on the golf course you shouldn't have any trouble with the gators, although they *can* wander away from their normal water source at times."

"Excuse me?" Taryn balked, eyes wide. "Gators? As in *alli*gators?"

"Oh yes, we're very proud of them. They're not to be worried over," Ellen assured her. "They're more afraid of you than you are of them."

Ha, Taryn shuddered. *Wanna bet?*

A few minutes later Taryn watched Steve and her new boss dart away in Ellen's little golf cart, her immaculate hair not even moving in the breeze.

"Lucky wench," Taryn muttered, shaking her head in mock jealousy.

Hands on her hips, she stood in front of the small house and smiled, nodding her head.

"Well," she whispered. "Here goes. Home sweet home."

CHAPTER 2

J ekyll Island, as a hotel and club, might have been developed as a playground and retreat for the very wealthy but the island's history was much older.

While the island was technically a tourist destination for anyone these days, and nobody had to arrive by boat anymore, it still wasn't cheap. Taryn discovered this upon trying to find something for dinner.

Although all the restaurants sounded good and she planned on trying each and every one at some point because eating was kind of her hobby, most of the menus boasted prices she'd consider a good night out back in Nashville.

Then again, Taryn *was* cheap.

She was starting to fear she'd need to stick to the gas station Dairy Queen if she wanted to dine out until she found the pizza place across from the beach. Sure, it was tucked in behind a mini-golf course and doubled as a golf cart rental center but the inside was old-world charming.

And it smelled heavenly.

"You waiting for someone?" the server, a skinny woman with bifocals, asked once Taryn climbed up on a barstool.

"Nope, just me," Taryn grinned. "I'm all alone."

"Getting a break from the family?" the server smiled sympathetically and handed her a menu. "I don't blame you."

Taryn started to explain that she didn't *have* a family but that sounded depressing. Instead, she returned the smile and scanned the menu. It didn't seem likely that she would eat an entire pizza by herself but it *had* been known to happen on occasion.

Matt started buzzing and setting her phone ablaze with text messages almost the minute her drink arrived. Taryn sighed and chewed on her lip. She needed to give him the contact information for where she was staying and let him know she'd arrived safely but she was also tired and didn't really feel like talking to anyone yet. Conversations with Matt were never short ones. She'd call him back when she returned to the house.

"Sorry dude," she said to the phone, setting it to "silent." "I'll call you back, I promise."

Her server raised an eyebrow as she walked by with a pitcher of water.

"It's the husband," Taryn explained wryly.

"Ha," the server called over her shoulder. "Leave a man alone with the kids for an hour and he doesn't know what to do. Ignore him and let *him* figure it out!"

Matt, of course, was not Taryn's husband. Sometimes "dating" even felt like too strong of a term for what they had going on. Their relationship was complicated.

Taryn had known Matt since they were children, for more than twenty years. As her best friend, and sometimes *only* friend, through the years he was the most constant thing she'd ever had in her life. Taryn's parents were both dead. Her grandmother, who she considered responsible for raising her, was gone as well. Her only other living relative, her Aunt Sarah, had died a year ago. Taryn hadn't seen her aunt in years and the guilt of not knowing she was even sick before her passing still ate at her.

Matt was all she had left.

For the majority of the time they'd known each other they'd simply been friends. Close friends, but just friends. That had changed in the past year and both were still trying to find their footing. Some days Taryn wasn't always sure the change was for the better. Their physical attraction to one another was astounding; Taryn had had no idea they'd be so wildly attracted to each other once they got over the initial awkwardness. And they were still best friends. Yet, there were times when she felt like something was missing. Or, that something *else* was there, overshadowing them.

Perhaps it was the ghosts.

There was no doubt that things had changed for Taryn in the past year. Seeing dead people would do that to a woman. Her beloved camera, Miss Dixie, had always been her partner in crime on her job sites. She used her photography as a way to get to know the buildings she painted, to get bring out their fine details and explore them. And while she'd always had a good imagination when it came to envisioning the past, Miss Dixie had helped bring the structures to life for her—something she could use in her work for her clients. But now Miss Dixie was revealing the past in other ways.

She was *showing* it to her.

When Taryn saw the first pictures she'd taken back at Windwood Farm in Kentucky, the vacant rooms suddenly filled with furniture from the past and the figure that shouldn't have been there, she'd been terrified yet intrigued.

At first she'd thought it was a fluke, just a one-time thing. After all, she'd had other jobs after Windwood and

19

nothing had happened. When it occurred again at Griffith Tavern in Indiana, however, and intensified when Matt accompanied her to a job site in northern Georgia, she knew it was here to stay.

And as much as she wanted to believe it, Taryn also knew that it wasn't Miss Dixie making it happen. Her camera was just the conduit. Now Taryn felt a presence almost everywhere she went. Echoes, fleeting images passing from the corner of her eyes, faint whispers...the dreams.

Taryn was surrounded by the dead who wanted to make themselves known to her. And, for whatever reason, not only was she seeing *them*, she was seeing their teacups and ottomans as well.

"That pizza good honey?" her server asked her with a wink.

Taryn nodded, her mouth full. She was already on her third piece. There might not be any leftovers to take back to the house.

While she attacked her pizza margherita with passion, Taryn flipped through a couple of books about the island she'd ordered online. The Jekyll Island Club Hotel represented a period she was fascinated with—the turn of the century. After the Civil War and before the stock market crash, the classes were still divided and the rich were frivolous and carefree. The men who made the money were inventive and sometimes scrupulous, the women savvy and headstrong. Even by today's standards they'd spent a ton of money on houses, clothes, and accessories. The Jekyll Island Club was a place to let loose, have fun, and flaunt their wealth to each other. It had been a tremendously gay time, and something that couldn't possibly last.

It hadn't.

*   *   *

"Darlin, you *sure* you don't need a box?"

Taryn was still smiling at the look of shock on her server's face when she'd realized that Taryn didn't have anything left to put into a box.

Now, back in her car and with her belly full, she decided to get to know her surroundings. She liked to jump into things headfirst and didn't believe in settling in when she first arrived. She wanted to hit the ground running.

Besides, she was still a little revved up after the agonizingly long drive.

"Georgia," she muttered as she turned onto the road, "why you gotta be so dang *long* and flat?"

Still, the ride down hadn't been as difficult on her as she, or her doctors, had worried. Taryn hadn't had the official diagnosis of Ehlers-Danlos Syndrome for even a year yet, but since it was a genetic condition she'd been born with it and suffered the symptoms all her life without knowing what they meant. The connective tissue disorder that caused her unstable joints to dislocate and sublux on a regular basis also caused her an immense about of pain. Her specialist had been afraid that sitting in the car for so long and doing the driving on her own would set her back. Any little thing could make her worse. She was also afraid of this but, so far, just felt tired. The excitement of being on the island, of starting a new job, overrode any weakness or pain.

Back in her car, Taryn took herself for a drive around the island, trying to see as much as she could from her car. She'd have plenty of time to get out in the golf cart or on the bike later, if she wanted. (And she *wanted*. A lot.)

George Strait sang about his exes living in Texas on the radio and she had a to-go cup full of Pepsi resting between her knees. It was still daylight and she'd received her second wind.

To her right, the twinkling Atlantic spread out before her, a vastness that both thrilled and terrified her. Taryn had a love-hate relationship with water. She wasn't so good in or on it. She loved watching it from the shore, though. It was one of the few times she felt like there was something bigger than herself out there in the universe.

The other times were when she saw the ghosts.

"Let's start with the big daddy of sights," she mumbled as she tried glancing down at her map and watching for cyclists and pedestrians at the same time.

Although there wasn't a sign for Driftwood Beach, the beach that boasted stark wreckages of trees and limbs that rose from the sand in skeletal monuments, she knew when she got there because of the amount of cars that were pulled over to the side of the road. She'd hoped she could catch a glimpse of the spectacle from her car but, alas, a thick grove of trees was in her way.

"Well. Damn." She'd have to save that for another day. Second wind or not, she didn't feel like going for a hike.

After passing a campground and RV park that looked pretty happening (Christmas tree lights strung through the trees, loud music pumping through the air, and the smell of charcoal) she rounded the corner and the so-called "tabby house" (officially known as the Horton House) came into view.

"Okay now, that's what I'm talking about," she sang, grinning as she drew upon it. If there was one thing that got her blood pumping, it was old houses. And this one was *old*.

Constructed of tabby in 1742, it was the oldest structure on the island and one of the oldest houses in the state of Georgia. For Taryn, it was a reminder that the Jekyll

Island Club Hotel might be what the island became famous for, but its history was a lot more varied. The house may have lacked a roof, walls, and floors but it *had* been standing since the 18th century.

She pulled over to the side of the road and studied it for a moment, appreciating the way the early evening light shone through the windows and danced upon the lawn. It had wonderful shadows now and she knew it would take terrific pictures.

"Mental note: return to Horton House," she reminded herself as she turned back onto the road again.

And then, after a few more minutes of driving with the river on her right this time, she was back around to the hotel again– the "historic village." Since she was planning on returning the next day for the official tour, she kept going.

"Plenty of time to get to know it..."

After passing through a breadth of road that didn't contain anything other than trees on both sides and a bike trail, she reached the water park. Taryn could see the tall water slides from the car and smiled. If she ever had a family she hoped she'd be the kind of parent who would round up the kids and take them to a place like that for the day. She envied the sunburnt and exhausted looking moms and dads she saw walking to their cars, carrying beach bags and screaming toddlers. Despite their tiredness and the heat they all looked so...*happy*.

The south end of the island was wilder, much less developed than the rest. She knew there were beaches nearby, like the one where the movie "Glory" was filmed, but she couldn't see them. Still, it was peaceful driving along the little road, windows rolled down and the hot summer sun warming her bare legs. As the lone car, she had the place to herself.

"This is going to be a good job, and a good place to stay," she said aloud. She could *feel* it.

The shadow that followed her flickered.

*   *   *

WITH HOUSES ON EITHER SIDE of her and several chain hotels nearby, Taryn hadn't expected the night to be so still. After slathering her legs with bug spray she pulled on her sweatshirt, grabbed a drink, and went out to the back patio to study the night sky and call Matt. He didn't answer so she left a quick message and then sat down on a chair, her aching legs stretched out in front of her.

There were *things* in the night but they didn't scare her. (Maybe the snakes and alligators scared her, but she wasn't going to think about those.)

One of Taryn's biggest secrets, and most embarrassing facts about herself, was that she was terrified of the dark. There was no rational explanation for her fear. But while it was true that the dark petrified her, it was only the artificial dark–the dark caused by turning out a light. She didn't mind the night sky, the darkness caused by *nature*.

Her backyard looked into the small woodland but thanks to the glare of the porch light she could only see to the edge of the patio. The world beyond was obscured by blackness, like a curtain had been dropped down to cut her off from the outside.

When her phone rang, she recoiled.

"Hey, I've been texting you. You okay?" It was Matt and he didn't sound happy.

"Sorry," she replied sheepishly. "I got here, met the manager, ate, and then took myself on a tour. I *just* finished unpacking, I swear."

She could feel Matt's sigh of relief rather than hear it.

"When I didn't hear from you I was afraid something bad happened, that you'd gotten sick somewhere along the way," he complained. "The last time you called me, you were in Atlanta."

"You mean the seventh layer of traffic hell," she corrected him and they laughed together.

"So, tell me all about it. What's it like?"

Taryn spent the next few minutes trying to describe what she'd seen so far. Matt listened attentively, asking all the right questions. When she was finished he said, "I might have to take a little vacation up there. I looked at the map and it's just a few hours away."

Maybe she was feeling exhausted and sentimental but the thought of her and Matt walking on the beach at sunset, sharing a pizza, and enjoying themselves on an island sounded wonderful and she suddenly wanted it desperately. They hadn't been on a vacation together yet, not as a couple anyway. They'd been on tons growing up.

"Oh, try if you can," she said. "I'd like that."

"Really?" Matt sounded pleased. "You would?"

"Why wouldn't I?"

"Because I'm usually the one showing up unannounced and weaseling in on your jobs," he confessed. "I'm not always sure you like that."

Well, it was true. He *did* have a habit of just showing up, especially when he thought she was in trouble. Which, granted, had been a lot lately.

"I don't know," she laughed. "I think I'm starting to depend on it now." She wasn't sure she liked that. Taryn had always been independent, even when she and Andrew lived together. And especially after Andrew died. She was trying to learn how to let go, though, and lean on Matt more.

Matt was now trying to explain to her something that had to do with his job at NASA. It was a complicated story but his even baritone was soothing so she leaned back and closed her eyes, trying to follow what he said.

And then something changed.

As long as she'd been sitting on the patio the air had been heavy with the early summer heat. The warmth had encircled her, loosening her muscles and washing over her like a blanket. The heady scent of the earth's natural musk from the trees, ocean, marsh, and lush vegetation had settled over her and reminded her of everything she loved about nature. She'd found it comforting.

Now, however, she caught a trace of something else– something potent and unpleasant. At the same time the scent hit her nose it reached her eyes and she found them watering, overflowing so that tears streaked down her cheeks and dripped on her jeans. As she wiped the water away with the sleeve of her sweatshirt she could feel her throat starting to tighten.

The air around her was suddenly full of thick, dirty smoke and as Taryn coughed violently into the phone she began to panic.

"You okay?" Matt asked with concern as she hacked and gasped, trying to hold the phone away from her mouth.

"Ye-yeah," she sputtered, momentarily able to catch her breath, but then gagged as the bitter poison slid down her throat and up her nose. "Smoke."

"Ew. Someone's smoking?" (If there was one thing Matt couldn't stand, it was cigarette smoke.)

"No," she heaved. It was getting worse by the second. "Fire. Fire smoke."

"Is the house okay?"

Taryn jumped up, waving her hand frantically in front of her face to push the fumes away. She was startled to see from her watery eyes that there was nothing there. The ugly cloud was gone but the odor lingered. She quickly turned and studied the house, half expecting to see it going up in flames.

It was fine.

"House okay," she stammered, retching in spite of the control she tried to maintain. Bile rose up but then slid back down again, mixing with the smoke and creating a vicious cycle.

It wasn't *just* the stench of the smoke now, though. As though someone had abruptly doused her with gasoline and flicked a match on her, her entire body was engulfed in an imaginary inferno as she felt the fever spread from the roots of her hair all the way down to her toes. With her skin on fire, burning from flames she couldn't see, she let out a blood curdling scream.

"Aakk!" Taryn cried, slapping at her skin and doing a panicky little dance on the patio stones. She thought she would surely die from the heat and the pain. She swatted at her head, her stomach, and at her legs–a hysterical woman doing a frenzied dance to music only she could hear.

Tossing her phone on the chair she tore off her sweatshirt, ripping it up the back in the process, and flung it out into the yard, leaving her standing in the open wearing nothing but her bra. Sweat rolled down her scorching arms and back, soaking her shorts. The heat was unbearable, blistering her skin and making her wail in agony. She went for her bottoms then and tried tugging them off as well but was blinded by the pain and couldn't get her fingers to function on the zipper.

"Taryn? Taryn!" Matt's muffled voice rose from the chair but she ignored it, panicked as she danced around and tried to rid herself of whatever was attacking her.

Then, as swiftly as it began, it all stopped.

The air around her cleared, her skin cooled rapidly, and she was left standing in her yard, half naked and wild-eyed.

Taryn, still hyperventilating, bent over at her waist and tried to gather her thoughts. "Breathe," she instructed herself. "Breathe."

In a trance-like state she walked back to the chair and picked up the phone. She could still hear Matt hollering at his end but he sounded very far away.

"It's gone," she whispered, her throat still raw. "The smoke is gone. But my whole body. It was on fire."

"Could it be the EDS?" Matt asked, his voice shaky but always quick to find the logical explanation when there was one. "Sometimes it's hard to regulate your body temperature."

Taryn nodded dully and walked out into the grass to gather her torn garments. Maybe she'd had a type of seizure or something. Didn't people sometimes smell smoke when that happened? And maybe it *was* a medical thing. The EDS caused all kinds of weird stuff. She was still learning about it herself.

"I'm okay," she whispered again. "Let me call you back in a little while. I need to get another drink and lay down."

But, as she let herself back into the house, she couldn't forget the last thing she saw before it had all come to a screeching halt: a wall of flames, towering over her, and drawing nearer at a dizzying speed.

CHAPTER 3

"I hope you enjoyed your first night on the island," Ellen Russo said.

Taryn was sitting in Ellen's office, a spacious room furnished with Art Deco style furniture. Once again, despite the crushing heat, Ellen sat before her looking cool as a cucumber.

"Yes, it was fine," Taryn smiled, trying to hide the shakiness she still felt at remembering the previous night. "The house is very nice. I'll enjoy staying there, I'm sure."

"Good. Well, I'm afraid I don't have a lot of time so I thought I'd give you a quick rundown of the hotel and then drive you to the locations you'll be working at. Amy was meant to be here but had to take the day off."

Taryn thought she noticed a note of impatience in Ellen's voice and she wasn't surprised. Ellen herself hadn't hired her; rather, the board of directors had. Out of all the cottages that were still standing, all but two had been renovated and were either open for tours or for meetings and accommodations. The last two cottages, Ivy House and Adena Cottage, would be renovated in the fall. Taryn would be working with the architect to come up with renderings.

She had a feeling that Ellen, like many people, probably considered Taryn's part of the project an unnecessary expense. After all, architects were paid to come up with sketches to show the big picture. What could Taryn possibly have to add to that?

Taryn may have suffered from nerves and the occasional annoying habit of wanting to please people too much, but she was confident in her abilities. She knew that what *she* offered was something more. She didn't just sketch or paint landscapes–she brought the buildings to life by recreating details and features that had been lost through the years. She showed what the structure would've looked like in its prime, when it was full of life and new. And, more than that, she captured the souls of the objects she painted until they were no longer *objects* at all.

Taryn was the closest thing they had to a vintage photograph which, incidentally, didn't really exist of the two cottages before their ruin.

Ellen and Taryn began their walk through the hotel first, with Ellen pointing out sights and details that were of both architectural and historical significance.

In the Riverfront Lobby Ellen paused. "The lobby bar here is something that everyone just *loves*," she remarked drily. "However, it's not original to the hotel. It was created as a set for a movie that was filmed here awhile back."

Taryn nodded and looked around. She'd seen *The Legend of Baggar Vance* and had liked it. And she could understand why people would like the lobby bar, regardless of its authenticity. With its fine wood finishing, old-fashioned bar top and stools, and chipper bartender in suit and tie she felt like she'd stepped back into the 1920's.

"This here is the Grand Dining Room," Ellen gestured proudly a few minutes later. "Meals are served here throughout the day, as well as a formal tea. There are three fireplaces we keep lit during the winter months, a pianist who comes in during the dinner meal, and impeccable service."

Taryn admired the large room with its beautiful crystal chandelier, grand piano covered in a display of roses, and delicate place settings on each table. Although a hostess stood at attention, there were only two tables inside with guests.

"It gets busier in the evenings," Ellen remarked. "And during special events, of course."

A long walkway took them past a courtyard, a deli with walls covered in movie posters of films shot there on location, and a ballroom. To Taryn's disappointment the ballroom was simply a large room with tables set up for a meeting. She was hoping for marble floors, an orchestra pit, and chandeliers everywhere. It did, however open to a nice courtyard.

"Well, we decorate it very well for events. It doesn't look like the same place then," Ellen laughed when Taryn questioned her. "You should see our New Year's Eve and Christmas parties."

Back in the golf cart with Ellen again, Taryn took a moment to admire the exterior of the hotel. The stark white paint set against the bright blue sky, expansive porch filled with rocking chairs, and strikingly curved walls made it look so much more glamorous than the nondescript interstate hotels she was used to seeing. The two wings spread out gloriously amongst the stunning oaks draped with their Spanish moss, and the imposing turret rose proudly into the sky, a symbol of wealth and prestige for those staying in the impressive Presidential Suite below it.

There was even a croquet court on the front lawn.

It was a short ride to the first cottage and Taryn took the time to appreciate the breeze. She'd have to learn to deal with the heat if she was going to work outside all summer. She'd also have to do something with her hair. Previously washed and styled, now it rested in limp curls against her wet neck and back.

Their first stop was Ivy House.

Ivy House was around 3,000 square feet, making the word "cottage" ironic. Construction began in the mid nineteenth century, making it one of the oldest cottages. It had once been a stately imposing structure but it had fallen into disrepair in the 1940's and had only been touched once since.

"We *did* try to renovate it two years ago," Ellen explained as they pulled up to it. Yellow tape surrounded the house, an attempt to keep trespassers out.

Taryn beheld the old cottage with sorrow. Built in a Queen Ann Style, it was as prissy as a wedding cake and boasted a charming turret. But one entire side had caved in, making it look like a giant had given it a good kick. It was difficult to tell what the original paint had been, although Taryn assumed it would've been colorful. Now it was a dull gray, bleached by the sun and salt air. The steps to the porch were overgrown with weeds, the floorboards caved in, and all the windows either road mapped with spider cracks or missing altogether.

Taryn, who believed houses had memories and some sort of soul, was saddened at the sight.

"What happened?" she asked, resisting the urge to whip out Miss Dixie and start working right then and there.

"Well, workers went in and began installing support beams in the parlor and..."

Ellen's voice trailed off, a bright pink blush coloring her cheeks.

"Yes?"

"Do you believe in ghosts, Miss Magill?" she asked curtly.

"I do," Taryn said. No reason to be coy about it. Besides, if they'd Googled her at all they would know what she'd been involved in. She'd developed a bit of a web presence after Windwood Farm.

"There are many locations on this island that are allegedly haunted. I am an educated woman but I don't shrink against the idea of there being something out there bigger than us. This," she gestured to the cottage, "is one of them. Workers spent three days in the house and it was nothing but chaos. Paint cans flew around the room, heavy footsteps could be heard tramping around upstairs when nobody was able to access it, and the men heard so much female laughter ringing through the walls that they said it was hard to hear each other talk. At last, the upstairs caved in on them. Injured two people. Nobody ever went back."

"What do you think it is? Or, whom, I should ask?"

Ellen pursed her lips. "The house was originally built by Steryl Lewis, a railroad magnate. His daughters inherited it upon his death and continued to live here until 1935. Apparently, before the eldest died, she informed everyone on the island that no matter what they did to it, it would be *hers*."

"I guess she doesn't like anyone touching it then," Taryn mused.

"Well, she best get over it because we have the money to fix it and we're going to," Ellen snapped.

As if in response, a shard of glass fell out of one of the upstairs windows and broke into a million tiny pieces on the ground not far from the women's feet. Taryn jumped back in surprise but Ellen just frowned and shook her head. "Oh, snap out of it Louisa," she barked. "We're not going to bother you. *Yet*."

Taryn looked at Ellen in growing admiration.

Adena Cottage, constructed in 1899, was in much worse shape. Although a photograph of it from 1953 did exist, it was only a partial view. And, regrettably, a tropical storm had almost ruined it completely three years later.

Taryn would have her work cut out for her with it.

"Are there any ghosts here?" she asked as they stood on the lawn and studied it. It looked peaceful enough, but you just never really knew.

"Not that we are aware of," Ellen answered. "We've never had any trouble with this one."

Back at the hotel Ellen had bottled water brought up for them while they went over the final paperwork. Once Taryn had signed all the contracts Ellen rose to her feet. "If there is anything you need, please let me know."

"Actually, I was going to ask about supplies. Groceries, paints, stuff like that," Taryn said. "Where do I need to go?"

"You'll find most of what you need in Brunswick, although if you need something specific you might have to travel down to Jacksonville," Ellen replied. "To be honest, however, if you're looking for good dining options I'd head over to St. Simon's Island."

"How long does it take to get there?"

Ellen laughed. "Well, not very long if you have a boat. Since you have a car, about half an hour if there's traffic. Two miles by sea, fifteen by land."

*   *   *

Taryn couldn't wait to get started on the initial photographing of the cottages, but first she needed to organize and then she needed supplies. She'd brought very little with her in terms of food, thinking there'd be a grocery store she could pop out to as soon as she arrived. She needed her late-night munchies; Taryn tended to stay up late working, and the night before had been brutal without something disgusting to snack on.

A seasoned gypsy, she packed light when it came to clothes. The majority of her summer clothes were lightweight and thin. They could easily be rolled up into her suitcase. She'd also brought her laptop, her external hard drive, and several lenses for Miss Dixie. These she set up on the dining room table, making herself a makeshift office.

To personalize the living room a bit she laid a handmade afghan, a birthday present from her grandmother, over the back of the couch. Her collection of sandals and boots were tucked away in the large closet in the house's only bedroom and her assortment of prescription medications and supplements she stored in the bathroom's medicine cabinet.

The last thing she did was place three photographs on the small dresser in the bedroom. The first was of her and Matt, taken when she was eleven. They'd bicycled to the lake that day, something she couldn't imagine kids that young doing outside of Nashville now, and had set up a little picnic. A stranger stopped and took their picture. Taryn was wearing a red T-shirt, blue jean shorts, and her messy red hair was in a side ponytail. Matt wore his usual somber expression with clothes that were a size too small.

The second was a photograph of her parents and maternal grandmother, all gathered around a Christmas tree. It was the last Christmas her parents had seen.

The third was one Taryn was still trying to process and wean herself from, but had failed as of yet. It was a single shot of Andrew, her fiancé, standing in front of a dilapidated antebellum home in Mississippi. His boyish grin lit up his face, the excitement he always felt around houses he loved evident through the lens. His car crash had been just weeks later. Sometimes she still told people he was her husband, and not her fiancé, as though rewriting history the way it should have been.

*   *   *

TARYN HAD SPENT MOST of the day trying to forget what happened the night before. Now that it was dark again however, and she was all alone, it was impossible to let it go.

Now, as she sat by herself in her temporary living room and tried staring at the television screen, she let herself remember another part of the hotel's history—the thing that nobody *ever* wanted to talk about.

The fire was the disaster that had almost brought it all to an abrupt end. New Year's Eve, 1907. During the celebration in the ballroom there were more than two hundred people inside dancing, drinking, and laughing. Nobody saw the flames or smelled the smoke until it was too late. A fire that started upstairs in one of the apartments quickly spread through the wooden walls. With the main door engulfed in flames, partygoers had smashed through windows to escape into the fresh night air. More than seventy-five people were seriously injured. There were forty deaths in total, including guests and staff. It was still considered one of the greatest tragedies in American history.

The majority of the original hotel burned to the ground, nothing but ashes. The apartments were all destroyed. Investigators determined that William Hawkins, a forty-year old attorney from New York, had started the fire in his apartment over the ballroom. The reason? To cover up the murder of his young wife, Rachel. William was tried for both the arson and the murder, found guilty in both cases, and sentenced to death. The story still resounded with historians, not only due to the nature of the tragedy but because a white man was hung. Fifteen of the deaths from the fire had been prominent businessmen and their wives. That fact had not boded well for William.

The hotel was rebuilt a year later, an exact replica of the original, although it would never be the same.

FOUR

*T*ryn had already been on Jekyll Island for four days and had yet to visit a beach.

It was official: she was pathetic.

It was funny how she had almost zero problems when it came to her professional life and yet her personal life was just one big procrastinated effort after another.

Although she needed to get over to the cottages and start taking her pictures she decided that today was the day she must explore at least one of the beaches. Her best photographs were taken in the morning or late afternoon and since she was rarely up for the morning light she still had plenty of time to take herself for a walk in the sand.

"This is why I took this job, remember?" she reminded her bathing suit as she fished it from her dresser. "To relax."

Taryn had honestly never been much of a beach person. Her mind never slowed down enough for her to kick back on the sand and zone out. Within minutes there would be a weird juxtaposition of song lyrics, movie reels, and bank figures dancing through her head. She loved watching the water, though, in all its forms. She'd never let her fear of what it could do detract from her enjoyment of watching it.

There were several beaches on Jekyll Island and the information pamphlet and map she'd picked up at the island's gate had recommended Great Dunes Park as a good place to start. When she pulled into the parking lot, however, it was packed. After circling it twice and nearly hitting a man carrying two folding chairs on his back and dragging a cooler she decided to take it as an omen that it wasn't the beach for her.

Getting back on the road she headed for Driftwood Beach

Driftwood Beach was named for the very thing it contained–driftwood. With visions of a normal sandy beach littered with a bunch of sticks, Taryn's expectations were low as she pulled over the side of the road and parked her car behind two minivans. Driftwood didn't have an official parking lot; you just kind of had to pull over where you could.

To reach the beach Taryn had to walk through a heavily wooded area. The narrow sandy path took her through a thick mess of trees, vines, and shrubs while mosquitoes and sand gnats flew around her head. She could barely see the ground for the undergrowth and had there not been a path there was no way she'd have been able to walk through the thicket. It looked like a jungle and for the first time since arriving Taryn had a better idea of what the original settlers might have been up against. She tried to imagine landing on the island and being met by the dense vegetation and sweltering heat, the mosquitoes swarming their heads and the fire ants below.

Had it looked like a paradise then, or hell?

Taryn was panting and swiping at the sweat burning her eyes when the trees opened up. Before her lay the Atlantic, wide and calm with just a hint of blue. A barge floated peacefully in the distance, its massive size barely a blip on the horizon. Straight in front of her, though, was something unlike anything she'd ever seen.

When she heard the word "driftwood" she expected logs, sticks, and pieces big enough to pick up. What she saw were the size of vehicles. It was as if entire trees had washed ashore and landed naked on the sand, creating a skeletal jungle. Their bare branches protruded upwards like emaciated arms reaching for the sky. They rose and twisted in impossible shapes, each one its own work of art, the shadows they left across the sand an intricate board game that made her feel like Alice in Wonderland.

Taryn walked amongst the monsters, stopping to examine tide pools and watch the dozens of sand crabs scurrying from her probing lens. When she got too hot she peeled off her tank top and walked around with her bathing suit sticking out of her shorts.

The beach was almost deserted. Although there were a few stragglers picking up shells and wading in the water, they were on the far end and nowhere near Taryn. She thought she had her part of the beach to herself so when a shadow loomed over her while she knelt to get a shot of tube worms covered in tiny shells, she flinched in surprise.

"Sorry to scare you!"

Taryn quickly rose to her feet and turned around. An elderly woman with a fanny pack and Birkenstocks stood facing her. "You kind of sneaked up on me there," Taryn laughed a little. Where in the world had she come from? Taryn could've sworn she wasn't there just a minute ago.

"I just wanted to ask you what kind of camera you were using," the woman said. "I'm in the business for a new one myself."

"Oh," Taryn replied, removing Miss Dixie from her neck. "Well, you can take a look if you want."

She didn't normally like anyone touching something so personal of hers but there was something about the woman that Taryn couldn't quite put her finger on, something familiar.

For several minutes the women talked about photography and their respective cameras. "I just doodle around myself," the woman said, handing Miss Dixie back to her. "I like nature photography. It gives me something to do. I don't have a lot to do these days."

"Do you come out here very often?" Taryn asked.

The woman looked out at the water and Taryn watched as her eyes glazed over. Although her face was craggy with lines and her hair brittle and sparse, her eyes were ocean blue and for a second Taryn thought she could almost see a glimpse of the beautiful young woman she used to be.

"I come when I can," she replied at last and offered nothing more.

"It's a beautiful beach," Taryn said politely. "I want to try to come back at sunrise one day and get some more shots."

"Just don't stay out too late or you might see Mary," the woman warned her.

"Who's Mary?"

"Why, she's one of our resident ghosts," the woman replied with a small smile. "She haunts this beach, and the beach on St. Simon's as well, if that can be believed."

"What's her story?" Taryn asked. "Who is she?"

The woman smiled and sat down on a log, turning her face so that she could watch the water. Taryn followed suit and sat beside her.

"Mary the Wanderer was an immigrant many years ago. Her family died on the boat ride over but one of the wealthy gentleman on St. Simon's offered her a job at his plantation. That's when the trouble started," the woman began.

Taryn nodded in encouragement.

49

"By all accounts she was happy there, although the gentleman was reportedly a hard man to like. Soon, however, she fell in love with the rich man's son. And he fell in love with her." A red glow spread across the woman's cheeks, much to Taryn's delight. She appreciated people who could get caught up in a love story. "As time went by Mary and her young man grew even closer. They were madly in love with one another and wanted to marry. Of course, that would not do. When the young man approached his father, his father was furious."

"Because she wasn't wealthy and was just a servant?"

The woman shook her head. "No, because *he* was in love with her as well!"

"Oh," Taryn said with a frown. "I guess that would put a kink in their plans."

"Yes, it did. When the young man found out he was furious as well. In his anger, he ran from the house and jumped onto his boat. He loved to sail and his boat was his pride and joy. He was just going for a little ride but a storm came on quickly. He didn't come home." Although Taryn assumed this story happened two centuries ago, the woman's eyes turned downward and she sighed, as though the tale was almost too painful. "Well, Mary went looking for him. When she reached one of the cliffs she looked down and saw his boat. It was beaten to death and in pieces. Floating next to the boat was her young man's lifeless body. In despair and hopelessness, she threw herself into the water. If she couldn't be with him life, she'd be with him in death."

"And now she haunts the beaches," Taryn finished for her.

"Yes, because suicides don't always turn out the way we'd hoped. She thought, once dead, they'd be together. They aren't, however. She's never found him and wanders the beaches each night, watching for his boat to come and take her away."

Taryn grimaced. "Oh my, well, that *is* sad. Poor thing."

"Mary the Wanderer is what they call her," the woman smiled, her eyes lighting back up. "Our resident ghost."

"Have you ever seen her?" Taryn asked.

The woman stood and readjusted her fanny pack. "When you get to be my age, dear, there isn't much you *haven't* seen."

*   *   *

ADENA COTTAGE SADDENED TARYN greatly. She didn't think she'd be so upset at the destruction of the cottages; after all, they were just vacation houses for rich folks a long time ago. It was just so darn sorry looking, though, that she couldn't help it. Taryn was a sucker for old houses of any

51

kind. Although Andrew had been the one obsessed with architecture, she had gone for the soul and had found it in everything from shotgun style cottages in New Orleans to antebellum mansions in Mississippi. For her, it was the ambiance of the place that was important, not how many rooms it had or how many fancy features.

And Adena Cottage had soul.

Taryn desperately wanted to slip inside the Jacobethan walls and see what the interior looked like, but the collapsed roof stopped her. Although the left side looked sturdy enough, the last thing she need to do was break her fool neck taking pictures. She'd have to be content with the exterior.

As she walked around the cottage, aiming Miss Dixie high and low, she tried to imagine what it would've looked like in its prime. The colors would have been vivid and bright, and there would've been many of them. This was no wallflower; Adena Cottage would've taken after her sisters and stood out like a proud peacock with its pseudo-Tudor style. The porch would've been full of small tables, comfortable chairs, and perhaps a swing. With its Flemish gables, patterned stone work, and fluted chimneys it was a true work of art. Its view of the river and the fact it faced west meant it would've been the perfect place to relax and watch the sunset.

Taryn was mindful of snakes as she knelt down by the porch to take a picture of what was left of the railings and spindles. She was watchful of spiders as she cupped her hands to her face and peered into the dusty windows.

In spite of its condition, the cottage almost preened under her scrutiny, standing proud and tall even with its current disability. Taryn imagined a grand dame in the midst of a scandal, putting on a brave face to those around her despite the turmoil she faced.

One of the upstairs windows still had a sliver of glass in it. It poked up from the window frame like a broken tooth in an otherwise empty mouth. The gummy smile was almost jaunty and Taryn laughed before snapping a picture.

"Look!" someone cried gaily, their voice full of enthusiasm. "Look!"

Taryn turned and saw a tourist group walking nearby, following a man holding up a big red umbrella. She wondered what was so exciting that someone felt the need to point it out to the others, but they all appeared to be quietly listening to the man leading the way.

She would've stuck around longer but the sun was sinking quickly now and she still needed to get to the other cottage. Tossing Adena a goodbye wave, Taryn hopped in her golf cart and made her way to the next one.

*   *   *

IVY HOUSE, WITH ITS GHOSTS AND LEGENDS, had onlookers when she arrived. As Taryn neared the group of men, women, and children she realized they weren't merely tourists out for a stroll but a tour group. Before them, a woman in a long white dress paced back and forth, waving her hands erratically and gesturing to the cottage behind her.

"She doesn't like anyone touching her and has been known to shriek and yell when workers get too close to changing something she likes," Taryn could hear the woman narrate as she drew closer. The tour group looked on with big eyes, some straining their necks looking over the house, perhaps trying to catch a glimpse of one of its deadly residents. On the road behind them a man sitting behind the wheel of a red trolley with the words "Ghost Tours-Jekyll Island" scrawled across the side sat back in his seat with his feet up on the dashboard. He flipped through a newspaper.

So as not to disturb the group, Taryn started at the back of the house.

She couldn't deny that there was something eerie about the place. While Adena set proud and regal, Ivy felt confrontational and hostile. Each time Taryn snapped a shot she imagined the house bristling, irritated at the attention.

This house was no life of the party. It wouldn't have made friends easily and, instead, would've sat critically in the corner, condemning the other guests for not living up to their expectations.

Taryn laughed at the thought and could've sworn she saw a window shade snap in disapproval.

By the time she made it to the front the tour group was gone, their trolley zipping on down the road. The guide was on a loudspeaker now and Taryn listened to the electronic hum until they went around a corner and were out of sight.

She was still nervous when it came to talking about her abilities (talent? gift? curse?). The first time she'd uploaded her photos and seen the furniture magically appear where it had not previously been she'd been scared out of her mind and questioned her sanity. She assumed others would as well.

She was wrong.

Instead, after a year of internet research, talking with others who knew much more about these things than she did, and consuming books about the topic as quickly as she could Taryn had learned one thing: the paranormal was hot.

Everyone seemed to either want to hear ghost stories, tell ghost stories, or experience their own ghost story. There were apparently even schools and workshops where people could go and learn how to hone their skills and become more sensitive.

You could find anything on the internet these days.

She was no longer as afraid to talk about what she did and saw, but the actual fear she felt during the experiences had still not left her. It had not become so second hat to her that she no longer got freaked out whenever she saw or heard something that shouldn't have been there.

And Ivy House definitely had *something*.

She was almost taken aback by the negative energy that poured from it, wrapping itself around her and squeezing. As the minutes wore on her scalp began tingling, the tiny hairs on the back of her neck standing at attention. Her fingers turned to ice and trembled; focusing her lens became a chore. With her heart pounding in her chest and her blood pounding in her ears Taryn finally gave up and went back to the golf cart.

Before she took off, however, she turned back to Ivy House. "You and I are going to have to work something out, old girl," she called. "Because I'm not working like this all summer."

For a split second the cottage seemed to grow taller and the long shadow it cast over Taryn felt like a slap in the face.

Taryn took it as a challenge.

IT WAS LATE, AND MOST OF THE ISLAND was already asleep, but it was Taryn's favorite time of the day: picture uploading time.

After a dinner at Dairy Queen and a stop at the gas station next door to pick up drinks and snacks, she'd gone back and talked to Matt on the phone for more than two hours. He was in rare form, talking a mile a minute and filling her in on his latest project and the new student interns they'd taken on. "My students are wonderful," he'd gushed. "I think I've assembled an excellent team this time and it looks like we're going to get a lot accomplished."

Taryn had asked the right questions, shown the right amount of interest, and generally said what he wanted to hear. The fact was, she knew nothing about astrophysics or aeronautics or anything else he did and his attempts to explain things to her left her even more confused. But she still supported him and was proud of him.

All the while they'd been on the phone Taryn had been uploading her photos to her laptop. She wanted to take a peek and it was killing her not to look but she knew that if she did, if only for a second, she'd get distracted and that wasn't fair to Matt. He deserved her attention.

Now, however, the time was hers.

After pouring herself a glass of juice Taryn settled herself at the dining room table and rubbed her hands together in anticipation, something she'd been doing since she was a child.

Her job was to paint the buildings and reconstruct them in a way that would show them in their prime. Before she ever started painting, however, she had to first get to know them. She'd never found a better way than with her camera. Miss Dixie was more than just an electronic device to capture images on—she was Taryn's other set of eyes. Between the two of them they could study the fine details and get a feel for the *real* heart of the place.

Once she had the pictures uploaded she would study them, taking the time to edit and manipulate them to learn their nuances. From there, once she felt like she understood the buildings' personalities, she'd start to paint. The pictures were for her, but they were necessary.

As she clicked on the folder to open the images and watched them spring to life in front of her she jumped back in her seat and gasped. She'd seen a lot over the past year, but wonders never ceased. She could still be shocked.

With a little laugh she got her bearings and leaned forward again, her nose just a few inches from the screen. "Well I'll be damned," she stammered. "*That* was unexpected."

FIVE

*I*t was after noon before Taryn woke up.

She didn't feel guilty about sleeping so late since she hadn't fallen asleep until daylight. Once she started working it was difficult for her to stop.

At first, the images had caught her off guard so much that she'd had trouble focusing. She knew Ivy House was haunted; the tour guide had talked about it, Ellen had told her, and she'd spent half an hour feeling its icy arms swatting her away. She was expecting unwelcoming ghosts and thought she'd prepared herself for the ghastly images that she might've captured on film. The Jekyll Island Club Hotel itself was known for being haunted—it was even famous for it.

That's why she was so shocked that on her screen Ivy House had looked as uninviting and homely as it did in real life while Adena had been fully restored to its glory, pink paint and all.

She'd prepared herself for Ivy House; she'd barely had a second thought about Adena. Yet, there she was, as handsome and proud as the day she was built.

The missing roof had been replaced, the shingles were straight and flat. The glass in all the windows glimmered in the bright summer sun as though they'd been recently washed, lacy curtains peeking through the glass. The porch, as she'd expected, held an array of white furniture with brightly colored pillows. A tray rested on a footstool with a silver pitcher in the center. The great front door was restored, a gold knocker in the shape of a horse head polished and shining in the middle. Flowers flourished along the pathway that wasn't there in present day.

The house didn't come through in all the pictures, just the ones taken from the front. From the back and sides, it was in just as much disorder as it was now.

Taryn studied the images for hours, zooming in on the details and even making notes when she saw something she thought could be useful. The thrill of seeing the past come to life again hadn't dimmed. She yearned to be able to walk through the picture, to be a part of the scene she was probing. She wanted to sit on that porch and drink coffee and watch the river, to walk through the front door and examine the rooms the way they used to be. But, if this was as close as she could get, she'd have to be content with that.

*   *   *

ALTHOUGH CURIOSITY WAS NEARLY killing her, she figured hunger might get her first. Taryn needed to eat. Since she'd done so well eating cheap so far she decided to treat herself to the main dining room at the hotel. She couldn't afford to eat there every day, but a few times wouldn't hurt.

Steve, the young valet she'd met on her first day, was standing at the front of the building when she pulled up on her golf cart.

"Hey," she laughed when he jogged down the steps to meet her. "You don't have to park me or anything. I just can't figure out where I'm supposed to dock this thing around here."

Steve smiled, a charming dimple revealing itself. She made him out to be around twenty-four years old. "I'll do it for you," he offered. "It's slow."

61

As she climbed out and grabbed her purse, he noticed Miss Dixie slung around Taryn's neck. "You here for the big event?" he asked.

"Your camera," he pointed. "I thought maybe you were here for the convention."

"Oh, no, I always carry her with me. What's going on?"

Steve shrugged. "It's the big ghost convention."

"Ghost convention?" Taryn immediately had an image of a bunch of spirits kicking back in chairs, listening to a demon do a Power Point presentation.

"Yeah, people come here and stay the weekend. Listen to people talk about ghosts and hauntings and stuff. At night they investigate the hotel, take their cameras with 'em and see if they can spot any orbs or whatever," he explained.

Taryn knew such things happened but had never actually been to one. From the way he described it, though, her *life* was a ghost convention. "Sounds fun."

"Yeah, well, they're usually good tippers. They don't bother me any," he shrugged again.

"You ever see a ghost here?"

Steve grinned. "Yes ma'am. Wouldn't be Jekyll Island if there weren't a few ghosts running around."

AFTER LUNCH, TARYN MADE her way over to Adena Cottage. She had to start there, of course. If the house was showing her and Miss Dixie its former glory then it obviously had something it wanted them to know.

After staring at the images of it fully restored it was a shock to her system to see it in person again, leaning to one side and half its roof missing.

"Poor old girl," Taryn mumbled as she set up her easel and high-back stool.

She sang to herself as she unwrapped her charcoal pencils and set up her canvas. She would sketch the front of the cottage first and then move to the back. She wouldn't start painting for at least a few more days. She knew some artists who dove right into it but it took Taryn a little more time. She still enjoyed painting, even though it was her vocation and no longer just a hobby, and she liked to have fun with it.

In the hours that she worked trolleys traveled past her, guides dictating narratives over loudspeakers to red-faced tourists. There was one every hour and by the third time it stopped she knew their spiel about Adena by heart.

Nobody paid her any attention; she blended in with the scenery after awhile.

When she got too hot or tired she'd stop, put her pencil down, and root around in her small cooler for a drink. She took several walks around the cottage, studying its walls and what was left of its windows. The cottage was quiet today, content with the fact that it had already done its part in revealing itself.

Taryn found herself staring at the lawn and trying to envision the pathway flanked by flowers, like what she'd seen in her pictures. Now it was just an empty expanse of grass– mowed and trimmed but otherwise unremarkable.

As she was wrapping things up for the day another trolley rocketed down the road and came to a stop in front of the cottage. She listened again as the guide, a young man in a top hat and tails, recited the history:

"If you'll look out the window to your left you'll see what's left of Adena Cottage. Adena was built in 1898 by Lowell McGovern. He owned a fleet of cargo ships out of New York City and, during his time, was one of the wealthiest people in the world. His daughter, Georgiana, was his only child and often accompanied him to their summer house here on Jekyll. When he passed away the house fell to her and she lived here full time for many years. Unfortunately, she didn't marry or have any heirs and when she died the house fell into disrepair. It's the only cottage that hasn't had any renovations done on it but that will change this fall."

As they picked up their speed and carried on down the road, Taryn looked up at the cottage and studied it again. Was it Georgiana who haunted it or Lowell? Or maybe someone else altogether? And what did they want from her?

Taryn sighed and carried the first load to her golf cart. She didn't know what they wanted but, as history had taught her, she'd probably learn soon enough.

SIX

*A*fter what had transpired during her job at Griffith Tavern Taryn hadn't been able to keep much of a low profile, at least not in the paranormal world.

The Friends of Griffith Tavern, the nonprofit organization set on saving the old stagecoach inn, had used her story to further their cause and gain publicity–as well as donations. She couldn't blame them. At least it meant the old building got saved.

However, it also meant that her name was suddenly showing up on paranormal blogs, in magazines, and in random supernatural-based forums. She'd been asked to appear on a few podcasts and radio shows as well, but had so far demurred. She knew that there was supposedly no such thing as "bad publicity." Still, she didn't think becoming an infamous psychic would do much for her freelance landscape painting career.

Still, despite her rise in popularity, sitting in the coffee shop at the Jekyll Island Club Hotel and getting ready for her day was the last place she thought she'd be recognized.

"It's Taryn Magill, right?" The man who towered over her had to be in his mid-to-late thirties but had a voice so deep and powerful that it made her table vibrate.

Assuming he was someone from the hotel, and probably someone she should know, she looked up and smiled politely. "Yes I am. Hello."

"Jerry Guillen ma'am," he said in that booming voice again, and stretched his hand to her. It was warm and soft but massive; it swallowed Taryn's tiny hand and she watched it disappear in fascination as he held onto it. "I'm a big fan of yours. Big fan. Just love what you do."

"Huh?" Completely confused now, Taryn was afraid he might have her mixed up with someone else. Unless he was into oils and watercolors and historical architecture she doubted he'd seen much of what she did. "My paintings?"

"Your *photography*!" Jerry grinned, wide-eyed. "Most of us in my field spend our lives imagining the past. The fact that you're able to *see* it is incredible."

It became clearer then and Taryn nodded. He still hadn't let go of her hand. "Oh, yes, well, it's...pretty incredible to me too sometimes," she finished lamely.

"I've read everything about your story that I can find," he said enthusiastically. "*Everything*! I know all about it."

She highly doubted that. Nothing, for instance, had been written about her time at Shaker Village of Pleasant Hill and people knew very little regarding her involvement in northern Georgia and the case of missing teenager Cheyenne Willoughby.

"Well, thank you. I think."

"Listen," Jerry began with marked enthusiasm, finally releasing her and pulling up a chair. "I'm one of the event organizers this weekend and we had a guest speaker cancel. Would you be interested in filling in maybe?"

Taryn paled. She wasn't terribly good at talking in front of crowds. The brief teaching stint she'd done had been awkward enough. "Um, I don't really have anything prepared for that kind of thing."

"Oh, you don't need anything formal! Just show up with some of your pictures. We'll hook you up to the computer, and you can do a slide show presentation or whatever. People will *love* it," he promised.

"Oh, I don't know. I am here on a job, and I don't know if that would be a conflict of interest or anything," she hedged.

"Don't worry about that. I'll talk to the manager. We could *really* use the help. People pay a lot of money to come to this and we strive to give them the best experience we possibly can. So, are you in?" He'd barely given her a chance to think about it.

Feeling pressured, Taryn caved. "Okay. When do you need me?"

"How about 9 o'clock tonight? We have a ghost hunt at 11:00 pm so you'd be finished in about an hour. And then you're welcome to come with us on the hunt. See if your camera can pick anything up?" he asked hopefully, looking like an eager puppy.

Taryn smiled. "Okay. I'll see you tonight. I can't promise that I'll be very good, though."

"You'll be terrific," Jerry assured her. "I have a feeling this will be the highlight of the weekend."

Taryn remained unconvinced.

*　　*　　*

IVY HOUSE REMAINED UNIMPRESSED by her presence. Taryn was bound and determined to make friends with it by the time she left but, at the moment, it was doing all it could to snub its nose at her. And it knew exactly what she was trying to do.

If she attempted to sketch the edge of the porch, a clump of Spanish moss would fall from the roof above and land on the exact spot that she was attempting to draw. If she noticed a particularly beautiful pattern of shadows across the curve of a column then the moment she began capturing them, clouds would suddenly block out the sun, and she'd lose it.

"I know what you're doing and you're not going to drive me away," she called out to the house, wagging her finger. "I need the money too much."

A crash rang out from the inside in answer.

When the tour groups with their history and ghost tales filed by, the house snubbed its nose at them as well. She imagined it crossing its arms and turning its back on everyone. Unlike Adena Cottage, Ivy House didn't yearn for attention or preen under watchful eyes. It wanted to be left alone.

Taryn didn't envy the people who would eventually have to work inside it for the restoration.

By the end of the afternoon she had a rough sketch of the front of the house and she was quite pleased with herself. While she worked, she'd stood under a large oak tree that offered plenty of shade, making the experience a tad more comfortable than the open lawn of Adena.

When she finished, she turned the sketch around and showed it to the house. "See? I think I did you justice."

The house seemed to consider her canvas for a moment and then, suddenly, a beautiful configuration of shadows fell across the front, providing mesmerizing contours and contrast.

Taryn laughed. "Well, you're welcome then." A woman passing by pushing a stroller with a sleepy toddler stopped in her tracks and glanced at Taryn before shaking her head in worry and quickly moving on.

"It's okay, ma'am," Taryn wanted to assure her. "I was just talking to the house." But she kept her mouth shut. If they couldn't hear it, they probably wouldn't understand.

*   *   *

SINCE SHE HAD A FEW HOURS BEFORE her speaking engagement, Taryn zipped back to her house to get ready for the evening. She needed to sort through her photos and find some that were worth sharing and discussing. Some were intensely personal to her and sharing them with anyone other than Matt felt like an invasion of privacy. Others, though, were okay. At least in a room full of amateur ghost hunters they'd probably be appreciated.

Taryn was surprised to see another vehicle in her driveway. The front door was open a crack so she knocked first before going in. When nobody answered she stepped just inside, ready to bolt in case it was someone who wanted to hit her over the head with something and drag her away.

When she heard the roar of the vacuum cleaner in the bedroom she knew she was safe. It was just the cleaning service.

Taryn let herself on into the house and closed the door behind her. Not wanting to disturb the woman who was pushing the vacuum and singing Madonna at the top of her lungs, Taryn stayed in the living room and fired up her laptop. She had thousands of photos saved on her external hard drive and it would take hours to get through all of them. She didn't have that much time. She was in desperate need of a better organization system. She tried creating folders and sub-folders and all of those good things but then she forgot what she'd labeled them.

Lost in her files, she didn't hear the roar of the vacuum stop or the footsteps coming into the living room.

"Oh my God!" the other woman screamed.

Taryn jumped a foot off the couch, knocking over the Coke that she'd set on the coffee table in front of her.

The terrified housekeeper dashed into the kitchen and returned with a roll of paper towels. Together they attempted to clean up the mess before it ran across the floor.

"I am *so* sorry," Taryn apologized. "I didn't want to bother you so I just thought I would stay in here. I figured you'd see me."

The other woman was in her mid-forties, very attractive, and had dark, curly brown hair that just skimmed her shoulders. Her face, tanned from the sun, was nearly the same shade of chocolate as her eyes.

"It's my fault," she replied as she gathered the wet paper towels in a plastic bag. "I had my ear buds in and got lost in my own little world. I'm Carla, by the way."

"Taryn," Taryn introduced herself. "And you certainly don't need to clean up after me. I can do it myself. Just sit down and take a break if you can't leave yet or whatever." The truth of the matter was, Taryn was a little embarrassed to have maid service where she was staying. At a hotel it would've been different but at the house it just felt lazy.

"You know, I don't mind if I do take a little rest," Carla laughed. "I'm trying to break in new shoes and they're killing me."

She took a seat in a chair across from Taryn and stretched her legs out in front of her. Her strappy sandals were cute but didn't look comfortable to work in.

"Gotta big date tomorrow night and wanted these all ready," she explained. "I usually wear tennis shoes but this is the only way I could get 'em turned in good."

Taryn nodded. "I understand. I collect cowboy boots. I love them but until I've worn them for a few weeks they're not the best to walk around in, especially if the heel is tall."

"So I see you're an artist," Carla said. "I saw your paint stuff."

Taryn nodded. "Yes, I am here to paint a couple of the cottages for the hotel."

"I've never met a real artist before. I mean, we get a lot of photographers in here who call themselves artists but I don't know about that," Carla said. "Seems like these days if you can afford yourself an expensive camera and editing software anyone can call themselves an artist."

Taryn knew what she meant. There were quite a few people she'd graduated from college with who were trained photographers and complained about the same thing. It was getting harder for them to make a living now since so many people were able to take their own pictures these days and make them look good.

"Some people don't exactly call *me* an artist either," Taryn explained. "They say my paintings are too literal, which is a nice way of saying I don't use my imagination and just paint things the way they are."

"Can *those* people paint?" Carla countered.

Taryn laughed. "Sometimes not."

The irony was that while Taryn might paint what was in front of her, rather than draw from inspiration, she did have to use her imagination for the majority of her work. She reconstructed things that were no longer there. But that was another can of worms.

"So do you live here on the island or do you commute?" Taryn asked.

Carla snorted and smoothed down her khaki shorts. Taryn envied her long, brown legs and decided then and there that she was going to make a better effort to get back to the beach.

"I can't afford to live here. I live over in Brunswick."

"Is it expensive here then? It's hard for me to judge since I am just a visitor."

"Housing is high," Carla said. "High here and high on St. Simon's next door. Didn't use to be. Used to be you could live in a pretty nice house with a yard for not much more than what things were going for in Brunswick. Now you pay twice, maybe three times as much."

"Who's living in these expensive homes?"

Carla grimaced and rolled her eyes. "Mostly people from out of the area. They come in and build these new developments over on St. Simon's. Put in their half million dollar homes, call them 'vacation' homes because they want to be a part of the island life, and then throw up big gates around them and close themselves off. They'd do it here, too, except they can't."

"Because it's protected?" Taryn asked.

Carla nodded. "Yeah, but they find ways around that. Did you see that big new hotel they're putting up by the water?"

Taryn said she had noticed it.

"Well, don't *even* let me get started on all the drama that's caused."

Long after Carla left, and as Taryn was going back through her pictures, she let her words replay themselves in her mind. It was interesting that the rich people were coming to the islands and buying things up. It seemed like someone was always after Jekyll and St. Simon's. The Native Americans had been there first and then they'd been run off by the first settlers. That first group had been run off by a second group, and then they'd fought for the island as well.

And then the glitterati of the nineteenth and early twentieth centuries. They'd come in and built their big fancy hotel and cottages. And now the upper middle class was taking over, building their big homes and hotels and chain restaurants.

Who else was left?

SEVEN

*T*ryn wasn't sure what she'd been expecting from the crowd of ghost hunters, but she was still surprised at what she saw.

As she looked out into the sea of faces she could feel nerves building in her stomach. The people before her were a mix of ages, races, and genders. There were more than a few elderly men and women, the ballroom lights casting ethereal lights on their white and silver hair. There were young men and women who looked college age, all appearing fashionably bored without trying to look too interested in what was going on around them. Then there were the average middle-class looking folks, mothers and fathers with rounded bellies, fanny packs, and coffees. Most of the audience members were dressed in regular clothing, slacks or shorts with sandals and pullovers. There were a few alternative members, however, and they stood out in their black tights, red and green streaks through their hair, and multiple piercings.

Apparently, there was no stereotype for ghost hunting. It was a free for all.

Taryn stood to the side of the small stage and waited while her introductions were made.

"Ladies and gentleman," Jerry, the man she'd met in the coffee shop earlier, announced, "I'd like you all to offer a warm welcome to Taryn Magill. Taryn is a special kind of psychic and we are all grateful to have her here with us tonight. Not only can Taryn act as a medium with the spirit world around us, she can also see it and capture it with her digital camera. She's helped solve several cases with her skills and has been written about in numerous publications. I'm sure you all are as excited as I am that she's with us now!"

And, the thing was, the audience *did* look excited to have her there.

Taryn stepped up to the microphone, her hands shaking. She didn't want to let anyone down and hoped she'd be as interesting as they were expecting her to be.

"Hi guys," she began. "I'm real excited to be here tonight. I brought some pictures to share with you all but I wanted to start by telling you a little bit about myself. In spite of the lovely introduction, I don't think I am a psychic or a medium. Most of what I've been able to do has been thanks to my camera and I am sure that, without it, I wouldn't be here today."

The audience members watched her and Taryn was startled to realize they were hanging onto her every word.

"The thing is," she continued, "I have always loved old houses. Old houses, old stores, old train stations...if it was built before I was born I'm almost certain to feel a bond with it. I think these buildings have stories to tell and even souls of their own. Maybe they get them from our energy or maybe, as they're built, they can create their own. But I've always felt a connection with them."

She could see a few people in the front nodding their heads in agreement. Sensing kindred spirits, Taryn felt her nerves ease up.

"In my job I recreate structures that are usually in disrepair. I help restore them to their former glory through my art. I've always had a huge imagination and been able to visualize these structures. Well, I took a lot of historical preservation and architecture classes in college, too. Those helped."

The audience gave her a round of polite laughter and Taryn's ears reddened.

"The best part about what I do is that now I can actually see some of the things I've imagined for years. And I guess, in a way, *that* part is a gift," she finished.

For the next half hour Taryn showed them more than twenty-five photographs, all featuring before and after shots of rooms that had once been bare and then suddenly filled with remnants from its past. She watched and listened as the onlookers gasped, laughed, and shook their heads in awe. Never before had Taryn felt so comfortable talking about this part of her life, expect for when she spoke to Matt and their mutual friend Rob. The people there were all strangers to her, but she could tell they were totally invested and interested in what she had to say.

When she was finished Jerry opened up the floor to questions and brought Taryn a chair to sit in on the stage while she answered them.

The first question was from a young woman in a long peasant skirt and hair that reached her waist. She had a loud, booming voice that carried across the room with ease. "Have you always been able to see and communicate with spirts?"

Taryn shook her head no. "This started fairly recently. A friend, and someone who is kind of an expert on these things, believes my thirtieth birthday might have been a factor. I did have some experiences as a child but I'd forgotten about them and written several off as something else."

The next question came from an elderly gentleman. His wife helped him stand and then continued holding his hand as he spoke. "Can you talk to the spirits yourself? Do they answer you?" His voice shook and he looked on the verge of tears. Taryn was troubled by the way his eyes bore into her, pleading.

"I don't know," she answered honestly. "I don't think some of them were actual spirits. I think they may have been leftover energy. But there have been others I communicated with and, at the time, it felt like they could understand me."

He continued to stand while his whole body quivered. "We lost our grandson in a fire last November. Have you ever tried contacting anyone on purpose?"

The hopeful look on his face just about broke Taryn's heart. She hadn't planned on that kind of question. "I've tried," she admitted. "I think it did work once, but it may have just been a coincidence. I lost my husband, well, my fiancé really, and I would like to contact him as well. I understand how you feel."

He nodded his head in disappointment and then slid back into his chair. Taryn watched as his wife wrapped her arm around him and nestled her head on his shoulder.

"Does this happen everywhere you go?" someone shouted from the back of the room.

"No," Taryn replied. "Not everywhere. And not even every time at the same place. For instance, I might take a picture of this room and see a party set up from one hundred years ago. An hour later I might stand in the same spot, take the same picture, and get nothing but an empty room."

"Can you try it and see?" Jerry asked, smiling.

Taryn bit her lip. If it didn't work, would they think her a fraud? She'd already taken dozens of pictures in the hotel and none of them had been unusual.

The rapturous applause following his question left her no choice. Jerry gestured to someone in the back and the overhead lights were flipped on, filling the room with artificial sunlight. "You're on the spot now, Miss Dixie," Taryn whispered as she turned her camera on. "No pressure."

Standing on the stage and facing the audience, Taryn aimed her camera at the middle of the room and snapped. She took three pictures in total, trying to visualize the past as she did. The ballroom was original to the first hotel. Although many people had died in the ballroom, it had been from smoke inhalation and not from flames. The flames had only destroyed one end of it, the end the stage was located on, since that's the part that was connected to the hotel. The rest had been damaged by smoke and water, but salvaged and restored.

As the audience waited impatiently, Taryn removed her memory card and inserted it into her laptop. Within moments the pictures had uploaded and they were looking at them on the big screen. The lights were dimmed again.

As the first image appeared the audience caught a glimpse of themselves from Taryn's viewpoint. The room was bright and cheerful, the expressions on people's faces nervous and excited.

In the next image, the round tables full of cardboard coffee cups, Coke cans, and digital cameras were a little harder to see. The room was darker, the expressions on faces difficult to make out.

At first, Taryn wasn't sure what she was looking at in the third. The tables were still there and still covered with drinks. The digital cameras had been replaced by plates and silverware, however. The audience was no longer standing. Some were running, some were lying limply on the ground, and some were clawing at their throats, eyes bulging and tongues protruding as they screamed in vain.

The excited and nervous expressions on their faces had been exchanged for sheer terror.

TARYN WAS SITTING AT THE BAR in the hotel lobby, sipping on a whiskey, when the elderly gentleman approached her. He was moving slowly, as though every step took effort, and his wife stayed at his side, holding onto his elbow. They walked in tandem, their movements together as fluid as water.

"Hello there young lady," he said as they neared her. "We've been looking for you."

"I needed a little something before going home," she apologized. She wondered how it looked, her sitting there alone at a bar with two whiskey glasses in front of her. She was already halfway finished with her second.

"Nothing wrong with a little something to whet your whistle," he said approvingly.

"Did you not want to go on the ghost hunt?" Taryn asked with a smile. Jerry had asked her to come along with them but she felt like she'd had enough excitement for the night.

"Oh no, no," the gentleman replied. "I'll just leave that to the young folks. I was wondering if, well..." His voice trailed off and his face flushed with embarrassment.

"He wants to know if you can try to contact our grandson," his wife offered. She lovingly ran her hand up his arm and smiled at him. "We've been to a psychic but she wasn't able to communicate with him. Bob has a good feeling about you, though."

"Oh, I don't know," Taryn answered. She didn't want to disappoint them and felt like if she tried contacting their grandson and failed it would be heartbreaking for all of them. "I've never tried for someone I don't know, just myself. I don't think I'd be any good at it."

"Please." It was one word and not even a question but the gentleman's desperation bled through. There was no way Taryn could refuse.

"I'll try," she vowed. "Do you have something of his?"

"Yes," the woman nodded. "In our room. If you'll come with us..."

Taryn finished off her drink, paid the bartender, and then set off with the couple. "I'm Charlene," Bob's wife said as they made their way down a long, thickly-carpeted corridor. "We've been married for fifty-five years. We come here every summer. Been coming for twenty-something years."

"We used to bring the grandkids," Bob explained with a slight smile. He stopped in front of a door and fished for his room key in his pants pocket. "After Timmy passed away, though, none of the others wanted to come back. He was the heart of our family, the one who kept us all going. This was his place. The others didn't care as much."

Charlene bobbed her head in agreement, her eyes watering. "We were given a gift with him. Everyone knew it. Our family hasn't been the same since."

"How old was he?" Taryn asked as they filed into the bedroom.

The room was extraordinarily neat. If not for the house shoes at the end of the bed and an Agatha Christie novel on the nightstand it wouldn't have been obvious anyone was staying in it. Taryn thought of the hurricane that she normally left behind in her wake and grinned. She really *could* make a mess in a short amount of time.

"He was eleven," Charlene replied. From the closet she produced a small framed picture while Bob picked up something from one of the room's wing-backed chairs. He returned to Taryn holding a stuffed neon orange elephant.

"This was his," he explained thinly, handing the stuffed animal to her. "Our daughter gave it to us. It's one of the few things that made it out of the fire."

Taryn balanced on the edge of their bed and studied the picture while holding the elephant in her lap. Timmy had been an elfin child with a sweet smile, slight build, and prominent ears. In the picture he leaned against a tree with a puppy at his feet.

"What happened?"

"His parents were out for the night and had hired a babysitter," Charlene said when it became clear that Bob wasn't going to answer. "It was cold and his room was drafty. The sitter put a space heater at the foot of his bed. He must have kicked off the covers in the middle of the night. A blanket landed on the heater, and it caught fire."

"I keep seeing him trying to get out the door," Bob mumbled, his eyes filling with tears. It had swollen shut so it would've been impossible to open it. "I see him crying and pulling at the knob."

"It keeps him up at night," Charlene added. Her own eyes were reddening as well. "He has trouble sleeping."

"What did the investigator say?" Taryn asked. "Was there any way to determined how he died? Where his body was, maybe?" Taryn felt horrible for asking the questions but the more she knew the more it might help.

Bob shook his head. "Our daughter didn't want to know the details. She was distraught. Her breakdown was so great that she had to be heavily medicated to attend the funeral. We don't want to ask her any questions. She's doing better now."

Taryn nodded. She understood. She hadn't wanted to know the details of Andrew's car wreck either but often wondered how long he'd suffered. She'd nearly driven herself insane imagining him lying on the side of the road, bleeding to death or even burning to death, while he waited for help. She'd never asked because she was afraid of the answers. It *was* enough to drive a person crazy.

Gesturing for the couple to have a seat on the chairs, Taryn stood up and placed the elephant on the bed. She propped the picture up beside him. Taryn sat down on the floor and made herself as comfortable as possible.

After turning Miss Dixie "on" Taryn closed her eyes and tried to focus on Timmy. It wasn't easy for Taryn to clear her mind, thanks to all the rubbish that danced around in her head at all times, but she imagined a blank screen and worked from there. Little by little she brought Timmy's face onto the screen. She focused on his sweet smile, his little hands, and his pointy ears. She saw him holding the elephant in his arms, his body tucked into the blankets.

Soon, the air around her began to change. It was a slight difference at first, just a small rise in temperature. Little beads of sweat began forming on her forehead, a warm flush spread throughout her body. It warmed the tips of her fingers, the ends of her toes, and filled her stomach like hot apple cider. Then the air was heavier, more concentrated around her. She found herself struggling to catch her breath, as though something heavy was sitting on her chest.

When she found herself beginning to panic Taryn opened her eyes, lifted Miss Dixie, and snapped a picture of the bed. One, two, three times she snapped. Something then, instinct maybe, had her turning to Bob and Charlene. Pointing the camera at them, she took one last shot before the air exploded from her chest and sent her reeling backward in a coughing fit.

"Are you okay?" Charlene cried, rushing to her side.

Taryn felt like her whole body was on fire. The fever coursing through her was still strong, her heart still racing. Slowly, as Charlene stroked her back, coolness washed over her. Her heavy breathing subsided and she was left lying on the floor, shivering like a fool.

"I'm sorry," Taryn apologized as she unsteadily rose to her feet. "I don't know what happened."

"It got damned hot in here for a minute, I can tell you that," Bob proclaimed.

"I don't know if I got anything or not," Taryn warned them, "but I'll look."

It didn't take long to find out.

The first shot of the bed was a perfectly normal one, if perhaps a little blurry. The orange elephant and picture were exactly where she placed them. In the second picture, however, a small boy lay on the pillow, his little arms wound tightly around the stuffed animal. The blanket sported a superhero image, not the generic hotel floral. In the third image the boy was still in the bed. The blanket was no longer on him, however; it had fallen to the floor. Flames encircled the bed, clawing at the ceiling and licking the walls. Thick, billowy smoke formed a cloud above and reached its tendril arms downward. Even in the somewhat grainy image you could see the boy's coloring had turned to pale blue. His eyes were still shut.

He had not died trying to escape. He had never been aware of what was happening to him.

As the implication hit Bob and Charlene they collapsed against one another. One of them, and Taryn was never sure which (and it could very well have been her), let out a sob.

They all grew still, however, when Taryn flipped to the last picture.

Bob and Charlene sat in the standard hotel room chairs. Both looked serious, anticipation on their faces. Charlene's hands were folded tightly in her lap. Bob's left leg was crossed over his right.

And between them, one hand on each shoulder, stood a small boy.

EIGHT

*S*till reeling from the events at the hotel, the ride back *to her* house was a sober one.

She'd left Bob and Charlene sitting on their bed, holding their grandson's picture. She'd waited until they'd stopped crying but the stark, wild looks in their eyes had almost been worse. She hoped that, in time, what they'd seen would bring them some amount of comfort.

One thing was for sure, however: Taryn was not cut out to be a professional psychic. She supposed that at the end of the day crossing off a prospective career choice was fairly productive.

It was after midnight as she chugged along the dark road in her little golf cart. She was the only vehicle on the road and felt silly for not driving her car. She also felt completely exposed; the sensation was unsettling. She'd had no idea how much comfort and sense of safety her vehicle offered with its enclosure. Although she liked the feel of the wind in her hair and the night air on her skin, there was little separating her from the outside world, and sometimes Taryn wanted that separation, that disconnection.

Lost in thought, she almost didn't see the faint flashing light as she pulled into her driveway. A second later and she would've rammed right into the cyclist and sent him flying through the air. As it was, she managed to slam on her brakes and swerve to avoid hitting him.

The crash of metal against pavement sickened her. Praying that nobody was hurt Taryn jumped out and ran towards the heap on the ground.

"Am I alive?" came the low moan.

"Oh my God, oh my God," Taryn chanted as she squatted down and took stock of the situation. A young man with long black hair down to his waist lay sprawled on the side of the road. His legs were twisted under his bike but his helmet was still on.

"I don't think I'm broken. Can you help me move the bike?" he asked.

Taryn gingerly pulled it out from under him and then helped him to his feet. He towered over her small frame and even in the darkness she could see the tight mass of muscles on his bare legs and arms. Dark spots had formed on his right knee and elbow, and she could smell the blood from where she stood.

"I am sooo sorry," she apologized. She could feel hot tears springing to her eyes; she thought she'd just about rather die than hurt someone. "I was daydreaming or something. I just didn't expect anyone to be out riding this late."

"Yeah, it's my fault," he said, dusting himself off and wincing. His accent was something she wasn't sure she'd ever heard before, curiously flat and yet still somehow musical. "I saw you coming and saw your turn signal and for some reason thought I could beat you."

"Well here, come inside and I'll give you some Band-Aids and something to drink," she offered. She knew she should've been concerned about having a strange man inside her house at that hour but since she'd almost killed him, it was the least she could do.

"Yeah, if you don't mind," he said gratefully.

Taryn waited while he walked the bike up to her porch. It looked okay, nothing damaged or broken, but he limped. Taryn was filled with guilt.

Once inside he made himself at home in her living room while she scurried around to find the Band-Aids, ointment, and a wet cloth. By the time she made it back to him the blood was dripping down his leg and arm and he was using a red bandana to mop it up.

"Here, this might help," she said, handing him the cloth. "I'll go get you something to drink. Coke okay?"

"That's fine," he replied. "We're connected now, you know."

Taryn stopped in her tracks and turned back around to face him. "Huh?"

"Your arm there."

Taryn glanced down and saw streaks blood on her arm. It was his.

"We've shared blood. So we're connected not," he smiled weakly.

He'd cleaned himself up and removed his helmet by the time she returned. His hair was longer than it had looked outside and reminded her of a sheet of black, glossy metal. From his dark skin and dark eyes, she pegged him as Native American, although she wasn't good at determining individual tribes. He looked around thirty years old, although his face was rugged, and his leathery hands could have made him older than he looked. Taryn could always appreciate a good-looking man, and this was one fine specimen.

She might have had a boyfriend, but she was human.

"So what *were* you doing out riding this late?" she asked, sitting down on a chair across from him. "And I'm Taryn, by the way."

"I like getting to know a place in all its clothing," he explained, wincing as he cleaned the wound. "It's difficult to get a feel for it if you only see it illuminated. Things change at night, don't you think?"

Taryn knew what he meant but still thought riding after dark was pushing it. "Couldn't you have gotten a feel for it in a nice air-conditioned car?"

The man chuckled revealing perfectly straight white teeth, a stark contrast to his dark skin. His laughter was melodious. "You're not connected to anything in a car. You can't feel the wind, smell the air, and *feel* the lay of the land under you."

Taryn shivered as she remembered the fact that she'd been thinking almost exactly the same thing right before she saw him.

"Oh, and I'm David. Do you live here year round?"

"No, I'm just here doing a job for the hotel. Just staying in this house until I'm finished. I take it you're here on vacation?" she asked.

"I'm here for work too, in a sense," David replied. "I work for the National Nonprofit for the Preservation of Native Lands. We call it the PNL."

"Is there a preservation effort going on here?" Taryn asked, surprised. She hadn't heard anything about it yet although, granted, she hadn't been out much.

"Not yet, but that's why I'm here. The Golden Isles haven't been as excavated as one might think. There was a problem over on St. Simon's awhile back, and now we're trying to ensure that it doesn't happen again," he explained.

Something clicked in Taryn's mind. "And with the new hotel development going up..."

"Right," he nodded. "We just want to make sure it's all going by the book and nothing gets disturbed that shouldn't be."

"Like they build their Holiday Inn or whatever it's going to be on top of an Indian burial ground," Taryn laughed. "I got you."

"You wouldn't believe how often that actually happens," David said ruefully. "Of course, it's better now than it used to be."

"How long will you be here?"

David shrugged. "As long as it takes to convince my boss that everything looks okay. They just started breaking ground two days ago. So far, so good. They're working with us well enough. I've talked to the site manager, Douglas Everson, a few times and he wants to do it all by the book. Things can change, though. People can get greedy when it comes to making deadlines and earning money."

Taryn knew that well enough. She'd seen people do all sorts of crazy things for money.

"So what's your job here?" he asked.

Taryn felt comfortable talking to him. He reminded her of Matt, perhaps because of the Native American connection. Matt also had Italian in him but had always looked more Indian to her. She briefly filled David in on her job at the hotel, omitting any of the supernatural elements.

"That's very interesting," he said when she concluded her spiel. "So I guess we're both here to do a little of the same–preserve the past."

Taryn smiled, happy to meet a cohort. "To the past," she said, raising her Coke can in the air.

David raised his as well. "And keeping it alive," he added.

Taryn shivered, chills racing up and down her arms. What was it her grandmother used to say?

Someone just walked over your grave...

*   *   *

IT WAS NEARLY THREE IN THE MORNING by the time she and David stopped talking. He'd resisted her offer to drive him and his bike home, claiming he was just staying a few houses down.

"We're neighbors," he'd smiled and she'd blushed.

The thought of him being so close by was both comforting and unsettling. On the one hand, she liked the idea of someone she could get along with being nearby, on the other hand she felt disloyal to Matt since that "someone" was so good looking.

Unable to sleep, and with Matt on her mind, Taryn sat down and composed an email to him. She could've waited and told him all about her evening when she talked to him later, but sometimes she preferred getting her thoughts down on paper. They'd been exchanging notes since they were in elementary school, often getting in trouble with their teachers for not paying attention in class. In fact, they'd been writing to one another for so long that sometimes she found herself composing mental notes to Matt, letters he'd never receive, as a way of processing what was going on around her. In many ways, Matt was her second brain in the same way that Miss Dixie was her second set of eyes.

Taryn found she still couldn't sleep, even after she was finished. There was nothing on television but infomercials and movies about animals taking over the world. She wasn't opposed to either (indeed, *Night of the Lepus* was one of her favorite truly bad horror films and her Magic Bullet was her favorite small appliance) but she wasn't in the mood for either.

Too tired to get out the canvases and paints and then clean it all up later she popped Miss Dixie's memory card into her laptop for some photo editing.

Ignoring the pictures she'd taken in Bob's hotel room because she just wasn't ready to face them yet, she brought up some of shots she'd taken earlier that evening. She'd use some of the shots of the audience in the ballroom for her website. She wasn't a great public speaker but some people made good money doing gigs. If she ever wanted to pay off her student loans then *she* might have to start doing them as well and just get over herself.

The rest of her pictures were of the hotel. They weren't great, but she hadn't been trying for professional shots, just something for herself and her scrapbook.

The hotel's entrance looked grand in the late evening sky. The wraparound porch was lined with white wicker furniture with bright red seat cushions; she could almost hear it calling out to guests to sit for a spell and sip on ice-cold lemonade. The steps leading up to the porch were flanked with potted flower arrangements, the blossoms spilling over their containers in colorful cascades. The lush green ferns that hung from the ceiling offered vibrant contrasts to the hotel's pristine white.

It was picture perfect, in spite of the pun, and every bit as lovely as the spreads she'd seen in magazines.

Still, something bothered her, but she couldn't put her finger on it. Maybe she was just tired.

"Shame that Steve's picture didn't turn out," she said aloud as she flipped through the ones taken of the exterior. She'd had a problem with Miss Dixie while he posed for her at his valet stand, all *GQ* smiles and apple pie dimples. The photo was missing completely now; there wasn't even a blurred or distorted version for her to study.

She liked Steve. He was handsome in an obvious, popular high school boy kind of way. He was also friendly and had a bit of a mischievous air about him too, though, and she appreciated that. He was the kind of man she could appreciate from afar, almost too perfect to truly take seriously.

David, though...David could be an issue. She felt her skin prickle just thinking about him.

Taryn was already up and starting into the kitchen for another drink when she realized what had been bugging her. Racing back to the desk she pulled up the pictures of the hotel again and began flipping through them. Nothing looked out of the ordinary. There was absolutely nothing foreboding or peculiar about any of her shots.

Or, at least, there wouldn't have been to most people.

As Taryn stared at them a second time, however, she saw that it wasn't just *Steve* missing from the pictures...his valet stand was missing as well. In the stand's current location there was now an enormous marble potting container, perennials spilling from it. And the bright red seat cushions on the white wicker furniture? They'd been blue for the past week.

Taryn realized then that she was *not* looking at the hotel as it was today, but as it had looked before the fire. For more than a dozen shots, Miss Dixie had transported her back to 1907.

*   *   *

SHE WAS FALLING THROUGH SPACE AND TIME, her body light as a feather. The weightlessness was alarming at first but soon Taryn grew fascinated by it and stretched out her arms to feel the air rushing past her. She was flying and reveled in the new freedom it brought.

Surrounded by darkness, she could see nothing. The blackness was thick and impenetrable, but its coolness was invigorating.

But suddenly she felt herself not flying but falling—spiraling downwards so quickly that she flailed her arms and clawed at the air, reaching for something she couldn't touch. When she landed on the hard floor, her head rattled and her bottom ached from the impact. Surely, if this were a dream, she would awaken. She'd never hit the ground in a dream before.

Am I dead now, she wondered to herself as she attempted to gain her bearings. Andrew, her parents, and her grandmother were nowhere to be seen, however.

Still, Taryn didn't recognize the space around her. It was still dark, but a trail of light filtered through a tiny hole, and revealed a patch of pine floor beneath her. She crawled towards the opening and put her face against it. It was a keyhole. On the other side she could see a large four-poster bed, a coverlet turned down neatly and an old-fashioned porcelain doll placed primly against a fluffy pillow. A fire burned cheerfully in the hearth, but the warmth didn't reach her. She was chilled and damp and suddenly realized with embarrassment that her bottom was wet, as though she'd sat in something. It smelled of urine.

Taryn felt around the space at once and exhaled with relief when her hand landed on a knob. To her dismay, however, when she turned it, nothing happened. It was locked.

Fear began creeping into her heart and as she pounded on the door in front of her, she found herself crying out for someone she didn't know. Taryn had always been a little claustrophobic, but this was much different. The small universe was closing in on her, and the suffocation threatened to seal her throat, making breathing difficult. Choking, she gasped for air, clawing at her skin and chest and brushing the rough fabric that clung to her aside.

NINE

*T*ryn had decided to allow herself one meal out a day.

Today, as a reward for getting up bright and early, that meal would be breakfast. She was actually enjoying grocery shopping in Brunswick and cooking in the house's modern, clean kitchen but sometimes a girl just didn't want to clean up after herself.

The small restaurant was attached to a hotel but it offered some of her favorite things: pancakes, biscuits, and grits. Her server was an older woman, Taryn judged her to be in her late sixties, and she was chatty.

When Taryn ordered nothing more than a pancake and sausage link, the server pursed her lips. "You sure you don't want something else to eat?" she asked dubiously.

"Later I'll probably regret not eating more but right now I'm still trying to wake up," Taryn explained.

The server didn't look convinced and shook her head as she walked away.

When she returned with Taryn's food she lingered for a moment. "You here on vacation?"

"Sort of," Taryn answered. "Kind of a working vacation."

"You been to Driftwood Beach yet? You should if you haven't."

Taryn nodded. "I went the other day, but I need to go back and take some more pictures. Is there anything else I should see while I'm here?"

"A lot of people like taking those guided tours. They do one of the historic area and a ghost tour, too. You might like that."

Taryn smothered butter and syrup all over her pancake and watched it sink in. "I've heard the ghost story about Mary the Wanderer. And about Ivy House being haunted. Are there other stories I should know?"

The server, whose nametag read "Eldean," nodded. "Oh yes, we have lots of ghosts here. Let's see...there's the pirate ship that sails up and down the island. They supposedly buried their treasure here and now can't remember where they put it. And then there are the ghosts of the Horton House. You can still hear drinking parties going on inside of it at night. Of course you know about Mary...What else? Oh! You might like the story about the haunted grave."

"The haunted grave?"

"Yes, that one is my favorite," Eldean smiled.

"Well let's hear that one," Taryn said. "If you have the time. I don't want to hold you up."

Eldean shrugged. "It's okay. Slow morning."

Making sure nobody was looking, she pulled up a chair and scooted in closer to Taryn. "So you know the story about William and how he murdered his wife and burnt the original hotel down?"

"Yes, I've heard that. And he was hung for his crimes, right?"

Eldean bobbed her head, her hair barely moving from all the Aqua Net holding it in place (Taryn had been around in the 1980s–she'd know that starchy fragrance anywhere). "Yes. Well, apparently while he was in jail he complained to anyone who would listen that he'd promised his wife never to leave her alone."

"Shouldn't he have thought about that before he killed her?" Taryn asked.

"That's what I've always said. At any rate, I guess he put up such a fuss that the jailer finally felt sorry for him. So each night up until the day he was hung Juniper, that was the jailer's name, carted William all the way across the island to her grave. When he got there William would light a candle and leave it burning. After he was hung, the light kept appearing from out of nowhere. Even now, on some nights, if you go over there you can still see the glow."

In spite of all the ghost stories Taryn had heard, she was chilled by the tale. It struck her as...sad. "Well that's kind of a nice story," she said at last.

Eldean stood to her feet and pushed back a lock of silver hair. "Yeah, I always thought so. If you take away the fact that he killed her and then committed arson to one of the nicest hotels in the south, it's almost a love story."

*   *   *

ADENA COTTAGE WAS HAPPY to see her, Taryn could feel it the moment she stepped from the golf cart, but she offered no clues that afternoon.

Taryn started off her day by walking around and taking more pictures. Though she studied her LCD screen after every shot, she was disappointed to find that they all came out normal–no shadows, no furniture that shouldn't be there, and no men or women sitting on the porch sipping their lemonade or tea or whatever it was they used to drink. Taryn was frustrated but that's just the way the ball rolled sometimes.

She got the feeling that Ivy House was glad to see her pass by. She'd felt the old cottage glaring in her direction as she'd zipped past it, barely tossing it a glance.

"Yeah, well, I'll get back to you later," she'd mumbled when it was out of ear shot. She was still determined to make that house like her, although it felt like a losing battle.

She spent most of the afternoon trying to find the shade. Too much sun caused her paint to thin and run, and that was making a mess. There were three trees in front of Adena and she'd been under all three of them, chasing the protection, if not the cool, of the shade they offered. She was about to wrap things up for the day when she heard the footsteps approaching her.

"Hey there," came the friendly voice behind her.

Paintbrush in hand, Taryn turned and saw Steve coming up behind her. "Hey," she called back.

His curly hair was frizzy from the humidity and she could see sweat stains on his gray T-shirt. He looked like he'd been out walking for a long time.

"I wanted to come say hello and see how you were doing," he explained as he drew nearer.

He stood by her easel for a moment and studied her painting and then broke out into a huge smile of admiration. "It's totally awesome! I mean it. How do you know what it used to look like?"

"A lot of research," she replied. "I've looked at the other cottages, studied the architectural style in books and online–you know, stuff like that. And I have a good imagination."

It wasn't the time or place to mention Miss Dixie.

"Well, it looks great. Hope they're paying you well," he said.

Taryn felt like he might be fishing for information, but she wasn't one to usually share income since it tended to cause more trouble than not. Instead, she just smiled. "Well, you know, it's not going to make me rich anytime soon but it pays the bills. Mostly. So what are you doing out today?"

"Oh, I have the afternoon off." Steve studied the ground for fire ant mounds and then plopped down at her feet and leaned back against the tree trunk. "Wasn't ready to go home so I thought I'd just take myself for a walk."

"Do you live around here?"

Now that she'd been interrupted it would be difficult to regain her momentum. She didn't mind stopping, though, so Taryn began putting away her supplies. She wrapped her brushes in wax paper and bound them with a rubber band. She'd wash them when she got back to the house.

"Ha," he snorted. "I live over in Brunswick. Just on the outskirts of the ghetto."

"I didn't know Brunswick had a ghetto," Taryn smiled. She'd been over there to go to Target and Walmart. It looked a lot like any other medium-sized southern town she'd been in. She'd heard good things about the downtown historic district but hadn't been there yet.

"That's just what I call it," he retorted. "It sucks being poor."

"Well, I can agree with what," Taryn said.

After following his lead and examining the ground for fire ant hills, she lowered herself to his side. In close proximity he smelled of some kind of young man's cologne and sweat. It wasn't an unpleasant odor at all. If she'd been about five years younger then his pretty face, lean build, and confidence were exactly the kinds of traits that would've attracted her.

"When I was a kid things didn't cost so much," he muttered. "Now it feels like only the rich people get to live on the islands or visit them."

"That's kind of the way they started though, wasn't it?" Taryn asked. "I mean after the settlers took over. It's kind of always been a rich man's playground."

"Yeah, maybe," he agreed reluctantly. "But it wasn't always as exclusive if you know what I mean. Have you seen the big gates going up on St. Simon's?"

She shook her head no. She hadn't been over there yet.

"Well, people come down from the north or over from Atlanta because they want to live on 'island time.' Then they build these big houses on top of each other and put up gates to, I don't know, protect themselves from the other rich people I guess," he snarked.

Taryn laughed in spite of herself. "People can be funny," she said. "Someone else was telling me the same thing."

"Sometimes it feels like no matter how hard I try I just can't get ahead," he complained.

"I know what you mean," Taryn said, patting him on the knee. "For me it's always felt like one step forward and two steps back. Have you thought about going someplace else with better job opportunities? Savannah maybe? Or Atlanta?"

"Atlanta is being run over with basketball players and rappers," Steve muttered. "Savannah's cool but, you know, I got my mama here. She's not doing so well. Going through chemo at the moment. Cancer started in her female parts but now it's all over."

"Oh, I'm sorry," Taryn said sympathetically. "That's difficult. I watched my grandmother get sick and pass away. It was awful. I was there when they removed the ventilator and feeding tube. I prayed she'd go right then but she held on another day. She was always a fighter. She basically raised me so I kind of know what you mean. I didn't want to leave her either."

"I always thought I'd do great things, and she'd be proud of me," he sighed. "But it doesn't look like she's going to see that."

"Well, you're a bright, intelligent young man," Taryn said. "It's not too late for you yet. I'd keep your eyes out for a better opportunity. Something is bound to come your way."

"Yeah," Steve said, a wry smile on his face. "I hope so. I really do."

*　　*　　*

The crowd gathered 'round was dense, and the current of excitement that ran through them was palpable.

As the bodies closed in tightly around her, she found herself fighting to push through, to get to the front. Nobody appeared to pay her struggle any mind or move aside for her. Instead, they just seemed to squeeze closer together, forming a wall of limbs and torsos.

She knew that the reason they gathered was for something bad, but had no idea why or how she knew it. She just knew that she had to make it to the front. On and on she pushed forward, arms outstretched, a frantic energy inside of her that drove her wild with anticipation. Time was of the essence.

Finally, up ahead, she could see the short stone wall, the wooden planks atop it. And then the man appeared. She knew it was a man because he wore trousers. And although she couldn't see his head for the covering wrapped tightly over his face, she knew it was her husband.

Anger surged inside of her now, anger and hatred as she stared at the small platform. The excitement of the crowd now coursed through her own body and lit her afire.

As the long rope was slipped around his neck the people around her cheered out, their voices reaching up into the sky as one. Some moved forward and were pushed back by guards waving pistols in the air, threatening them. Their movements pushed her forward as well, but nobody shooed her away. They seemed not even to notice her at all.

As the voice merged into a single chant, steadily growing and growing until it became too much for her, she raised her hands and covered her ears.

And then, in one swift movement, the bottom was opened. She watched as her once beloved descended with a jolt, his legs frantically kicking back and forth as though he were running through air. A deep gurgling noise came from the cloth over his face; even through the deafening noise of the crowd she could hear it.

She was so close to him that she could reach out her arms and touch his legs as they dangled there, trying to locate a foothold they'd never find. And she did that now—she reached out her hand to grasp his foot. As she watched in horror, however, her hand slipped right through it; it was nothing but fog.

She tried again, this time with more urgency. He'd stopped moving now, and she simply wanted to feel him one last time. But, again, her hand melted through the solidity of his body.

In horror, she snatched her hand away and turned to face the crowd. The scream she let out rose above their chants and cheering, it carried itself up into the sky and wrapped around the trees and clouds and burst onto the rays of the sun.

But nobody could hear her. She was dead.

TEN

T *he soft breeze was cool on her cheeks, a welcomed relief from* the house's stuffiness.

Sometime during the night, probably about the time she was watching someone drop to their death from a noose in her dream, her air conditioning went out. With the interior temperature steadily climbing to 95 degrees she had no desire to cozy down under the covers and sleep in. In fact, Taryn thought it might be awhile before she wanted to sleep again.

Like many of her dreams, this one had felt too real. She'd felt the surge of energy from the crowd, smelled their sweat and excitement, saw the glint of anticipation in their eyes...it hadn't been pleasant.

Now, however, on her bicycle, she rode across the island on the well-marked bike path, the wind whipping her hair back out of her face. In the clear light of day everything looked so much brighter and friendlier. It was hard to believe there was anything malevolent or evil in the world when the sun was out and there wasn't a cloud in the sky.

It was true what they said about riding a bike. She had barely lost her balance in the half hour she'd been on it.

Soon Taryn passed the construction site and group of trailers that acted as temporary storefronts. She passed the roundabout and convention center and chain motels and found herself bordered by trees, not a building in sight.

Proud of herself for riding as far as she'd gone, even if it wasn't a difficult ride since the whole island didn't rise more than four feet, Taryn pedaled onwards. She didn't have a particular destination in mind; she just wanted to feel the island around her and to see how far she could go.

On her iPod she plugged in Angaleena Presley and sang along with "Ain't No Man" as loud as she could. Nobody was around to hear her sing off-key. When the road came up to a water tower on her right Taryn slowed down. There were three cars pulled off to the side of the road across from it and a small sandy path wound through the trees.

"Huh," Taryn mused, popping her earbuds out and turning off her iPod. "I wonder if this is another way to get to Glory Beach."

Since nobody was there to answer her, she walked her bike across the road and leaned it up against a tree. There had to be something through the trees, or else there wouldn't have been cars pulled over to the side like that.

Grabbing Miss Dixie and a water bottle from her bike's basket she began trudging up the sandy path, momentarily taking comfort in the brief shade the trees overhead offered her. She was going to be in shape by the time she left; she swore it. She was already venturing farther and farther every day and that *had* to be worth something, right?

When she reached a rise, she clamored upwards and huffed and puffed until she reached the top and then Taryn stopped in her tracks, her mouth slackening.

It was quite possibly the most beautiful sight she'd ever seen.

Before her the white sandy beach stretched on for what looked like miles without a single soul in view. There were no children on picnic blankets, no coolers filled with soft drinks and sandwiches, no shirtless fishermen with tanned skin and dirty hats...nothing but her and the water.

The dunes rose up around here, some of them flanked with poles that documented sea turtle eggs. Signs were posted to keep off the dunes, but they were the only signs of human activity. Wherever the other vehicles' occupants were, she couldn't see them. She had the entire place to herself.

Shaking with happiness, Taryn flew down the embankment like a little girl, losing her sandals along the way. By the time she reached the water's edge her eyes were burning brightly and her cheeks hurt from the force of her wide grin. With her feet planted firmly in the water, she closed her eyes and let the ocean lap at her ankles, shifting the sand beneath her feet and digging her deeper and deeper into the earth. The winds were night and somewhere above her a kingfisher squawked in unsteady flight. She ignored it.

When she nearly lost her balance, Taryn walked along the water's edge, kicking at the crystal clear waves as they broke on the shore. There were sand dollars in abundance on the ground–the first time she'd ever seen any outside of a tourist shop. She was squatting down to collect one when a voice called out from behind her.

"Taryn!"

Startled, she turned around, annoyed at having her peace interrupted. She softened when she saw David's long black hair and tanned arms swinging in the sun.

Yeah, well, I guess he can come here too, she thought wryly.

"It's the best place on the island, isn't it?" he asked as he drew nearer.

"So far," she agreed. "I can't believe nobody's here."

"Yeah, well, it seems to be off the beaten path," he shrugged. "I've been coming out here about every day. Sometimes I run into people from the Sea Turtle Center, checking on the eggs."

"So what are you up to today?" Since her peace was broken she figured she might as well enjoy the company. In fact, now that he was close to her, she felt her blood bubbling.

Stop it, she commanded herself. *He's just a man and you've already got a very nice one.*

"I have a meeting with the site manager over at the hotel in about two hours," he replied. "I've gone over my notes so many times that I'm starting to forget them. I needed to get out for awhile."

"I understand," Taryn laughed. "Sometimes I also have to get out of my head to work."

"So how's the painting going?"

"It's going..." she answered slowly.

She was aching to tell someone about Adena Cottage, about Ivy House, and about her dreams and what had gone on after the ghost hunters' meeting. So far Matt had been too busy to invest much time in her ramblings but she understood. He was in the middle of a big project himself and couldn't just tear himself away to listen to her.

"Anything wrong?" The look of concern on David's face boosted her spirits, but there was no way she was going to unleash all her thoughts on a perfect stranger.

"Oh, it's fine. I just didn't sleep well last night. Bad dream," she added casually.

David bowed his head and looked like the weight of the world was on his shoulders. "Yes, I've been having them since arriving on the island myself. I assumed it was because I am Creek, and it was the Creeks who settled the island for many years."

"So you have a connection to it?" she asked.

David smiled. "Yes. So what about you? What's your connection to it?"

"I don't know," Taryn said. "That's what I am trying to figure out."

David turned away from her and faced the water. She watched the sunlight touch his face and seem to glide over him, wrapping itself around his body. She wished she could feel as peaceful as he looked. Finally, he turned back to Taryn. "There are many things on this island, many lives and histories. It is possible that one of those histories has found you and is reaching out to a kindred spirit."

"It's happened before," Taryn admitted. "Several times actually."

"It's not a bad thing, not when you can learn how to control your doorway. It's letting everyone in that can be the problem."

Taryn smiled wryly and took a long drink of water. "But if you open the door for the good, aren't you also letting in the bad?"

Placing a friendly hand on her shoulder David leaned in and looked her in the eye. Their faces were only a few inches apart, and Taryn could feel something snap in the air between them. "Be careful with this," he said softly. "Not all histories are meant to be remembered or brought back."

Taryn bit her lip and nodded. But what happened when they just wouldn't let you go? What were you supposed to do then?

*   *   *

SINCE HER FIRST EXPERIENCE with Miss Dixie's knack for the past at Windwood Farm, Taryn had faced an extreme amount of confusion in regards to what she was supposed to do about the things she saw. Even more confusing was IF she was even meant to do anything at all.

She'd talked extensively to Matt about this, as well as their mutual friend Rob who owned New Age Gifts and More in Lexington, Kentucky. She'd learned along the way that just because she saw ghosts and occasionally took a walk through the virtual past didn't necessarily mean that she needed to do anything about them. She had to learn to control her emotions and feelings.

That was not easy.

Taryn didn't have much control over anything she did, from gorging on ice cream or watching multiple episodes of *Designing Women* and *The Golden Girls* when she was meant to be working.

So far she'd been pretty proud of herself for not going off the deep end with what she'd seen and felt at the cottages.

"It's okay," she muttered to herself as she walked along the path to the bookstore. "Just because I see a ghost, and the ghost knows I am there too, doesn't mean there's a big mystery to solve or that it needs my help..."

She was talking to herself more and more these days. She really *did* need to make some friends. It was hard making friends, though, when she was almost constantly on the road.

The bookstore had been many things in the past, but now the circular historical building held lots of goodies, from new releases to photographic and historical collections of the Golden Isles. Taryn might have been able to brush off what she'd experienced at the cottage, and even chalked up what happened at the hotel as another aspect of her ability, but she couldn't ignore the dream.

The hanging had felt real. She'd seen it as clearly as if she'd actually been there herself. The fact that she saw it through a ghost's eyes was unnerving, but she was now convinced that she was meant to do something about it.

"The hanging has to have something to do with one of the cottages," she whispered as she slipped through the door.

It didn't take her long to find the "local" section of the shop. Soon, she was sitting on the floor, her back against a shelf, with a stack of books at her side. She'd purchase the ones that were most useful but for the moment she needed to check things out and see what they offered. Around her were the sounds of quiet shoppers, silently removing books and flipping through their pages, the only real sound being the cash register and fluttering of paper. She enjoyed the fact that some people treated bookstores as reverently as they did places of worship.

The first few books were mostly technical; Taryn had a hard time focusing on the words. Another was full of beautiful photographs, but they were all recent and therefore unhelpful.

At last, she discovered a volume that wasn't just about Jekyll Island, but about the entire Glynn County area. She briefly read about the early settlements with the Creek Indians, the Spanish, the French, and the English. A few passages caught her eye and made her stop and catch her breath. A letter Sir Francis Drake sent to Queen Elizabeth in 1587 about the English reaching Cumberland Island to the south and what they did before moving their sights to Jekyll was one passage she'd never forget. She found herself shivering in horror as she read:

"On the 17th we took an observation, and found ourselves in latitude 30 deg. 30 min. N., and near a large island, which we felt sure was the land where we had information of a Spanish settlement of magnitude.

Seeing some log houses, we decided to make a landing.

We unfurled the standard of Saint George and approached the shore in great force, that we might impress the enemy with the great puissance of your Majesty.

The accursed Spaniards, concealed behind the trees, fired upon us, and a sore and cruel fight seemed pendent, when the enemy, stricken with fear, incontinently fled to their homes, with their habiliments of war.

One of our men was gravely wounded by the Spanish Captain, whom we presently made prisoner, and, having set up a gallows, we there hanged him in a chain by the middle, and afterwards consumed with fire, gallows and all. "To us was the good God most merciful and gracious, in that he permitted us to kill eighteen Spaniards, bitter enemies of your sweet Majesty.

We further wasted the country and brought it to utter ruin.

We burned their houses and killed their few horses, mules and cattle, eating what we could of the fresh beef and carrying the rest aboard our ships.

Having in mind the merciful disposition of your gracious Majesty, we did not kill the women and children, but having destroyed upon the island all their provisions and property, and taken away all their weapons, we left them to starve."

"Damn," Taryn said, forgetting to lower her voice. "That's harsh."

The next few sentences were even worse:

"The women were most ungracious, sullen and obstinate, perchance from their husbands having been killed before their eyes, and wickedly refused to answer us; but after we had burned a hole with a hot iron through the tongue of the most venomous of their number, they eftsoons told us that there were no Spaniards upon other island..."

"'Sullen' and obstinate' because their husbands were killed? No shit," Taryn declared loudly again. An overweight man with two cameras slung around his neck turned and glared at her and she lowered her head again and continued reading. Making a silent commitment to watch her language and volume.

There were a few mentions of the pirates and how, for many years, people still believed there might be buried treasure on the island. Taryn stopped, looked up, and grinned at that part.

How awesome would that *be*, she thought to herself, remembering that not everyone needed to hear her ruminations.

When she finally got to the part about the millionaires and the Jekyll Island Club Hotel she made sure to pay careful attention.

The images of the cottages in their prime were enjoyable and fascinating, but she'd already seen those. Of more interest now were the descriptions of how the men and women spent their leisure time on the island and these accounts provided some amusing insights to a world Taryn couldn't even fathom.

Taryn's parents were successful, but nothing more than upper middle class (although her mother, at least, took great pleasure in the "upper" part of that). In their prime her grandparents had been working class people who squirreled away money all their lives to buy the old farm house and acreage outside of Nashville they loved so much.

Taryn herself often scrambled to make her miserly bills and lived on a budget that she almost always had to be creative with. She couldn't imagine taking a month or more off at a time to jaunt down to her private island to sit on the porch of her mansion (er, "cottage"). Spending all day drinking alcohol, playing cards, and gossiping with her lady friends while her husband had animals shipped in to hunt.

Although, to be clear, she wasn't opposed to giving it a try.

It didn't take long to get to the fire.

"William Hawkins was instantaneously accused of creating the fire that killed not only his young wife Rachel, but more than forty of the hotel guests on New Year's Eve.

Hawkins was discovered with traces of accelerant on his clothing and was witnessed running down the hallway from the room he shared with his wife shortly before the rest of the floor burst into flames.

Throughout the trial Hawkins did not move to offer an alibi of any kind, other than to consistently declare he'd been outside on the grounds "enjoying the night air".

By reports from other witnesses at the celebration, Rachel Hawkins had retired early from the evening's entertainment and it was speculated that he had joined her in their rooms where an argument ensued. One of the most critical pieces of evidence came from the testimony of a Mrs. Lucinda Moorer who was housed in a suite of rooms across the corridor from the Hawkins' and testified that moments before smoke filled the floor she heard Rachel Hawkins "crying and whimpering."

Hawkins was incarcerated in the Brunswick jail for six months before his trial began. According to Juniper Willis, guard, Hawkins only made two requests during his incarceration—to visit his late wife's gravesite and to keep his family Bible in his cell at all times. Both requests were honored. Hawkins had one visitor during his incarceration, a member of the Jekyll Island Club. He was found guilty after only two hours of deliberation. He was hanged three days later at the gallows which is now the site of..."

Taryn stopped reading then and looked up from the book.

Huh, she thought, *why wouldn't he have tried to at least make up some sort of solid alibi?*

Seemed odd to her, especially since he knew he'd probably be hung. Hell, they were rich. He probably could've paid someone off to vouch for him.

Taking everything she'd read and what she knew about human behavior into consideration, Taryn felt like the case was pretty much closed. He probably *was* guilty. No miscarriage of justice there, except for the party goers who had died in the fire. Yikes. If there was one thing Taryn had learned it was that people did crazy things for crazy reasons *all the damn time.*

The book went on for several more pages. It spent a little more time talking about William, Rachel, the monetary damage the fire caused, and the rebuilding. Although it was all interesting and she knew she could read for hours, she closed the book and stood and stretched.

She'd found what she wanted. Now she had work to do.

*　　*　　*

IT WAS DARK BY THE TIME she finished. Without any interruptions from tourists or other employees she'd worked steadily all afternoon, getting more accomplished than she usually did. It was only in the high eighties that day as well and the humidity hadn't been terrible. It was much easier to work when she wasn't worried about sweat running down into her eyes or dying of heat stroke.

As the last few drops of sunset faded into the dark sky she loaded the rest of her supplies into the golf cart and took off. Ivy House had been quiet all day. She hadn't felt any niceties oozing from it but she didn't feel like it wanted to open its mouth and swallow her whole, either, so that was a start.

When she got to the part of the road where she'd usually turn right to head to her house, she continued straight, heading towards the north end of the island. There was a small cemetery there, the one where Rachel was buried, and the ghost story the server told her had been weighing on her mind.

North Riverview Road was eerily quiet, deserted and isolated as it usually felt away from the hotels when it was dark. There were never many people out on it at night. The longer she drove, the more she second guessed her intentions.

"Don't be a wuss," she chided herself when the shadow from a tree made her jump in her seat. "If people can go out bike riding at night you can skirt along in a golf cart."

As she neared the shell of the Horton House, she slowed down and pulled over to the side. The one lonely streetlamp did little to brighten her surroundings and, if anything, made the small woods around her even darker. Rummaging in her knapsack she fished out the small flashlight Matt had bought her a few months earlier.

"If you're going to be traipsing around spooky places after dark then you at least need some good light," he'd complained after handing it to her.

And, in typical Matt fashion, he had diligently researched flashlights for at least a week online before picking out the right one for her. Not only was it rechargeable, have a power beam, and doubled as a screwdriver–it was also bright pink.

Now she turned it on and sprinted across the road to the small cemetery that lay just beyond the tree line. She'd driven past it a time or two and had seen the headstones rising from the ground but hadn't yet explored it.

"You're nuttier than a fruitcake," she lectured herself as she disappeared into the shadowy canopy. "Can't you ever do anything strange in the daytime? You're worse than the Scooby Doo people."

But she wasn't truly frightened. Taryn *liked* cemeteries. She thought they were peaceful and comforting. Even as a child she'd enjoyed wandering around the graves, careful not to step on anyone and to act in a respectful manner as she read the inscriptions and ran her fingers over the smooth stones.

The tiny area was enclosed by a tabby wall that came up to her chest. The black wrought iron gate was open so she slipped through and entered quietly. When the gate closed firmly behind her, the sound of metal on stone had her jumping, nearly dropping her flashlight.

"Jesus!" she shouted and then cackled at her skittishness. "Some ghost hunter I am."

It was hilarious that the people on the internet were starting to think of her as this tough paranormal expert who, in their minds, investigated old houses and walked around a la Nancy Drew solving mysteries. A week didn't go by where she didn't get an email from someone asking her to poke around their haunted house.

In reality, Taryn was afraid of the dark and about as jumpy as they came. To be fair, thanks to the insane things that had happened to her over the past year, she *was* starting to think of her life and jobs in terms of book titles: *Taryn and the Mystery of the Old Farm House, Taryn and the Mystery of Shaker Village, Taryn and the Mystery of the Missing Girl...*

It gave her something to do on long car rides.

It only took a couple of seconds to find Rachel's grave; there were only a few. As she knelt down beside it, the flashlight balanced on her knee, she read aloud the words written in stone:

"there shall be no night there; and they need no candle, neither light of the sun; for the Lord God giveth them light: and they shall reign for ever and ever"

Taryn sat back on her heels and chewed on her bottom lip. Frankly, considering how the poor woman had died, she found the Revelations quote to be in poor taste. Wasn't she meant to have died because she burned to death?

Taryn wasn't completely sure why she was even there. Adena Cottage had nothing to do with William and Rachel. Their story was closed. He'd started the fire to cover her murder and he'd paid for it. Justice was served. Adena had belonged to Georgiana and her father. She'd found no connection between that cottage, that family, and the hotel fire.

Besides, as she continued to find out, there were lots of stories about the island. She could be connecting to any number of them.

Shaking her head, Taryn started to stand but as she was rising to her feet she paused, all of her senses on high alert. The only sounds were that of crickets and some obnoxiously loud tree frogs. How something so little could make suck a racket was beyond her. And yet...

Taryn had the distinct feeling that she wasn't alone. She continued to straighten, keeping her flashlight trained on the ground at her feet. There was no movement in the darkness, so no sound of footsteps, no cars on the road behind her, yet Taryn knew someone else was there with her. It was a prickling at the back of her skull, a faint rash of coldness that seeped down her neck and into the top of her shirt.

Without turning, Taryn closed her eyes and tightened her grip on the small flashlight. "Hello?" she asked quietly, struggling to keep her voice steady. Her instinct was to make a mad dash to her golf cart and get out of there as quickly as possible.

Whatever was behind her crept closer, its icy hand closing over her left shoulder. Taryn felt the weight if not the solidity of the appendage. Then, as though it had the weight of the world on *its* shoulder, an enormous sigh pervaded the air around her, a sound tinged with disappointment, longing, and frustration.

Taryn bit back a scream and willed herself not to pass out.

What had to be only milliseconds later, the weight of the hand was lifted and she knew that she was alone again. The last thing she saw before she fled from the enclosure and raced across the darkened road was the faint glow on the ground by the headstone, just the size of a small candle.

ELEVEN

*T*ryn read through the letter three times before *picking up* the phone and calling Matt.

      She'd had a night full of bad dreams again. Once again she'd been in a locked room, dark and dusty and cramped. A small beam of light had shone through a tiny hole but the miniature ray was only enough to be mocking. She'd thrown herself against the sides that closed in around her and cried, scratching at the wood until she felt her fingernails break and her fingers bleed. Nobody had come to help her.

When she'd finally woken up, drenched in sweat, she'd turned on every light in the house. Then she'd sat in the living room for hours, just flipping through the television stations, one channel after another.

And then the letter came.

Matt picked up on the second ring.

"Hello?" Taryn thought he sounded distracted. She figured she must have caught him on his way out the door and felt guilty about bothering him with more of her problems.

"Hey, you got a minute?" she asked.

"Yes, for you. What's up my queen?" As a child she'd pretended she was the Queen of Sweden, having no authority on the Swedish royal family, or if there even was one at all.

"I got a letter from that attorney up in New Hampshire," she replied. "Aunt Sarah's house?"

"Everything okay?"

Taryn sighed; the piece of paper still caught between her fingers. "There was a storm and some damage from trees. He gave me an estimate to have it fixed, but I can't afford it. I don't have any money. I don't know that I will ever have that kind of money."

"How much do you need? I've got some," Matt replied casually.

Taryn was mortified. "Good Lord, Matt, I wasn't calling you for money. To be honest, I thought I might want to just go ahead and sell it. I can't get it fixed and I don't want to let it sit there and fall into ruin."

The idea made her miserable, though. She'd loved her aunt, possibly one of the only people in her family who'd ever understood her, other than her grandmother. Sarah had been a bit of an enigma. She was her mother's sister, a woman who rarely socialized and lived in her big old farm house alone in the "New Hampshire wilderness," as Taryn's father referred to it. Taryn hadn't seen her in years but had fond memories of visiting her aunt as a child. She'd meant to return as an adult but put it off year after year until she'd received the letter from the attorney, informing her of her aunt's death and how she was sole inheritor.

Sarah had died a year ago, but Taryn still hadn't been up to the house. A property manager was taking care of it and it had been winterized while vacant. Now she knew it was time to do something about the place, though. The idea of letting it go, of having nothing of her family's that belonged to her, bothered Taryn greatly. No bank in their right mind was going to lend her any money with the kind of job she had, though, so a loan was most certainly out. The only thing she owned was her car and it was on its last legs, so to speak.

"Let me think about it," Matt said at last. "I might be able to come up with something."

"I think I should go up there and at least look at it," Taryn replied. "See what all has happened to it myself. Maybe it's not as bad as he made it out to be."

"I think it would be good for you to visit her house and get some closure," he agreed.

Taryn realized with a start that she desperately needed that connection with her family. It was ironic that she spent her time chasing ghosts and visiting graves of people she'd never known and yet had done virtually nothing about her own family member's passing.

"I'll look at some airline tickets and see if I can't take some time off," she replied. "You want to fly up there with me?"

"It depends on when you go," Matt said. "We're kind of knee deep in this project at the moment, and I just don't want to go off and leave my students right now. They have a good grasp of what we're doing but they're not there quite yet—not where I'm comfortable with them being."

Taryn had to laugh to herself. Matt's "students" were only a year or two younger than him and yet he'd always acted older and wiser than everyone else. It was both charming and annoying.

"I'll call you later," she said. "I've got to get out of the house for a little while and try to work. I think I'm going to be done in about two weeks if all goes well."

"Alright. I'll be here. I love you!" he sang cheerfully.

"Um, you too," she replied awkwardly.

Matt, not caring so much *how* she said it as long as she did, happily hung up on his end.

Taryn had never been great at telling anyone how she felt. Her parents were aloof and distant when they were alive and for the majority of the time her connection with her grandmother had allowed them to communicate without the use of words. Now, twisting the ring on her finger that belonged to the woman who'd mostly raised her, Taryn could feel her eyes swimming with tears.

"I wish you were still here," she murmured aloud the words that she thought at least a dozen times a day.

*　　*　　*

IVY HOUSE WAS STARTING TO ACCEPT HER, Taryn firmly believed it. It might not be rolling out the "Welcome" mat for her, but it wasn't slamming doors or breaking glass in her direction anymore and that was an improvement.

"So what's your secret?" she asked loudly, dipping her brush into a smudge of blue on her palette. "What do you guys want from me?"

"Are you talking to your paint or your canvas?"

Taryn recognized David's voice at once and looked up and smiled. He moved with an almost unnatural grace, light as a feather despite his height and muscles.

"To whatever will answer me I guess," Taryn replied, smiling.

David walked up to her and studied her work. "Nice! You *do* have a talent for this."

"Well, that's why they pay me the big bucks," she joked. "So what brings you here?"

"Just trying to walk off some steam," he replied, shaking his head.

She could see the flashes of frustration in his eyes and winced. "Bad day?" she asked sympathetically, thinking of the attorney's letter.

"I don't know. You at a stopping point or anything? I could use a friendly ear."

She really *wasn't* at a "stopping point" but had so few friends that she hated to turn down a request for something that might momentarily offer her companionship, even if it was artificial.

It took her a few minutes to wrap everything up and cover her canvas but soon they were walking along the path by the river, dodging bicycles and sweltering tourists.

"So what's up?" Taryn asked when they came to a bench and he motioned her to sit. The marsh spread out before them, lush and green. Once again Taryn was struck by the vividness of everything on the island.

"I had that meeting with the project manager that I was telling you about," David began.

"And I'm assuming that it didn't go well?" Taryn prodded.

David shrugged and swept back his long hair until it fell down behind them, nearly touching the ground. "It *should* have. He said all the right things, acted in all the right ways..."

"But you don't believe him."

David exhaled loudly, his brow furrowing in deep lines. "Not in the slightest. Most of these companies? They don't care about the history, about what they might be uncovering or disturbing. Sure, they make their donations to the museums, usually just for the big tax write-offs, and *claim* to be environmentalists or whatever but...I don't know.

You know those sea turtle signs you see all around here and how they tell us not to bother the eggs?"

Taryn nodded. She'd seen a lot of them on the beach.

"You know that if they were out there digging around and came across a nest of eggs they'd probably cover them up. Or else they'd throw them away instead of telling someone if they thought it would cost them an hour or two of work."

"My, my, you're a cynical one," Taryn laughed in spite of herself.

David snorted. "Yeah, well, I've seen a lot. You know that airport over on St. Simon's Island?"

"Yeah." She didn't, not really, but thought she'd go with it.

David grimaced. "When they were digging up the ground to build it they found a Native burial site and village with thousands of artifacts. Just dug them up and put them in a big pile. No official excavation was done at the time. Who knows what else could be under there. Of course, that was back before we had certain laws and regulations but still..."

"I know," Taryn said. "I see it a lot in my work, too. They just kind of keep quiet and move on. Makes you wonder what the future generations are going to do with *our* graveyards."

"Well, in my family we're cremated and given back to the earth we came from," David explained. "I like to think that's also the environmentalist in us talking."

"So are you going to leave now that you've met with him?"

David pursed his lips and stared straight ahead. She could feel a mixture of sadness, irritation, and excited energy radiating from him. It was the first time in a long time she'd met someone who felt so...alive. A small shrimp boat was gliding past them, the nets raised up in the air. It looked like a picture and Taryn had the urge to paint it. There were lots of things on the island she'd like to paint, but first had to finish the job she was actually being paid for.

"Not yet," he replied at last. "I've got at least another week or two here. They just broke ground, and I want to be on hand in case anything turns up. It's a small island and people will talk, whether they want them to or not. If I have to stay on for awhile even without being paid I will."

Taryn appreciated his stubbornness. She also had a fairly good feel for people, though, and while she wasn't as sensitive as she'd like to be, there was still something about David that she couldn't put her finger on. She got the distinct feeling that he wasn't telling her everything. "Are you expecting to find something?" she teased him. "Are you aware of something that's there and just not sharing it with the rest of us?"

David laughed then, a full rich sound that carried through the air. "No, no, I don't know anything right now. I swear. But I have a hunch. Haven't you ever had one about a place?"

He turned and looked at her then, a searing gaze that made her uncomfortable. She could have sworn that he was looking *into* her and not just *at* her. Changing the subject at once, she moved on to the books she'd bought the day before and what she'd learned so far.

"And anyway," she finished after a lengthy rambling on the early history of the settlers, "this island has seen an awful lot."

"Well that's for sure," he agreed, his face more relaxed now. "Is that the book you bought?" He pointed at the edge of the volume sticking out from her knapsack.

"Yep, that's it."

"I've read it; it's a good one.

"It's wild to think that at one time this was almost a jungle and yet these prim and proper people were over here trying to build mansions and cultivate a proper society out of it," Taryn mused. "We always want to turn a new place into what we're familiar with instead of learning to adapt to what we find."

"And then there were people who did learn to adapt and swing the other way," David said with a glint in his eyes.

"Huh?"

"Well," David laughed, "a long time ago when this *was* a true wilderness people were swayed to do things they might have never done otherwise. Let me see that book of yours."

Taryn handed him the thick volume and watched with curiosity as he thumbed through it. "I know you're not as interested in the early history of the island as you are with the later stuff, but check this out. This is from a letter Lady Oglethorpe wrote her husband in 1734:

"Since your departure, my dearest husband, all the pigs have escaped into the dreadful wilderness about us, and we fear daily that thay will be captured and eaten by the savages. The Chief, Altamaha, and his band, are still upon the island, and yesterday he came and begged tobacco and sugar, and also demanded of me our maid servant Elizabeth as his wife, much to her astonishment and terror. He was dressed in all his barbaric finery, painted and bedaubed in as many colors as the coat of Joseph, and decorated with feathers, bear's claws, and bright colored shells, as befitted a man equipped for female conquest. The wretched pagan has already three wives, whom he treats worse than beasts of burden, and I think this somewhat

influenced Elizabeth, as, had he been unmarried, the prospect of being a queen, even of the wild and savage Tuscaroras, might have moved her."

"Ha, ha, ha," Taryn snickered, the force of the gaiety shaking her and almost making her double over. "I can totally envision that. This woman being aghast at the marriage proposal from this 'savage' and yet, at the same time, thinking '*Heeeyyy*! Maybe I'll get to be Savage Queen!'"

David closed the book with a smirk. "People don't change much. The lure of riches and position can sway just about anyone."

"Boy, isn't that the truth," Taryn agreed, settling back onto the bench and looking out at the water again. The sun was high in the sky, the rays soaking into her skin, but instead of the heat being oppressive she felt relaxed and at peace. She'd do her best to enjoy it, no matter how brief the sensation was.

*   *   *

SHE WAS NERVOUS WHEN ELLEN called her to her office that next morning. One of the things Taryn liked best about her job was that she didn't have to deal with the people who hired her very often. Most would stop in from time to time to check on her work and say hello but, for the most part, they left her alone. Taryn preferred to work by herself and didn't like someone hanging over her shoulder. Getting called in for a meeting was a bit like getting called to the principal's office.

Steve was standing at the valet stand when she walked up the steps. "Hey," she whispered, sidling up to him. "Have you seen the boss lady today?"

"For a few minutes about an hour ago," he whispered back. "Why are we whispering?"

"Because I've got a meeting with her and I don't want to be blindsided by something bad," Taryn kept her voice low and her head close to his. "Did she seem like she was in a bad mood?"

"Nah," he winked. "I think you're good. Matter of fact, I heard her bragging on your landscape of Adena to someone this morning."

"Awesome." Taryn gave him the thumbs up and went on inside.

Ellen was waiting for her in her perfectly cool and organized office when Taryn entered. After motioning her to sit Ellen pulled out a large leather-bound ledger from a shelf behind her desk and placed it in front of Taryn. "I know you're doing a splendid job with recreating the cottages, but I did find something a few days ago I thought might help," she began.

Taryn opened the heavy cover with care and peered inside. It was a scrapbook of sorts, full of photos, illustrations, old maps, newspaper clippings, and handwritten notes. She carefully flipped through the pages, taking in the contents with interest while attempting to keep her ears open to what Ellen was saying to her.

"This is one of the many scrapbooks once kept here at the Clubhouse over the years. Unfortunately, this is one of only two that survived the great fire. The other is much more fragile and I'm afraid I can't bring it out. I thought you might be able to garner some inspiration from it," Ellen continued formally.

It was, indeed, fascinating. In enthrallment, Taryn read in detail a dinner menu that included roast beef, duck, corn soufflé, and dozens of other items that all made her tummy rumble. When she looked at the date at the top, she was startled to realize it was dated December 31st, the night of the fire.

"This is great, thank you," Taryn said. "May I sit here and go through it?"

"By all means," Ellen replied, sweeping her arms out in front of her. "Spend as much time as you need. Only three photographs of Adena Cottage and Ivy House exist, and two are of the interiors. Still, sometimes getting a feel for the environment as a whole can help you understand the specific parts, don't you agree?"

Taryn nodded; she *did* agree. That's why she took her photographs and why Miss Dixie was special to her even before she'd allowed her to see the past.

"Are you experiencing any...*trouble*?" Ellen lowered her voice and her cheeks reddened somewhat–the first time Taryn had seen her come close to losing her near perfect composure.

Taryn looked up and was surprised to see soft pink spots appear on her current boss's cheeks.

"N-no," Taryn replied. "I don't think so."

"The cottages are tolerable then?" Ellen prodded. Her tone was gentle, yet still demanding. Taryn felt like she was being interviewed for an important position by Mrs. Claus.

"Well, yes, they're fine. They're–" Taryn stopped then, at last understanding to what Ellen was alluding. "Oh, I see. Well, it has taken some time to adjust to Ivy House but I believe we've reached an understanding."

Ellen nodded and pursed her thin lips. "I am going to say this and I don't want you to be offended."

"Okay," Taryn promised. "I'll do my best."

"You weren't our first choice to come and paint our beautiful buildings," Ellen stated, raising her chin up a bit in near-defiance.

Despite what Taryn had promised, she felt the beginning of spikes and, to her shame, her cheeks flushed with embarrassment. "Wha–"

"What I mean is," Ellen continued, interrupting her, "that we had hired someone else first. They were here for several weeks doing what we thought was their job. As it so happened, several days went by without anyone seeing the young man at either one of the cottages. When those few days became a week I sent my assistant to check on him. He'd apparently holed up in his room here at the hotel and refused to leave, even to step out into the corridor. He claimed that the 'ghosts' had followed him from the cottages, Adena specifically which is interesting since it's not the one that's haunted, and were holding him prisoner. He'd not eaten a thing and was visibly weak with a terrible pallor. We had to call the doctor. It was an ugly affair." Ellen trembled at the memory and shook her head in regret.

"Oh," Taryn replied, at a loss for words. "I'm sorry." That was quite a bit to process, although she *had* wanted to jump in there and inform Ellen that Adena had more going on with it than she may have thought.

"So you see, I had concerns when it came to hiring anyone else. It was my assistant who discovered you online," Ellen explained. "Amy has read about your...adventures, shall we say?"

Taryn nodded without expression.

"We hoped that with both of your backgrounds at play that working in such an environment would not prove to be an issue for you," Ellen finished. There was quiet steel in her voice and no warmth in her eyes as she gazed at Taryn.

"It's fine," Taryn assured her, attempting to keep her face impassive. "I don't scare easily."

(Eh, what she didn't know wouldn't hurt her. At least, so far, the ghosts had mostly liked her. None had tried to hold her prisoner, at any rate.)

Ellen nodded, satisfied. "You see, my dear, I am a practical woman. I hold several degrees and have worked in some capacity with this facility for thirty years. It's my *home* as much as my job. I'm educated and good at what I do, as well as any man. I know we have spirits, however. I know there is something special about this island, something that I don't think exists anywhere else in the world. I do not think a belief in these things and an educated mind have to be contradictory."

"Neither do I," Taryn said.

"I also believe that many people do not treat these matters with the gravity they deserve. And they end up suffering for it," Ellen added. "I have a feeling about you. You're no fool, my dear. I've watched you. I have a touch of this, scent, myself. You're what we needed here."

Taryn slumped back in her leather chair and pulled the scrapbook closer to her. "Ellen, am I here for a different reason? I mean, besides the paintings?"

Ellen stood and walked towards the door. "I don't know," she said, stopping halfway to the door. "Are you? I have another appointment right now. Please, take all the time you need and then just leave the book on my desk when you're finished."

Now confounded with muddled thoughts, Taryn returned to the book. She spent the next half hour leafing through the thick pages, stopping to study the images and read bits and pieces that caught her interest.

The interior picture of Adena Cottage showed a jovial robust man standing in what looked like a parlor. To his left was a tall, good-looking blond man who appeared to be in his forties. He wore a suit, his white dress shirt radiant in the lamp light.

The younger man's arm was draped around a rather drab looking, much younger woman. Her weak smile appeared forced, and she slumped into the young man as though he was holding her up. Her tiny frame was almost childlike. With her flat chest, skinny arms, and tiny hands her evening dress made her look like she was playing dress-up in her mother's clothing.

To the right of the older gentleman was a beautiful blond, her face full of gaiety and her blond hair piled atop her head in ringlets. Her mouth was open in a laugh and the jewels on her fingers and at her neck and ears sparkled. She was the only one not looking at the camera. Instead, she was gazing at the young man. Taryn recognized that look. She'd often looked at Andrew the same way–like she wanted to crawl under his skin.

The caption read: Rachel Hawkins, William Hawkins, Lowell McGovern, & Georgiana McGovern. Adena Cottage.

"Huh," Taryn said out loud. "Well, that's interesting. Miss Rachel wasn't much of a looker. He must have married her for some reason, though. And looks like Georgiana had the hots for him. Wonder how he felt about *that*..."

The last two pages of the scrapbook were full of newspaper clippings. Taryn glossed over them, as most concerned financial information about the members of the Club. On the last page, however, something caught her eye and made her take another look. The headline read "Local Ghost Makes New Appearance." Fascinated, Taryn pored over the article (something that looked like it might have come from a gossip section) and read aloud:

"Mary-the-Wanderer appeared to several members of a hunting party last weekend on Jekyll Island. Mary, who has

been identified on both Jekyll and St. Simon's, was walking along the sand in the moonlight when members of the party saw her from a distance. She wore her traditional white evening gown and, as one spectator reported, appeared to be 'floating in the air.'"

Taryn stopped and grinned. She wondered if such a thing would be reported as "news" these days.

"The members of the party were startled at first but carried on, assuming she meant no harm to come to them. 'It startled me but I wasn't particularly affronted,' stated another member of the party. 'A spirit isn't meant to hurt a human soul. They're just lost and wandering.' Will this be the last sighting of Mary on the islands?"

Taryn finished reading and put the book down but then immediately snatched it up again. Someone had taken the time to sketch the image of "Mary the Wanderer" at the bottom. Although it was only a sketch, and the young woman with the long, flowing hair and big dark eyes was at least fifty years younger in the newspaper, Taryn instantly recognized her as the old woman she'd met on Driftwood Beach.

"Well I'll be damned," she swore. "Mary's still out there and has upgraded herself from a long, flowing gown to a fanny pack and sandals."

Taryn knew, and not for the first time, that she would never cease being shocked by the things she saw.

TWELVE

"I was thinking I'd try to drive up this weekend," Matt said.

Taryn had been working all morning, trying to get in as much outside work as she could before the heat became too oppressive. She'd been feeling bad for the past two days, like every joint in her body was being hammered by a dull object over and over again. Her usual treatments offered little relief. The heat made it worse, but she didn't want to get too far behind and tried to bear it, although there was no grinning involved.

"That would be nice," she replied absently, as she dipped her brush into the paint again and studied her canvas. The windows were giving her problems today. She didn't know why. Ivy House was gorgeous in the morning light. Maybe she just wasn't feeling it.

"Do you not want me to come?" Matt asked quietly.

"Hmmm?" It was the color, she decided at last. The color was making her shading off. She'd mixed too much green in this time. Sighing, she laid her brush down and dropped to the ground.

"If you think I'm going to cramp your style or take up too much of your time I can come next week." Taryn was taken aback at the soft sadness in Matt's voice and felt promptly ashamed for not giving him her full attention.

"Oh Matt, it's not that I don't want you to come. I'm just having trouble with this cottage. I was distracted. Of *course* I want you to come up here," she said, trying to put more enthusiasm in her voice.

"Are you sure? I'd really, *really* like to see you," he replied, sounding hopeful.

"Yes, I'm sure. There's a lot of sightseeing I haven't done yet, and it will be nice to have some company," she assured him.

"Or we could not go out at all and just stay in. There's some sightseeing of my own I wouldn't mind doing," he teased her.

Taryn blushed, despite the fact that nobody could hear them. She didn't know when Matt had learned the art of flirtation–it wasn't in high school or even college–but it was fun *now*.

"Well, you should have plenty of time to take in some of the local stuff," she said with a smile.

"I may have some good news to share with you as well..."

Taryn watched as the shadows over Ivy House slowly drew back, a testament to the sun rising higher in the sky. She'd lose her shade soon. Not only did her bones ache, she felt a heaviness on her shoulders, a great weight pushing her down. It wasn't just the heat and fatigue she usually felt but something else. Taryn felt like she was pushing through the days, fighting against something she couldn't see. Everything was taking more and more effort.

All of a sudden she realized Matt had been talking for several minutes and she hadn't heard a single word he'd said. "Uh huh," she murmured, hoping her general, non-committal sound would not be mistaken for the elusiveness it was.

"Okay, well, I can talk to you about it more when I see you. I'll leave tomorrow afternoon and should be there by seven at the latest."

"Do you want me to text or email you the directions?" she asked.

"Nope. I already have the address plugged into the GPS, the car is gassed up, and I've packed a weekend bag," he sang.

Taryn bit her lip and shook her head. And if she'd said it wasn't a good time? It wouldn't have mattered. Matt had always had a sixth sense about what was going to happen when it came to the two of them.

*   *   *

ONCE SHE HUNG UP WITH MATT, Taryn was unable to get back into the zone again. Since it was getting too hot she decided just to call it a day and return to the house.

Of course, once she reached the house and took medication for the swelling and inflammation in her legs and hips she had nothing to do other than flip through the television channels.

Nothing suited her.

"Well, I can't just sit around here all day and enjoy my pain medication," she murmured. "I'll fry my brain between the internet and the bad TV."

She considered taking a nap but that seemed like a waste of a perfectly good day. Instead, she hobbled to her bedroom, tugged on her bathing suit (one piece because she was getting a little tummy and nobody needed to be exposed to that), and grabbed a towel and sunblock. If she was going to be miserable then she might as well be miserable in the sand.

"I will learn to be a beach person," she stated. "I'll learn to relax in the sand if it kills me."

Taryn wanted to go back to the beach that offered more privacy but didn't think she could do even the short amount of walking that was required to reach that glorious stretch of sand. Instead, she settled on the main beach across from the miniature golf course and pizza place.

Since it was still early in the afternoon, and low tide. The beach was crowded with families and young people. The former barked orders and slathered creamy lotion onto wriggling children while the latter tried desperately hard to check each other out without being obvious.

Taryn found herself a spot that wasn't too close to anyone else and spread out her towel. It was a pleasant afternoon. There weren't any bugs biting on her at her toes, no gale-force wind blowing sand in her face, nobody pumping rap in her ears at a raucous level... She'd brought a trashy romance novel with her since it was the beach and that's what you were apparently supposed to do but she left it in her beach bag and opted to try the water first.

"Saltwater cures everything," Dr. Culver, her primary doctor back in Nashville, had joked when she informed her of her new assignment. "You might come back a new person—new bones and joints and everything!"

It was just a joke, of course, since there was no cure for what she had, but the water *was* lessening some of the pressure off her joints and it was easier to move around. The Atlantic Ocean was surprisingly warm so early in the summer and the waves were small and gentle. Wary of jellyfish and other things under the murky depths she stayed close to the shore and waded up to her chest, sometimes pausing to float on her back and enjoy looking up at the sky.

When she looked at the sunny beach, the happy vacationers, and the modern hotel buildings and shops in the distance it was easy to forget the other stuff about the island's history. It was easy to forget the pillaging of the early settlers, the fighting, the greed, the fire, the deaths...the hanging that would come. And then there was the horrible tragedy involving the slaves who were illegally shipped there after slavery was outlawed. She'd just read about that the night before, about how they'd jumped into the water and thrown their chains from their bodies as they struggled for the shore. Some said you could still see some of the chains when the water was at the right level.

Taryn shuddered just thinking about it.

"You okay there?" The woman next to Taryn was heavyset and wearing a two-piece suit in shocking yellow. Her pale skin was almost blinding and with it set against her wavy black hair she reminded Taryn of a Goth pinup.

"Yeah, just thinking about something," Taryn said. "Sorry about that."

"You looked like a ghost walked over your grave just then," the woman smiled. Taryn was taken aback, remembering that the same phrase had slipped into her mind just a few days before.

The other woman appeared to be in her early fifties. Although she was up to her neck in the ocean she was still wearing rhinestone earrings (or maybe they *were* diamonds, Taryn couldn't tell the difference sometimes), a thick gold necklace, and half a dozen flashing rings. She was also in full makeup, from her hard liquid eyeliner to her coral lipstick.

"My grandmother used to say that," Taryn replied. "I was just thinking about the history of the island and it gave me a chill."

The woman nodded solemnly and adjusted her top, almost causing a show. It looked to be at least one size too small and her heavy breasts were straining against it. Taryn hoped a big wave didn't come.

"Yes," she said, pursing her lips together. "Some awful stuff here on the island for sure. You here on vacation?"

Taryn shook her head. "A little work, a little vacation. I'm trying to take some time to enjoy myself while I can."

"Good for you!" When the woman beamed she looked much younger. "We're up here from Jacksonville with the grandkids. The beach is just better. Cleaner, if you know what I mean. Not a bunch of partying going on. Sorry, no offense if you're into that."

Taryn laughed. "My idea of a party these days is a gallon of ice cream and some Brad Pitt movies. Usually by myself."

"Now that's my kind of party," the woman agreed. "By the way, my name's April. It's nice to talk to someone who isn't related to me. I love my family, but I've gotten sick of them after not seeing anyone else for a week."

The two women bobbed companionably in the water together, just a few feet apart. Considering they didn't know one another, it was strangely intimate being so close to someone who wore such few articles of clothing. "Do you come up here a lot?"

April nodded, her earrings catching the sunlight and making lights dance across the water. "Yep. Every summer for fifteen years now."

Sensing an opportunity, Taryn pounced on it. "Has it changed a lot?"

"Yes and no. The people seem to change more than anything else. It goes through phases I guess you could say. Sometimes it's families who all want to come here. And then it's retirees like me and my Murray. St. Simon's gets a lot of the younger people, the ones looking for action and to be seen. The ones who come here want to get lost."

Taryn could understand that. "It *does* have a special kind of feel to it," she agreed.

"Oh honey, it has more than that. If this island calls to you then you *know* it. It shows itself in different ways. My daughter? She won't step foot on it. Says there's evil here, that there are things hiding or crawling around the island that she can feel but can't see. My husband Murray?"

April gestured to a chair on the beach occupied by a skinny bald man with thick glasses and a can of beer in each hand. He alternated taking drinks from each can, both different brands, while he appeared to keep his eyes on a group of twentysomething women giggling with each other on a nearby blanket. "He's never felt nothing but goodness here. Says it's the most peaceful place he's ever seen."

"What about you?"

April shrugged. "I know what my daughter means, but I'm able to ignore it. I can put it aside and tell myself it doesn't concern me."

Taryn wished she were better at doing that. Building upon the rapport they seemed to be establishing Taryn pushed harder. "I've been engrossed in the hotel's history, especially the fire and what happened at the turn of the century."

April shivered dramatically. "Ooooh! That! What a terrible, terrible thing. All those people scurrying, trying to get out. Trampling each other. They said that by the time the rescue workers came over from Brunswick to help with the flames the whole front lawn was just littered with bodies. They couldn't tell who was alive and who was dead. All those fine suits and evening gowns covered in soot and ashes and grass stains...just terrible."

Taryn could envision it even then and for a moment could swear she caught the scent of smoke but then she shook her head clear of it. It was just her imagination acting up on her.

"And all of that just to get rid of his poor wife," April continued, shaking her head in sorrow.

"So why do you think he did it?" Taryn asked.

"Money," April replied. "Although I don't know why. Back then the man pretty much held the purse strings anyway, even if she was the one who came into the marriage with the cash."

Taryn nodded in agreement. She was right, of course.

"Of course," April lowered her voice to a whisper and bounced closer to Taryn in the water. "Of course there are those who think there may have been something more sinister going on."

Taryn bent her head forward and whispered back. "What do you mean?"

"All those rich men here, all those wanting to protect their assets. Some think they weren't just here to shoot ducks and enjoy the view, if you know what I mean."

Taryn looked at her in confusion. No, she really *didn't* know what she meant. "Sorry, I'm not following..."

April giggled. "Well, I've never been one to keep up with these sorts of things but there is a very substantial rumor that several years later some of those same Club members came back and held a secret meeting amongst themselves and that's when the Federal Reserve was created. It was all clandestine of course, very cloak and dagger."

"And maybe William had something to do with that?" Taryn pondered aloud.

April straightened and patted her hair primly, her rings glittering again. Taryn was struck by her cherry red fingernail polish and the little rhinestone nail art on each finger. "Weelllll....Not everyone was on board with it or liked what was going on. And some of those people met a very unfortunate demise."

"What do you mean? Other people were murdered?"

April laughed, a girlish sound that belied her years. "Oh my dear, just look what happened to the Titanic and who all was on board! Think about *that* for a minute and how some of those men had more than enough dough to buy their way off on a lifeboat but went down anyway..."

The skinny man in the chair stood then and called out to her. Both women turned towards the sand and Taryn saw him folding up his chair and gathering the towels. "Well my dear, it appears that I am being summoned. I must depart!"

Taryn said her goodbyes but continued to stand in the water, ignoring the tickle of ting fish fins against her legs. A fire that nearly knocked off half the country's richest men? Secret meetings from Club members? The Federal Reserve? Murder? The Titanic? Taryn's head was swimming more than her body; she was beginning to feel the start of an oncoming headache.

What the hell had *happened* on this island?

*   *   *

"You don't honestly believe that the men on Jekyll Island had something to do with the sinking of the Titanic do you?"

Taryn could tell that Matt was trying to humor her but she also knew that he was about two seconds away from

170

breaking out into hysterical laughter. She recognized that tone.

"I don't know," she muttered. "I watched this documentary on You Tube and–"

"Taryn? Really?" he asked, controlled patience edging his voice.

Taryn stopped pacing around her living room and slumped her shoulders. "Okay. Well, it made sense while I was watching it."

"I think you're getting spooked and your mind is getting cluttered," he said. "Why don't you take a step back and regroup and go back to the beginning."

Taryn sighed and plopped down on the couch. Dangling her feet off the armrest she stared up at the popcorn ceiling and started at the point where she'd met the woman in the ocean. She laughed herself. "Okay, so I can see where I went astray. There's just so much history here that it's hard to keep it all straight. I can see what you mean about things being cluttered, though."

"Well, I did a little sleuthing of my own and found some information about the hanging. I'm going to bring up with me tomorrow when I come," Matt told her. "I think you should focus on the fire. With what you felt at the house with the smoke and fire and what you saw in the hotel room..."

"You think that had something to do with the fire at the hotel?" she asked. "But that couple's grandson didn't die there."

"I don't think it necessarily matters," Matt replied. "I think one of the reasons you picked up on it is because of the fire that happened at the hotel. You know, maybe the receptors were more active or something."

"Yeah, okay, that makes sense," Taryn conceded. "So you think maybe it's Rachel haunting me, trying to tell me something? Maybe seeking revenge or wanting help?"

"I think that makes more sense than anything else," Matt agreed.

"But what about the cottages? Ivy House and Adena? How do they play into it?"

"I don't think they do at all," Matt said. "Taryn, we talk about this all the time. Just because a place is haunted doesn't mean it has anything to do with you or that you're meant to do anything about it."

Taryn later hung up the phone but continued to stay on the couch. It was growing dark out and the shadows were moving across the room but she made no move to get up. Something was nagging at her. She should've been comforted by Matt's words, but she wasn't.

Matt was wrong. She wasn't sure about which part, exactly, but she knew in her gut that something wasn't right.

UPSET AND ANXIOUS, Taryn threw on a light jacket and long pants and headed out–this time in her car. It was almost midnight and most everyone would be up for the night. She'd never been to the beach after dark before, though, and wanted to see the water.

Mindful of alligators and other night critters Taryn chose a spot on Great Dune beach and spread out her blanket, her back resting on a hill of sand. The new hotel was going up not far from where she sat and she could see steel beams rising from the ground. During the day you could hear clanging and banging around as the workers rushed to finish their job. Now, however, it was quiet. It was just Taryn and the ocean.

The water looked black at night. The stretch of sand that acted as the beach was smaller now than it was during the day and she wondered how safe it was sitting in her location. The waves rolled in with gentle speed and lapped at her feet, coming close to touching but never quite reaching her. The full moon rose high above her, its light reflecting on the water and illuminating the beach.

"Well, it *is* a little eerie," she said aloud and then grinned. She could almost imagine seeing a young Mary the Wanderer, strolling through the sand, her white gown billowing. The woman she'd met at Driftwood had shared Mary's eyes and smile. Her cheekbones and chin. But she'd been very real.

Taryn was enjoying the serenity of the water, letting the pull of the moon calm her, when something caught her eye. About fifteen feet to her left there was a glimmer in the moonlight, something struggling in the sand. She watched it for a moment, at first thinking that a piece of garbage had flown over from the hotel. When the clouds parted and the beach grew lighter, however, she realized it wasn't a grocery bag blowing in the wind, but a shell.

"Oh shit," Taryn cried, jumping to her feet. "Damn it..."

She muttered to herself as she crossed the sand towards the baby sea turtle. Upon close inspection she could see that it was trapped in a hole, a plastic pop can ring tied around it. Taryn's first instinct was to carefully lift it up and free it but then she remembered what she'd read and heard about the turtles. She wasn't meant to touch them at all, she was supposed to call the Sea Turtle Center if there was a problem

Rummaging around in her knapsack while still keeping an eye on the little guy she fished for the brochure with the phone number. It rang twice before a man who was way too chirpy for that time of night answered. "Y'ello!" he called into the phone. "How can I help you?"

"Hi," Taryn replied, kneeling down to get a better look at its predicament. Maybe if she could at least get the plastic off... "I'm on the beach and I found a baby sea turtle. I think it's in trouble."

The man's voice turned serious then. "Give me your location and I'll be there in fifteen minutes," he promised.

Taryn rattled off her general whereabouts and then hung up. "Well, it's just you and me little guy, at least for a few minutes."

The turtle looked up at her and moved its tiny head up and down.

"Please don't die on my watch," Taryn pleaded.

Settling in next to the hole, Taryn made herself at home while she waited. She knew she wasn't supposed to touch him but if a wave came or he got more wrapped up she was going to do whatever she had to do.

Left alone with the turtle, Taryn sighed. It was always something.

A noise came then, the slight sound of laughter behind her. She started to rise to her feet, the words, "Well that was fast" on her lips. Something made her stop, though, and she fell back to the ground. Taryn was protected by a dune to her back but could now clearly hear the sounds of several men joking and laughing with one another.

"Probably just some guys looking for fun," she assured the turtle. "They won't bother us." A black-crowned night heron screeched just then and Taryn jumped.

"Geeze, I'm getting skittish," she laughed nervously. Being a female alone on the sand, though, made her nervous. Suppose the other men had been drinking or doing something illegal?

One of them laughed and then Taryn heard the sound of metal. *They were at the hotel site, then,* she thought to herself. Maybe they'd forgotten something. She strained her ears harder as she listened to their laughter.

"Just don't drop it for Christ's sake," one of them muttered. His voice was raspy, like maybe he smoked a lot.

"Did anyone even look at it?" another one laughed. He sounded younger than the other one. "How the hell do we even know what's in here?"

"We don't," a third man replied. "We don't ask and they don't tell. Just walk!"

Taryn slowly brought herself to her knees and peered over the tall sea grass. She was shielded from their view but realized with a start that they were only about ten feet away. They worked in the dark and Taryn watched in fascination as they lifted a box heavy enough that all three of them had to lift.

"One, two, three!" the smoker cried and they all raised the box high in the air. Straining from the effort, they carried it to a nearby truck and slid it onto the bed. "One more!"

Taryn watched again as they went back to the spot near her and lifted another one from the ground and carried it back to the truck.

"What they don't know won't hurt 'em," a skinny man in a baseball cap laughed.

"Hey, is this the turtle?" Taryn jumped and spun around. At the same time, she heard the men above her running across the grass and jumping into the truck. As it took off Taryn watched as the older gentleman walked towards her.

"Uh, yeah, this is it," she pointed nervously.

The man appeared to be in his late sixties but walked with a lift in his step. He moved with little effort through the sand, a container that looked like a cooler in his hands.

Taryn watched as he gently pried the plastic off the baby and then lowered it into the container. "I'll take him back to the hospital and let them check him out," he promised. "Thanks for calling."

"Can I come check on him later?" Taryn asked. Now that she wasn't alone she didn't feel as spooked, but she hadn't yet recovered from what she'd just seen the men do.

"Sure!" he smiled, his teeth sparkling in the night. "Just come on over tomorrow and we'll give you an update."

Taryn walked back up to the parking lot with him. It was only after she was back in the safety of her house that she let herself accept the truth.

Just before she'd turned around she'd made definite eye contact with the man in the baseball cap. She wasn't sure he could pick her out of a lineup, what with the moon behind her and the tall sea grass between them, but *she'd* be able to pick *him* out of anything.

THIRTEEN

"You weren't supposed to be here until tonight," Taryn *cried*, pleasant surprise filling her.

Matt stood on her front porch, a small rolling suitcase behind him. His midnight-black hair was soft and shiny, his dark skin smooth without a single line. He beamed at Taryn, his smile stretching from ear to ear as he reached out and engulfed her in an embrace. "I couldn't wait," he mumbled into her hair.

Taryn, who'd only just woken up when she heard the pounding on the door, was wearing a ratty T-shirt with her hair sticking out every which way from her head. She knew her breath was not nice.

"Come on in," she said, trying to shield her mouth with her hand. "I'll be right back."

"Are you trying to hide your morning breath?" Matt laughed as she darted off into the bathroom.

"No!" Taryn cried as she frantically scrubbed at her teeth with one hand and pulled a brush through her tangled mess of hair with the other.

By the time she came back out Matt had made himself at home on her couch and was flipping through her pictures on her laptop. "These are fantastic," he said, zooming in on the shots she'd taken off inside the hotel.

"Thanks," Taryn answered, settling down beside him. She snuggled into his side and then took his arm and put it around her. "I'm glad you're here."

Matt leaned back against the couch, bringing Taryn with him. "Me too. I didn't think I could last another day. And I'm digging your bedroom attire."

Taryn, aware that her T-shirt was riding up her legs and bunching around her waist giggled, a rare sound for her. "I wore it just for you."

"Hey, isn't that my T-shirt from high school?"

Taryn nodded and snuggled in close. "Yep."

"I've been missing that for, oh, fifteen years or something," he mused.

"Yep."

They might have found other ways to entertain themselves, but a few minutes later the housekeeper strolled through the front door.

"Oh!" she shrieked and jumped when she saw Matt and Taryn cuddled on the couch. "I'm sorry! I'll come back."

Taryn laughed at the way she tried to shield her eyes and look the other way. "It's okay. I've got to get dressed and we're going out. Please, don't let us keep you. I know you want to get this done and go home."

Carla grinned sheepishly and nodded at Matt. "It's true. This is my easiest house. Taryn doesn't do much of anything in here."

"Is that so? Things must have changed from the packrat I know," Matt teased her.

Matt continued to go through her photos when Taryn excused herself to get dressed. When she emerged a few minutes later, she found Carla mopping the kitchen floor, her earbuds stuffed in her ear and iPod on.

"Hey, I want to tell you about something that happened last night," Taryn said as she slipped on her sandals.

"What's up? And will you need your camera? I can put the battery back in if you want," Matt gestured to where it was charging in the wall.

"Yeah, sure. Can't leave Miss Dixie behind," Taryn replied. "So last night I went for a walk on the beach and…"

When she finished Matt studied her and frowned. "I don't know," he said at last. "Sounds like something illegal was going on. You're lucky they didn't try to hurt you."

"Oh, I was fine," she admonished him but inside she agreed. She'd been nervous herself.

"Look, I'd just keep it to yourself, okay?" Matt looked worried for her sake. "I know I'm usually all about calling authorities and doing things by the book but I don't like you being here alone and thinking something might happen."

"Well, normally I'd be all about putting my nose into places where it doesn't belong but on this point I agree with you," Taryn said. "The last thing I need is more trouble."

With both of them ready to leave the house Taryn threw her hand up in a wave towards Carla. "See you later Carla," she bellowed.

The housekeeper didn't look up.

"Bye Carla!" Taryn tried again.

This time Carla jerked her head up from the mop and fiddled with a button on her iPod. "Bye-bye girl," she waved. "See you next week!"

Once they were settled into the golf cart and Taryn was whizzing down the road Matt chuckled to himself.

"What are you laughing about?" she asked.

"Your maid," he answered. "You do realize that she didn't have that iPod on, right?"

"What?" Taryn asked in confusion.

Matt shrugged. "No idea why. It hadn't been on since she started working. She was just pretending not to hear you there at the end."

Taryn pursed her lips and picked up the speed. Now she had something else to worry her.

*   *   *

"So what are we looking for?"

Matt held up a bulging file folder and flipped through the loose papers inside. "It's a little hard to know where to start."

Taryn, sitting crossed-legged in the middle of the dusty room, held up her folder. "We're looking for records on

William and Rachel," she replied. "Back then they would've kept records of when they stayed, what they did while they were here, and maybe even more detailed information about who they were. You know, so that they could provide the best service."

"And you think that will help?" Matt mused, settling in beside her so that their shoulders were touching.

"It can't hurt. There's been almost nothing about either one of them online. It seems that except for the fact they were rich and lived in New York City with some of these other guys there wasn't anything notable about either one of them. He didn't invent anything, she was an heiress but not, like, an important one."

Matt grunted, his concentration keen on the files.

"And I promise, Matt, that tonight we'll do something fun," Taryn promised. "I swear."

"Oh yeah, we will," he agreed. "Why else you think I follow you around in dirty rooms and spend hours digging my nose into the lives of people who have been dead for a hundred years?"

Taryn swatted him with a century-old hotel receipt and smiled.

Ellen hadn't been surprised when Taryn asked to see the records. She let her assume that the more she knew about the place, the easier it was to work. "Now it's hot and stuffy up here," Ellen's assistant, Amy, had warned them as they climbed the stairs in the back of the hotel, "so you might want to crack those windows."

She was right. It *was* hot and stuffy. And the lone light bulb that dangled from the ceiling did very little to brighten it up. Still, once she'd gotten into the work Taryn forgot about those things.

Taryn was fascinated with the history of the hotel and turn of the century period in general. She could've spent hours poring over the records, letters, and newspaper clippings. She spent about ten minutes reading in detail all the items someone had ordered from the mainland, from flour to shoe polish, for instance. It had nothing to do with what she was looking for but even the smallest of details gave her insight on the inner workings of the island.

Matt, who looked up on occasion and shook his head at her rapturous attention to such things, claimed she missed her calling as an anthropologist.

"Okay, got one," Matt said after about an hour. "Right here. They checked in here for the first time. There's a note by their names."

Taryn took the piece of paper and studied it. "Hmmm...so this is dated more than a year before the fire burned everything. So I guess that tells us that they weren't newcomers. People obviously knew who they were."

Matt went back to his folder and continued making a neat stack of everything he'd looked at already. Just a few seconds went by before he spoke again. "Okay, here's something else. Very interesting."

"Huh?" Taryn was lost again, this time in notes on the construction of Adena Cottage.

"Look here. It says that they were moved. They apparently spent two nights in this room," Matt pointed to the first location in the note, "and then requested to move to another one for the rest of their stay."

"Does it give a reason?" Taryn asked, peering over his arm.

"Yeah. It says they wanted something that caught the morning light. Kind of strange," Matt said.

"Maybe not. Some people like the sunrise," Taryn shrugged. "It's the best light to paint in. I just never get up that early. Maybe Rachel was a painter herself."

"I don't think that's it," Matt continued, "because it also makes a note to say that they've requested extra lamps."

Taryn placed her folder on the floor and rose to her feet. The small window they'd opened to ease the stuffiness was at the other end of the room. She faced it now. It was afternoon, and although the sun was high in the sky, long dark shadows raced across the floor.

"Were they in this building at first?" she asked as she walked towards the window.

Matt nodded and told her the room number.

When she reached the window she gazed outside. The grounds on this side of the hotel were darker, full of trees that had been there for centuries. This entire part of the hotel was cast in shadows and somehow gloomier than the rest. William and Rachel's room would've faced that direction.

"That explains that, then," Taryn nodded.

"What?"

She looked back and pursed her lips. "I think one of them was afraid of the dark..."

*   *   *

STEVE AND THE OTHER VALETS were standing on the steps, heads bent together, when Matt and Taryn walked out.

"You guys planning a heist or something?" Taryn teased them.

The four men looked up with sheepish grins and laughed. "Naw, there's a race going on," Steve explained. "We've all got bets going. The pot's big this time."

"Hey, I heard you found a baby turtle last night," one of the guys said to Taryn. She'd seen him around but didn't know his name. They hadn't actually spoken to one another yet.

"Yeah, how did you know?"

The man, who could've been anything from twenty to fifty, shrugged. "My uncle was the one on call. When he said your name I knew who you were."

"Do you know anything about the turtle? We were getting ready to go over there and check on him."

"Sorry," the man shook his head. "I haven't heard anything."

"Where'd you find him at?" Steve asked, leaning back against his wooden stand.

"On the beach by where the new hotel is going up," Taryn replied.

"Huh. It's good you found him instead of some kid," Steve said.

"Well, it was late at night," Taryn explained. "I was the only one out there."

She hadn't meant to share that with anyone but felt put on the spot.

"My uncle said it was wound up in some garbage, so it's a good thing you were out there that late. It wouldn't have survived at all if you hadn't seen him and called," the other valet spoke up.

Taryn nodded and started on down to the sidewalk, Matt beside her. "Well, I think we'll go over there and see how he's doing," she said. "See you guys later!"

Once they were out of earshot Taryn sighed. "Damn it, I wasn't going to announce to the world that I was out on the beach alone like that."

"I think you're fine with that group," Matt chuckled and reached for her hand.

*　　*　　*

"See, I told you I'd take you out and treat you right," Taryn said, lightly punching Matt on the arm.

Nodding in agreement, Matt leaned back on the park bench and took a bite of his frozen yogurt concoction. "This is wonderful."

"Yeah, well, nothing's too good for my baby. I can buy you the best fro-yo money can get," Taryn grinned.

It was nice, though; he was right.

After a dinner of crab cakes and rolls at Barbara Jean's they were sitting in the park, simultaneously people watching and gazing at the water as the sun set. St. Simon's Island was vastly different from Jekyll Island. Where Jekyll was quiet and laid back and moved at a serene pace, St. Simon's was vibrant and full of life.

The pier was full of teenagers showing off to one another, couples strolling hand in hand eating ice cream, and families barking orders at their children to not "get too close to the edge." Grizzled fishermen cast lines into the ocean, buckets beside them full of their catches. The scent from the fish washing station drifted through the air and mixed with the heat of the day and the salt of the ocean.

Clothing boutiques, small restaurants, ice cream stores, and toy shops peppered the small village. There were surprisingly few souvenir places and Taryn appreciated that. It was still a tourist destination; that much was obvious, yet managed to look like a quaint seaside town.

Of course, Taryn had driven around the roundabout twice before she figured out how to get off. It annoyed her that a traffic circle had beaten her but she was up and ready for round two on the way back.

"I think I'd like to live here," Taryn said suddenly.

Matt turned and looked at her, surprise etching his face. "Really? It's not too crowded?"

"Kind of the right kind of crowded, I think," she answered, watching a group of toddlers playing on a live oak. Its limbs reached all the way to the ground, and the little ones were riding one of the limbs like a horse, giggling and shouting with glee. Taryn thought she felt her uterus jump a little.

"You'd move here, without there being any historical homes or big abandoned place to buy and fix up?" he teased her.

She'd thought about that already.

"I thought you didn't do ranch houses," Matt added.

Well, that was true enough and St. Simon's seemed to have something against two story homes. And gutters. There were no gutters. What was up with that?

"I don't know," she shrugged. The quiet tree-lined streets we saw, the kids playing out on their bikes, the clean beaches, the nice restaurants, the history...Maybe I could give up my old houses for all those things."

"And me?" He asked it teasingly, but his soft tone had Taryn looking at him. For a moment she thought he looked sad but then his eyes softened and she figured it must have been a trick of the moonlight that was taking over.

"You'd be welcome to visit anytime you wanted," she assured him.

"Every night?"

Used to feeling cold chills when something supernatural was about to happen, now Taryn felt cold chills of another kind creep across her neck. "Sure. *Any*time."

"Will you marry me?" Matt asked abruptly.

Taryn, who was mid-bite, found her spoon flying from her hand and landing in the dirt. "Uh...are you proposing?"

Matt laughed and patted her on the knee. "No, not yet. You'll know when I am. I am just asking *will* you, when the time comes?"

Taryn put her cup of chocolate yogurt down beside her and snuggled into Matt's arm. "I couldn't imagine life without you," she answered with total honesty.

The ride back to Jekyll Island only took them fifteen minutes and Taryn was pleased with herself for not letting the roundabout get the best of her again.

In contrast to St. Simon's light and activity, Jekyll was dark and quiet. An oppressive mood settled over Taryn as they got out of the car and started into the house. She'd felt so much lighter on the other island. Now she felt depressed.

"The ghosts must be getting to me," she mumbled, as she started towards the bedroom.

"What?" Matt called from the kitchen where he was bringing down a pitcher of tea he'd left sunning in the window all day.

"Nothing. Just talking to myself," Taryn hollered back.

Feeling grimy and sweaty she considered hopping in the shower but decided she was too tired. Instead, she slipped on her nightgown, brushed her hair, and scrubbed her face. Matt's toiletries took up almost as much space as her own on the bathroom sink and this made her smile. She also grinned at the sight of his bathrobe hanging on the back of the bathroom door and his towel folded neatly on the edge of the bathtub. Matt always traveled with his own bath towel, even to five-star hotels.

When she finished she returned to the bedroom. While Matt puttered around in the kitchen Taryn busied herself in the bedroom. She turned on the lamp on the nightstand, stacked the throw pillows neatly on the floor, and removed the afghan at the bottom of the bed. When she reached for the blankets to pull them down, however, something extraordinarily red under the snowy white duvet caught her eye.

Not altogether comprehending what was before her, Taryn flung the covers back with gusto. The angry and frightened snake that slithered towards her at a lightning-fast speed might not have been very long at only two feet but when its tiny tongue flew out in a livid "hisssss" Taryn dropped straight to the ground in a dead faint.

FOURTEEN

Fr the fifth time in less than an hour the *grandfatherly* officer assured Matt that he'd done the right thing.

"I've never killed a living creature before. I even catch mice and take them out to fields," Matt worried. "But when I saw that thing slithering around her, I didn't even think twice."

"You did the right thing," the elderly gentleman replied. "If it had've been my own wife, I'd have beat that thing to a bloody pulp for touching her."

"It already bit her once. Are they supposed to go back again for another try?" Matt asked in wonder.

Taryn, propped up in a hospital gown, opened her eyes and looked around in a glassy daze. Her calf throbbed with an ache that wasn't part of her "normal" pain and her head felt thick. She thought she might vomit and reached for the bowl next to her bed. Both Matt and the officer reached for it at once and handed it to her together.

In embarrassment, Taryn emptied her stomach into the plastic container and tried to ignore the fact that there were people watching her. It was mostly bile that spewed forth, but it was bitter on her tongue, and that alone had her gagging a second time.

When she was finished Matt took the bowl from her and set it on the other side of the room, knowing that having it close would make her even sicker to her stomach. After he'd washed her face off with a cloth he dampened in the sink, he turned back to the officer.

"So that wasn't normal, right?"

"Well, even those coral snakes won't usually strike unless they feel threatened," he agreed.

"And we don't know if it bit her before or after she passed out," Matt said.

"I don't remember," Taryn croaked, finding her throat sore. "I just remember seeing it. Why am I so sick?"

"It might be the antidote," Matt replied. "We're in Brunswick. We got you here pretty fast, but the doctor thinks that because of your EDS it hit you harder."

"EDS?" the officer asked.

"Ehlers-Danlos Syndrome," Matt explained. "It's a connective tissue disorder. Pretty serious. It's basically like her body is a house and the bricks are all defective. It affects all of her systems and sometimes things that wouldn't hurt people like us just strike her harder."

"I'm sorry to hear that ma'am," the officer remarked, looking grave. "I would like to ask you a few questions, though."

"I'll try," Taryn answered weakly. She felt sick, like she had the flu. She just wanted to go back to sleep, but she also didn't want Matt leaving her.

"Have you had any trouble with anyone on the island?"

"Me? No," Taryn smiled thinly. "I don't interact with many people. I work most of the time and keep to myself."

"What about friends?" he pressed.

"I haven't made any," Taryn stated drily. Now she felt sorry for herself. She'd been there for weeks and hadn't made even a real acquaintance, other than David. "Oh, wait, I did make a little bit of a friend. His name is David. We've been hanging out. I haven't seen him in a few days though."

Matt turned and looked at her, his eyes full of questions. She could feel his mind probing at hers, seeking answers. He'd always been able to do that. She tried to ignore it now and let him search.

"Any chance he's upset with you?"

Taryn laughed. "No, no. We're on the same side."

The officer, who'd been making notes in a small booklet, snapped his head up and gazed at her. "'Same side'? What do you mean by that?"

"Oh, not that there are sides or anything. It's just that he works in historic preservation, in a sense, and that's my area as well. I recreate historic structures through my paintings. We both love history is what I meant."

"Are you thinking that someone did this to her on purpose?" Matt asked narrowing his eyes.

"Oh well, we don't want to go that far. We just like to cover our bases."

"How else could the snake have gotten in the house?" Matt pressed, moving closer to Taryn and taking her hand. The IV point was sore, and the pain raced all the way up her arm but she didn't want to let go.

The officer shrugged. "Well, they're small fellers. Could've come in through a hole you don't even know you have. Or sneaked in when you left the door open bringing in groceries or something. They can live like that for days before coming out and making themselves known."

Taryn shuddered at the idea of having lived with a snake for "days" and not knowing it.

"Well, if you can think of anything else, just let me know," the officer said, snapping his notebook closed. "I'm sure this is just an accident. My names Juniper and I've left my number with your husband here."

Taryn closed her eyes and nodded, not bothering to correct him. "That's the name of the guard who took him to the cemetery..." she mumbled groggily.

"What?" Matt and Juniper asked in unison.

Taryn shook her head. "Never mind."

When he was gone Matt pulled a chair up to her bedside and took her hand again. "They said you can go home tomorrow probably. I'm going to leave here in a little bit and make a clean sweep of the house just in case that guy has some friends hiding out."

"My grandmother always said 'where there's one, there's two,'" Taryn agreed. She was slurring her words, unable to keep her eyes open. She felt like she could sleep for a week.

"You want me to go back now? I could bring you a change of clothes, your hairbrush or something," he offered.

"Can you just stay here awhile?" Taryn mumbled, snuggling down into her flat hospital pillow. "Don't leave me by myself for awhile."

He leaned over and brushed the hair back from her face and then let his hand rest against her cheek. "I'm not going anywhere," he answered.

Taryn let herself drift off, trying to convince herself that what she'd seen and heard on the beach had nothing to do with what had happened earlier that night.

*   *   *

"How 'ya feeling?"

Taryn glanced over at Matt and rolled her eyes. It was the sixth time he'd asked her that in an hour. She tried to remind herself that he didn't *mean* to be annoying; he was just concerned.

"Not so bad," she answered, barely looking up from her painting. She hadn't felt like going to either cottage so she'd set her easel up in the back yard. Matt had pulled a fold-up chair near her and was flipping through a Terry Pratchett book. "Good to be busy."

"Anything hurt?"

"Not any more than usual," came her curt reply.

She'd ended up staying in the hospital for two days, much to her aggravation. Three jobs in the past year had put her in the hospital. Her insurance company was just going to *love* her. She grimaced now, thinking about the bills that would probably beat her home.

"You got more flowers delivered," Matt spoke up again. "I put them in your kitchen."

"Yeah? Who they from?"

"The woman over at the hotel."

"Oh," Taryn paused, paintbrush mid-air. "Well that was nice."

Ellen, of course, had been horrified. "What a terrible, *terrible* accident," she'd cried, yet still hadn't managed to lose her composure.

Matt was still convinced that it was no "accident."

"Hey, I was talking to this waitress over at that restaurant last night? Eldean? She said she'd waited on you."

Taryn sighed and put her paintbrush down. It was becoming clear that she would get little work done. Matt was unusually chatty this afternoon.

"Yeah. What did she say?"

Matt shrugged. "She told me about the airport over on the other island and how, when they put it in, they found all those Indian graves."

Taryn frowned. "I knew about that. Had I not told you?" She felt like her memory was getting worse and worse these days.

"Yeah, I remembered you telling me but Eldean said that for a long time nobody knew about the skeletons. That the airport was already in and by that time nobody wanted to dig it up," Matt explained.

"So then there are probably more graves under it..." Taryn found herself shivering, thinking about how disrespectful it was to have take-offs and landings over a final resting place.

"Well, I was thinking about what you saw the other night. What if they found a gravesite and was trying to clear it out?"

Taryn turned her chair around to face Matt and considered. "That had crossed my mind as well. Interesting. It would definitely delay construction if they found something," she mused. "And from what I understand, which granted is very little, it could set them back a lot of money to stop construction and have the archaeologists and anthropologists come in."

"So it makes sense," Matt agreed.

"Wouldn't it be funny if they'd found the pirate gold or something?" Taryn laughed. "I mean, it didn't *look* like your average treasure chest with skulls painted on it but you never know."

"You never know," Matt assented. "I still don't think you should talk to anyone else about this. They're obviously up to something, and that snake was no accident. Somebody put it there. Be careful, Taryn. If they put an alligator in your bed you might be on your own." With that, he picked his book back up again and began reading.

Ha, Taryn thought to herself, *just like a man. I stop working to talk to him and as soon as she's finished he tunes me out.*

She started to turn back around when something bright by the corner of the house caught her eye. Flinching, and bracing herself for another unwelcomed reptile attack, she laughed in relief when David moved forward.

"Hey, sorry about that," he laughed. "I heard about what happened and wanted to come see how you were."

Matt looked back up and scowled at the long-haired man standing before them. Taryn was taken aback by their similarities. She knew that not all Native Americans looked alike, but Matt and David had strikingly similar features, from the shapes of their noses and chins to the golden shade of their skin. They even moved with a similar grace.

Oh good, Taryn thought with relief. *Maybe* that's *why I've been attracted to him...because he looks like Matt and I've been missing him.*

"Matt, David. David, Matt," Taryn quickly made the introductions.

In a rare form of insolence, Matt glowered at David and narrowed his eyes. "How long have *you* been standing there?"

Matt!" Taryn hissed, shocked and embarrassed. Matt was usually the politest person she knew. He was even courteous when she personally thought the situation called for something more redneck.

David, however, was nonplussed. "I just got here," he laughed. "Just wanted to check on our girl. She's the only person I've had the chance to get to know since being here."

Taryn felt her face burn at the "our girl" part and saw Matt's scowl deepen.

"Well," Matt replied, "she's doing great. *I've* been taking care of her."

Taryn groaned inwardly and resisted the urge to roll her eyes at this uncommon show of jealousy. "Have a seat," she gestured to her own chair and stood. "I'll go get me another one."

Both men moved toward her at once. "I'll get it," they insisted in unison and then looked at one another, one with a grimace and the other in amusement.

"I'll be fine, I'll be fine," she muttered with a smile and strolled off. Shaking her head, she walked around the house to the front porch to grab another chair, leaving the two men alone.

"Well," she said aloud, "this is going to be awkward."

And maybe a little fun, she added silently. After all, she *was* female.

*   *   *

"I still say he's been standing there listening to us the whole time," Matt insisted.

"Dude, let it go," she laughed. "Just let it go."

She'd felt fine when they left the house. She even drove the golf cart herself, despite Matt's insistence of letting him give it a spin. Now that they were at Adena Cottage, however, Taryn was exhausted. She'd broken into a sweat and her legs felt heavy. The beginning of a headache was annoying her. Still, she wanted to get out and show Matt her job sites. She'd been a terrible hostess. He was meant to return home that evening but had opted to stay one more night to ensure she was over the worst of it. Now Taryn was worried about his job. How long would NASA put up with that? Weren't they already on thin ice budget wise?

"You *sure* you're feeling up to this?" Matt asked in concern, glancing over at her as they wandered through grass.

"Yeah, yeah. I'm fine," she swore, though she knew she was pale and had never truly been able to fool Matt—not even when they were kids. "Besides, we're just going to walk around a house. We're not swimming the rapids or climbing Kilimanjaro."

Standing before the derelict cottage, Matt frowned. "You're right. It's not in very good condition."

"Yeah, well, they're going to start working on it in the fall," Taryn retorted. She felt defensive of the aging beauty. It wasn't her fault nobody had maintained her. "She'll be a real showstopper then."

"I'm sure she will," he concurred, but his almost condescending tone had Taryn's hackles rising.

"Here, just look up there at that turret," she pointed. "Isn't it magnificent?"

Matt tried to look appreciative but failed. "I'm sorry, Taryn, I know you love those features but I'm more of a simple guy myself. It' all a little much for me. I'm probably more of a brick ranch house on St. Simon's, to be honest."

Taryn was inexplicably disappointed. She knew they didn't have to have everything in common and that there were couples who were complete opposites and still managed to have totally healthy relationships. Still, the old houses and architecture were more than just a love and hobby for her– they were an essential *part* of her.

"Well, you can at least appreciate the porch, right?" she asked hopefully. "I mean, with a swing and some white wicker chairs...It would look pretty wouldn't it?"

Maybe feeling like he'd disappointed her enough he slipped his arm around her shoulder. "It's a fantastic porch," Matt said. "It will be a great place to enjoy the sunset, drink lemonade, and relax. I do love a good porch on a house."

Feeling pitifully better, and hating herself for feeling like she needed his approval, Taryn moved and began walking around the edge of the house, being careful not to get too close.

"I'd love to go inside but this is in bad shape, even for me," she explained when they stopped by a large window.

"Considering your luck I don't think it would be a great idea," Matt agreed. "She might just get mad and fall down on you."

"Oh no, Adena wouldn't do that to me," Taryn proclaimed. There was that defensiveness again. "She *likes* me. It's Ivy House who has a problem with me, although we're working on that. I think she's caving, no pun intended."

Matt didn't say anything, just smiled.

Taryn, overcome with an exhaustion of a different kind, fiddled with Miss Dixie's settings and cleaned the lens with a cloth she kept in her knapsack. "Listen, I'm going to take some shots of what's left of the roof," she said. "I'm having some trouble with it back at the house and I want to see if I missed anything."

"Okay," Matt sang cheerfully. "I'll just mosey on around the property myself."

Left alone, Taryn sighed and went to work. She was being too hard on Matt. He didn't have to like and appreciate everything she did. The important thing was that he supported her, right?

"Right," she assured herself out loud.

But she still wasn't entirely convinced.

*　　*　　*

"Let me see that again," Matt demanded, moving in to look at Taryn's computer screen.

"See?" she pointed at the top left-hand corner. "I missed it the first few times myself. But it's obvious now. Can't you see his face?"

Matt pursed his lips and studied the image. "Yeah, I see it. Definitely a man."

"And look..." Taryn brought up a copy of the image taken in front of Adena Cottage, the one containing Rachel, William, Georgiana, and her father. Taryn had taken a picture of the image while thumbing through the book in Ellen's office. "It's definitely him. It's William."

"I see it," Matt agreed. "And it does look like William. You're right about the house, too. It was attractive before it started falling apart."

In spite of their individual feelings towards the older homes, they both took a moment to sit back and admire the beauty of the once-grand vacation cottage. In the picture Taryn took of the back of the house, it was perfectly intact. "Yeah. It did look good," she said.

"So what do you think this means?" Matt asked, continuing to study the image, zooming in on the other windows to see if anything else stood out.

Taryn was ready with an answer. She'd been working on it for the past hour. "I think it means that William was having an affair with Georgiana. It explains why he didn't have a solid alibi for that night. Or it explains why he killed his wife in the first place. It was her money and if he divorced her he wouldn't get the cash. He tried to make it look like an accident."

"And then, once an acceptable amount of time went by, he could marry the other woman?" Matt ventured.

"Yes! Or else he was sleeping with her at the time of the fire and it really was an accident," Taryn mused. "But the fact that he's upstairs in what has to be a bedroom and kind of lurking around, see that weird look on his face, means something."

Matt nodded his head and considered this.

"And why else would he supposedly return to her grave every night put a candle on it?" Taryn asked with triumph.

"Love."

"Guilt!"

Both answered in unison and then laughed at one another.

"Well," Matt remarked drily. "It's easy to see who the cynic is between us."

"You've always been a romantic, dear," Taryn said fondly, patting him on the leg.

"I don't want to be a fly in this ointment, but you're assuming that was Georgiana's room. What if it were her father's? What if in this picture he'd been called up to talk to him?"

Matt's question was reasonable enough but Taryn didn't think that was it. To her, it was obvious that Rachel's ghost had sent her the image to prove that her late husband had been fooling around with another woman. After all, it had to be Rachel who was sending her the messages and haunting her.

Taryn was sure of that.

FIFTEEN

"I promise you'll like the beach," Taryn coaxed Matt, all but dragging him up the steep rise of sand. "This one is different."

"I live very close to the beach at home," he complained but continue to follow, lugging the beach bag that contained their drinks, blankets, and sunscreen.

"This is different," she promised. "You live near Daytona Beach. Since you don't really drink, never go to clubs, don't like loud noises, and think driving a car or four-wheeler on the sand is profane you've never fully appreciated the area you live in. You'll *like* this."

Matt may have grumbled, but he'd go along with just about anything Taryn wanted and she often used this to her advantage. She knew what Matt would like, and what he wouldn't, and this was something he needed to see.

When they crested the rise and stood looking out over the water, Taryn could feel Matt's exhale, a sigh of relief. "Okay," he relented with a grin. "You were right."

"I knew you'd see it that way. Now come on," she cried, running towards the water and leaving a spray of sand in her wake.

"Of course *you* can run. You're not carrying anything," he complained, but his mood was lifted.

Lately it seemed like when they were together they had little fun. Their time was mostly spent talking about work (his or hers) or him attempting to solve the many problems that plagued Taryn since her abilities deepened. The enjoyment of each other's company they'd experienced as children and young adults often felt pushed to the wayside, ignored in favor of "real world" life and issues. For the first time in a long while they were able to relax, play in the sand, chase each other around, and act like they were a real couple.

While Matt floated on his back, enjoying his weightlessness in the salt water and the expanse of blue sky above him, Taryn walked along the shoreline, picking up shells and sand dollars. Occasionally they'd meet back on their blanket and apply liberal amounts of sunscreen to one another, sharing drinks and nibbling on fruit. They body surfed on the gentle waves together, Taryn always careful not to get too far out and Matt keeping his eye on her at all times, knowing she wasn't a strong swimmer.

When the sun was high in the sky they returned to their blanket to rest, the back of Taryn's head resting on his flat stomach so that she could watch the clouds. He brushed back her wet hair from her face with one hand and played with her fingers with the other. Taryn felt content and safe in a way that she rarely did when surrounded by people. The beach was quiet and empty. There wasn't a single person in sight.

"It's funny that the water bothers you sometimes, considering that you're a water sign," Matt mused at last.

"What? I like the water," Taryn insisted. "I think it's peaceful."

"You like looking at it," he corrected. "You don't like being out on a boat, you definitely don't like the big choppy waves when it storms, and you're not big on swimming. You just like to kind of bob around in it."

Well, that was true enough.

"Maybe I drowned in a past life," she suggested. "Or something."

"Have you ever considered the fact that you're more drawn to fire than you are to water?"

Taryn turned on her side to face him. From that angle she thought he looked like a little kid again. It was both comforting and unnerving. "You think?"

"Sure," he nodded. "When Nana used to burn her trash you'd always stand there and stare at the fire. I remember coming out of the house once with more boxes, and you were just standing there, not five feet away from the monstrous flames, and your hair was flying back out of your face. You were staring at it, kind of like 'bring it on!' You looked like the Firestarter or something. When I got up next to you the heat was so awful I had to take a few steps back. I don't know how you stood it; you hadn't even broken a sweat."

"I don't remember that," Taryn frowned. Although, to be fair, her grandmother had burned her garbage a lot. Back then nobody cared as much. And Matt was always around offering to help out.

"And any time we've stayed someplace with a fireplace you always fall asleep in front of it, watching the logs," he continued. "You have trouble sleeping alone and hate the dark but start a fire and you're out like a baby."

"Yeah, that's true enough."

"So maybe water is your birth sign but fire is your life sign. Or something," he offered. "I don't know a lot about those things."

"You think that's why I am so drawn to what happened at the hotel?" Taryn asked.

"Maybe. Or maybe that's why it's so drawn to you."

Taryn would have to think about that some more.

"Hey, I have to get back and change and then run over to the hotel for a few minutes. You want to have a quickie here on the beach?" Taryn wagged her eyebrows up and down suggestively and traced a line over his chest with her finger.

The look of horror that flashed across Matt's face had her laughing. "Here? In public?"

"Yes Matt, in front of all these people..." She gestured to the expanse of empty sand.

"I don't know...all that sand everywhere..."

"Okay, but don't say I didn't ask," she warned him, rising to her feet. "I wanted to have sex, but you didn't..."

"Hey now, that's not fair," he complained. "You knew I'd say no."

They were still laughing and teasing one another after they'd packed up their bag and were walking through the woods back to her car.

Behind them, someone stood over the indentions they'd left in the sand. Fury permeated and bounced off them, creating waves of anger that rolled out in all directions. Overhead a seagull squawked in fear and decided against landing on that particular stretch of beach. The figure seethed and simmered, resentment filling them. And then they were gone.

*   *   *

"Thanks for stopping by Taryn," Ellen thanked her as she walked her down to the hotel lobby. "I hope you're feeling better."

"I am," Taryn agreed. "I just wanted to let you know that I'd be gone for a few days but that the paintings are still on schedule and will be delivered in time."

"Do you need anything?" Amy, Ellen's assistant asked. She was pert young woman with a haircut that left her looking like a pixie and big blue eyes. Taryn was reminded of Rosemary Woodhouse.

"No, I'm fine. I'm going to drive up to the airport in Savannah and leave my car there," she answered.

"I live in Savannah. What time's your flight? I could take you," Amy offered. "Save on parking."

"Actually, that would be nice," Taryn assented. "I'll email you the itinerary when I get back to the house."

It was the start of the "magic hour" when Taryn made it outside and the hotel was lit up with a rosy glow. Without any cars in the circular driveway or people in modern clothing milling around going in and out it reminded Taryn of what the hotel would've looked like back when it was first constructed. It was nice to be able to see a glimpse of the past in person, rather than having to rely on Miss Dixie's talents, and Taryn found herself enjoying a quiet moment. She wanted to throw on a white tea dress, straw hat, and stroll the front porch.

Maybe I'll do that soon, she smiled.

With all the talk of death, fires, murder, and mysteries it was getting harder and harder to see places for the good and gentle times they'd experienced. She had to remind herself that the hotel had been a treasure, and still was, regardless of the terrible incident that had cost so many their lives.

Wanting to capture the moment Taryn turned Miss Dixie on and snapped several photos of the front lawn, circular porch, and curving driveway. Then, with the sky a glorious blaze of color, she walked down to the river and snapped a shot of a shrimp boat docking at the rickety wooden pier.

It was a picture-perfect scene.

Taryn didn't know then that it would be one of the last peaceful moments she'd have on the island.

*   *   *

"Why didn't you tell me that you were going up to New Hampshire?" Matt demanded.

"I talked to you about it already," Taryn sniffed. "I even asked you to go with me. You said you couldn't, that you couldn't leave your project."

"I don't want you going up there alone," Matt said, his face reddening. He stalked around her living room, picking up blankets and folding them, rearranging sofa cushions, stacking magazines on the coffee table–typical things Matt tended to do when he was frustrated or nervous. "I won't let you."

"*Let me*," Taryn snorted. "Please."

"You've had too much happen to you, Taryn. What if something happens up there? What am I supposed to do?"

Taryn tried hard to keep her composure. They'd been arguing about this for two hours. She knew this was Matt's way of showing that he cared but it was making her angry and she also knew that any minute she was liable to explode and say something she shouldn't.

"I am just going to fly up there, rent a car, look at Aunt Sarah's house, and meet with the lawyer. Then I'm coming back. I'm only spending one night!"

"Then I'll call work and get a few more days off. I'll go with you."

Taryn smiled thinly and closed her eyes to gather her thoughts. "Look, I truly appreciate it but this may be something that I have to do on my own. I should've gone up there months ago. I'll be fine. I can't expect you to protect me always."

Matt did not look happy. "You're never going to really let me in, are you?" he asked sadly. "Whenever I have helped you it's because I've invited myself or just shown up. You don't need me do you?"

"Aw, Matty." Taryn gazed him with guilt. She'd hurt his feelings, she could see that written all over his face, and she felt terribly guilty for doing so. "You're my best friend. I don't know what I would do without you. But you have to let me—"

"Go?" he finished for her.

"No," she corrected him. "You have to let me make mistakes sometimes and do things alone."

Matt lowered his eyes and focused on a spot on the area rug. Taryn, feeling sorry that they were arguing when they didn't have much time left together, put her hand on his leg.

"What's the matter, Matt?" she asked. "You've seemed a little off since you've been here?"

"I don't think I like what I'm doing anymore," he confessed softly. "Not with you, not with work, not with my house..."

Taryn felt like the bottom of her stomach dropped out. "What do you mean with me? Do you want to stop seeing me?"

"No!" he cried, looking up, eyes hot. "The opposite actually. The panic I feel about something happening to us makes me crazy. I want more. I'm just not happy."

"You've wanted to work at NASA your whole life," she pointed out. "What else would you do?"

"I don't know," he shrugged. "I might enjoy teaching. And I do have an engineering degree. I've always been interested in bridges."

She tried to imagine Matt working in something that didn't involve space but couldn't. Still, he looked like the little boy she'd known as a child, his eyes big and sad. He was depressed. She could feel it. And she didn't know how to help him.

"I don't think you *need* me," Matt said as he stood and began pacing the room. "Clarissa *needed* me. I felt like my presence added something to her life. Even her parents talked about how much better her life was with me in it."

Taryn, whose burst of sympathy suddenly waned slightly, wasn't sure if she should roll her eyes, snort, or laugh. If only he were joking...

"Matt, comparing me to your ex-girlfriend, the one who dumped *you* by the way, isn't going to win me over. I need you in a different way. I've known you longer than I haven't known you and I can't really fathom a life without you in it in some way. But I still need my independence. I still need to do things my own way. That's just who I am."

Matt broke his gaze and lowered his eyes. "But with Clarissa–"

"I don't mind talking about our future or your current job or your new job or whatever else we have going on right now, but I don't want to talk about an ex-girlfriend who never treated you well to begin with," Taryn fumed.

"You bring up Andrew all the time," Matt pointed out. "And he's been dead for, what, six years?"

"Andrew didn't leave me on purpose," Taryn nearly shouted. "He *died*! And you know you're the only person I've tried to make a relationship work with since."

"Things with Clarissa were just so much different and–"

"Oh my God, Matt!" Taryn jumped to her feet and stalked the living room, looking for her shoes. When she found her beat-up sandals, she slipped them on and headed the door. "I'm going out for a few minutes."

"Where are you going?" Matt cried, looking at her in panic.

"To ride my bike. I'll be back in a few minutes."

Taryn tried hard not to slam the front door behind her, but she was boiling. That was at least the fifth time Matt had brought up Clarissa's name over the course of his visit. Taryn knew they were getting close to the anniversary of Matt's breakup and that, for that reason, she was probably on his mind more than ever but Taryn was sick of it. Clarissa graduated at the top of her class, Clarissa's family had invited him for all the major holidays and even sprung for his plane ticket, Clarissa had constantly complimented him…

Yet she couldn't have been *that* perfect and their relationship so great. After all, she had dumped him just weeks before the wedding. Taryn herself had flown down to comfort him, drag his behind out of the house when he started to pale, done his grocery shopping and cooked his meals…She'd done her part to take care of him and listen. She thought she'd done enough.

Besides, she thought as she pedaled her bike furiously down Old Plantation Road and then through the quiet streets, *it wasn't anything like what had happened to Andrew.*

He'd died and left Taryn alone. Clarissa had just found someone else.

It was hard with Matt, she tried to remind herself, because they were so in tune with each other. She could be miles away and know that something was going on with him. They shared literal dreams with one another, often seeing the same landscape in their sleep. They were bound to have arguments.

Sometimes she just needed distance.

In spite of the late hour, Taryn wasn't the only one out for a night ride. She passed several men and women on their beach cruisers, their night lights flashing into the blackness. They sent polite waves to one another as they passed on the bike trail but nobody spoke. She sensed that she was the only one out for a leisure ride. Everyone else looked red and tired, their baskets stuffed with blankets and beach gear, as though they were returning home after a long day out on the sand.

Taryn rode for more than hour, going up and down residential streets before darting back out to the main road. Some of the rental houses had their lights on and curtains open. She caught glimpses of families sitting around dining room tables playing board games, of cartoons on the big-screen televisions, of parents laughing while the kids tried to swirl spaghetti strands around their forks. Everyone appeared so happy and relaxed, together as a family.

Taryn had never had that.

Of course, she knew that she wasn't getting the whole picture–it was easy enough to look happy and relaxed while you were on vacation.

Although she was cooling off now she was still frustrated with Matt. Part of her found his possessiveness endearing but the other part was angry. He wouldn't "let" her go to New Hampshire? Comparing her to an old girlfriend? Perhaps transitioning from best friend to boyfriend hadn't been as smooth as she'd thought. In the past it had been simple enough listening to him moan and groan about his relationships and their demise. She's sympathized with him, held his hand, and supported him. Now, though, she just didn't want to hear it. She didn't want to think he was comparing her to someone else and that she might be coming up short.

Realizing she was starting to work herself up again, Taryn stopped pedaling and slowed to a stop. Looking around, she saw that she was on a part of the island she'd never been on before. There was a pond before her and it glistened in the moonlight as prettily as the ocean did. A wide path led down to the edge. Although she was wary of things that lurked in the dark there, two streetlights overhead illuminated the path all the way down to the water. She could see the entire circumference, as well as the water's surface, and nothing appeared to be moving or slithering about.

Letting her bike fall gently to its side, Taryn slipped down the small embankment and strolled towards the edge of the water. A park bench had been planted there and she stopped and rested on it, letting her feet dangle in the air.

"Well that's just great," she scolded herself. "He's leaving in the morning and you're out here riding your bike by yourself and leaving him at the house."

Several cars drove by above, and this comforted her. At least she wasn't out there alone. People were still out and about.

Angry now, she fell back against the bench and sulked. Taryn didn't have much of a temper, but she *had* been known to cut off her nose to spite her face.

It was hormonal, she decided. She was tired and stressed and being unreasonable. She was worried about what had been happening on the island with the ghosts, still sick from the snakebite and antidote, and apprehensive about her upcoming trip to New Hampshire. The Clarissa thing had just been the last straw and not something that would've normally set her off.

Matt wasn't always the easiest person to deal with either. Although he was sensible most of the time, he had a stubborn and selfish streak in him, as well as a one-track mind.

And a *very* small understanding of women.

Groaning in weariness, Taryn realized she was finished with her bike ride and needed to get back to the house. She wasn't accomplishing anything out there alone, although she felt slightly better. The minute she rose from the bench, however, a noise from atop the rise had her taking a step back. It crunched and rustled, the sound of bushes moving aside and sticks breaking from something moving through and over them. Something *large*.

Taryn froze in her tracks and tried to peer up the small hill. She could still see her bike but was almost certain it was leaning on the ground more than a few feet away from where she'd left it. Taking a tentative step forward and holding her breath, Taryn moved slowly, her eyes darting all around her.

"Hello?" she called out in a hoarse voice. "Anyone there?"

Nobody answered, although the faint rustling continued, this time sounding much closer.

Hoping it was just another visitor out for a night stroll she picked up her pace, moving up the slight incline in several bounds.

The road spread out before her, dark and empty. She looked both ways but couldn't see headlights in any direction, nor were there any bikes or vehicles pulled over to the side. To her surprise, however, her bicycle helmet was laying several feet from the bike, close to a bush that was nearly as tall as she was.

Having distinctly remembered clasping it around her handlebars, Taryn froze in fright, her blood running cold through her veins. The straps were unclasped and spread out neatly to the sides, as though someone had placed it there intentionally.

"Hello?" she asked again, this time a tremble in her voice.

Taryn gently lifted her bike and kicked the kick stand, leaving it standing. The push to just *go, go, go* was strong in her, but the helmet had cost her $30 she hadn't really had and she was damned if she was going to leave it behind.

Creeping softly towards the bush where her helmet lay, Taryn twisted her fingers together and bit her lips, the blood pumping through her with rapid speed and her heart's pounding visible under her shirt.

When she was a foot away from the sparkly pink plastic helmet, she squatted down to pick it up, relief coursing through her that she could now make haste and get out of there. It was at that moment, however, that a sound she'd never heard before exploded from the bush just inches from her face. With her hand on the helmet she glanced up and found herself face-to-face with the long, scaly snout of an alligator.

Later she wouldn't be able to explain how she'd managed to pick up the helmet, run to her bike, and take off down the road so quickly. It was all so blurry. She'd moved with the speed of lightning, her feet barely touching the ground.

She would always, however, remember the sound of the four strong legs on the pavement, running behind her. In fact, she'd continue to hear that sound in her sleep for a very long time.

She's read about alligators and their speed. She knew how quickly they could move. She knew how short her legs were. There was no way she could outrun an alligator. When she looked back and saw it rambling towards her, much faster than what its bulky body should allow, she'd screamed—a wild sound that filled the air and pierced her lungs and yet was still swallowed by the towering pines and night sky.

On and on she'd cried as she'd ridden, a cold sweat making her handlebars slick. Once she'd lost her grip and nearly tumbled to the ground. Blinded by rage and fear, she'd lost sight of what was in front of her or where she was going, her only thought being to put as much distance between it and her as she could.

When her voice was hoarse and her body so heavy with fatigue she thought she'd faint, a truck pulled up beside her and honked, its sound barely registering with her. Ignoring it, she kept on riding wildly, her legs throbbing with pain and her arms and shoulders weak from exhaustion.

"Hey!" came a familiar voice. The truck had pulled up next to her again.

Glancing over she saw the familiar face of David, his mouth lined with concern. "You okay?"

"It's there, it's there! It's after me!" she cried, unwilling to slow down.

"What's after you?" he asked, glancing behind him.

"The gator! It's chasing me!"

Tears flowed down her face and were brushed away by the wind. Her nose was running and spittle caked her chin from where she'd been riding with her mouth open.

"There's no one there, Taryn. Nothing there," he hollered back. "Just stop. Get in the truck. I'll get your bike."

"No!"

"Taryn, get in. I promise it's gone."

Finally, Taryn came to a complete stop. In total exhaustion she flung her arms and head over her handlebars and wept, the sobs rolling off her in waves. She heard David get out of his truck and then felt him lift her from her bike. She let him carry her to the passenger side. Once in, she immediately locked the door and fell up against it, still sobbing.

Once he had her bike securely in the truck bed, he sped off.

"Tell me what happened," he demanded.

Through her tears she explained what she'd seen and heard.

"That's odd," he mused. "The gators here don't normally go after people. Maybe there were eggs or something nearby and it saw you as a threat." He didn't sound convinced, however.

Once at the house he picked her up and carried her to the door where Matt met them. "Here you go," David said, handing Taryn to a startled Matt. "I'll get her bike and explain in a minute."

Matt reached out and gathered Taryn up in his arms and carried her to the bedroom where he deposited her on the comforter. "Be right back," he promised, kissing her on the head.

Taryn dozed from exhaustion, drifting in and out of sleep. She could hear the men talking in the living room but their words sounded very far away. One thing, however, caught her attention and had her sitting up in bed.

"Gators don't normally chase people here," she heard David explaining, "but now I know why this one did."

"What was it?"

"She had pieces of fresh meat stuck in her wheels. It's a wonder that thing didn't catch up with her and tear her to pieces. All over her helmet, too. She must've grabbed it so fast she didn't see it."

Taryn fell back onto the bed, stunned.

I'm dreaming, she thought as she drifted off to sleep. *This is just a bad dream. That's not what he said at all.*

SIXTEEN

"You should just leave," Matt declared as he smoothly rolled up another T-shirt and stuffed it into his suitcase. "Come on home with me and finish your painting there. You can work from the house. You're nearly finished anyway."

Taryn nodded miserably. Sitting cross-legged on the bed, watching him pack, she felt that he might be right. First the snake, now the alligator. Someone clearly didn't want her there.

"You may be right," she sighed in resignation. "Maybe I just can't hack it here. Even if it wasn't a person who caused all of this, maybe it was just a sign that I am not supposed to be here."

"Oh, it was a person all right," he huffed. "Need I remind you who suddenly came to your rescue?"

"David? Oh please. He likes going for night drives. He told me."

"Humph," Matt grumbled.

"I get a good feeling from him. I don't think he'd hurt me," she insisted stubbornly.

Matt ignored her and continued packing.

Taryn was conflicted. She was still scared out of her mind about what had happened and the idea of something worse was terrifying...but she didn't like the idea of someone running her off.

"The Universe really might be trying to tell you something," Matt declared. "You should listen to these things. I do."

Taryn nodded. She believed in signs.

"Yeah, maybe I'll go home with you. I'm going to turn off the computer and stuff. When you leaving?"

"About an hour," he answered.

Of course, she'd have to change her airline ticket to fly from Florida and explain to Ellen why she was leaving and hope she didn't lose her job...but it probably was for the best.

Her memory card was still in the drive. She'd forgotten the pictures she'd taken at the hotel the last time she was there and that she'd started uploading them. They were finished by now, of course, and the folder was highlighted.

Taryn started to shut everything down but, at the last second, decided to flip through her last shots of the Jekyll Island Club Hotel. "Eh, why the hell not?" she muttered.

She was glad she did.

She'd started taking the pictures at sunset. By the time she'd finished it had been dark. The first few shots showed the hotel lit up by the pinks, reds, and oranges of dusk. The hotel shimmered in the late afternoon sky, the colors dying the white-washed walls a rainbow. The hotel in *those* pictures appeared exactly as it was today, perfectly rebuilt after the fire.

And then there were the ones taken *after* dark.

The flames blazed in all their glory, reaching high into the heavens and licking at the stars and full moon. Taryn could almost feel the heat even now. The fire raged white in some areas, its power and fury undeniable even one hundred years later. The pressure caused the windows to shatter on the top floor and a spray of glass flew through the air, like silver droplets of rain falling to the ground. Smoke billowed from every direction, so black in some places she could barely make it out against the dark sky and pearly white in others.

It was the hotel guests, however, that had her trembling.

Their cries were silent through the virtual images, but she could still hear them in her mind—the screams, the cries, the moans, the whimpers... Their anguish was evident as they poured from the windows and doors, running from the porch and through the lawn. The women, with their evening dresses ripped and covered in black soot, clinging to them to keep from falling. Their hair tumbling from diamond combs and pins, tangled curls matted in the wind as they ran. Makeup streaked across tear-stained faces.

The men with torn dinner jackets, stumbling in confusion through the grass, eyes wild. Some carrying women or dragging them by their waists as their arms outstretched towards the inferno, reaching for someone who might still be inside.

Taryn felt fat teardrops fall from her eyes as she realized that flames clung to some of the partygoers and climbed their pant legs and tops, spreading through their hair. These people, confused and stunned, continued to race through the darkness, thinking they could outrun the blazes that clung to them.

The worst of it, though, were the ones who *weren't* moving. What was now the croquet court was littered with bodies, dozens of bodies that lay motionless.

It was a sea of devastation. Annihilation.

*   *   *

MATT WASN'T HAPPY TO LEAVE HER BEHIND.

"I'm sorry," she apologized again after he'd loaded his suitcase in the trunk. "I know I'm meant to be here and I need to finish this."

"You have to start learning to think about yourself, Taryn," he'd complained. "These people have been dead for a long time. They're not your concern. They're especially not your concern when your life and health begin suffering."

Taryn was stubborn, however. "I don't think I'd be seeing these things if I wasn't meant to. I'm seeing them for a reason and I have to know the rest of the story. It's for me, too."

Matt nodded then and kissed her goodbye.

Once he was gone Taryn felt a heaviness in the pit of her stomach. She was alone again and it hurt. In spite of the fact that she'd gotten irritated with Matt more than once, she enjoyed his presence and missed him when he was gone. She normally didn't mind being alone. Taryn *liked* her own company, in general, but there were times when it really hit her that there wasn't a soul in the world who truly cared about her other than Matt.

Sometimes that hurt.

What would she *do* if something happened to him? He complained that she didn't need him, but that wasn't true at all.

Still, she didn't have time to stand around and depress herself. She was leaving for New Hampshire the next morning and wanted to get as much done before she left as she could.

Taryn wasn't particularly in the mood for Ivy House and her moods that day so she headed back to Adena. She hadn't returned since seeing William in the window.

There were people milling around taking pictures when she arrived so Taryn waited in the golf cart before setting up. The onlookers stood in front of it, arms around each other, posing for pictures. Taryn felt uncomfortable for the poor house who loomed behind them in sad disrepair. She wondered if houses embarrassed.

Once they'd all moved on she got out and started setting up. The sky was overcast and she wasn't sure how long she'd be able to stay out. It liked to rain around 3:00 pm every day, and since it was already after two she figured she could get in at least a good forty-five minutes before the skies opened.

As the clouds rolled in overhead Taryn painted furiously, filling in the details for the roof that had been giving her trouble. The Adena Cottage on her canvas was much statelier than the one that rose up before her. She was proud of her work.

"Don't worry old girl," she said to the house as the first boom of thunder rolled in. "They'll have you fixed up good as new soon!"

When the tiny drops began falling Taryn put her paintbrush down and wrapped the canvas in its waterproof case. These she secured in a plastic tub with lid and stowed in her golf cart.

The rain was really coming down by the time she had it loaded up and as she sprinted back across the lawn to her easel she squealed from the cold drops that slid down her warm back.

It only took a minute to fold up her easel and stool and wrap up her brushes. When she began her mad dash back to the golf cart, however, the sounds of laughter behind her made her pause.

Expecting to see another tour group out braving the rain, Taryn turned with a companionable smile ready on her face. They were, after all, kindred spirits in the wetness.

There wasn't anyone there.

Shrugging, she ran on across the wet grass and finished loading everything up. As she tied the last plastic tub in place, the laughter came again. It was undoubtedly female, the soft echo flirty and friendly as it spilled out over the grounds.

The laughter was coming from *within* the house.

More curious than spooked, Taryn watched the cottage in fascination. There were no physical signs the house had come to life; it was still in poor condition–looking even worse thanks to the rain pouring down on it and the gray clouds that hovered above.

With her hair plastered to her head and water squishing between the toes in her sandals with each step she took, Taryn plodded across the lawn towards the house. The laughter came again then, sweet and delicate. A male voice followed it, low and pleasant.

The music started when she was but five feet from the porch. A rolling melody pounded out on the ivory keys of a piano, the sound swelling through the once-cavernous room and making its way out the cracked windows to where Taryn stood. The tune was an old one and not something she recognized, but it was fast-paced and lighthearted. Soon, voices joined in and she could almost make out the words as the invisible partygoers sang along, laughing and clapping their hands in time to the music.

In spite of the timid fear creeping up her spine, Taryn was riveted and more than a little jealous. Whoever had been there was having a jolly time of it. Taryn was almost certain

239

she could make out the clinking of glasses, the scent of cigar smoke, and the sound of dancing feet. She'd *never* been to a party that sounded as much fun as this one. Most of the parties Taryn was invited to found her hanging out at the buffet or hidden in a corner, hoping someone would talk to her.

For a moment Taryn closed her eyes and allowed herself to forget the fact that they'd been dead for a long, long time and were no longer in that house celebrating. She imagined herself with them, in an old-fashioned party dress, standing in the middle of the room with a dashing stranger. She saw herself touching his upper arm and patting her hair in flirtation as her face blushed prettily from his flattery. She felt herself spinning around the room in a frenzy, dancing until her feet ached. Singing along with the tune and raising her glass up in the air when the others did, cheering and stomping her feet.

Oh, if only she could actually be there and *see* it.

When the music and laughter stopped Taryn was back on the grass, wet and cold. She was a drowned rat, her clothes and hair stuck to her body. The house was silent and sad, gazing at her with the same longing she felt.

Walking away with her head bent down from the rain, Taryn sighed with regret. Sometimes her "gift" was just cruel.

CARLA WAS BUSY WIPING DOWN the kitchen cabinets when Taryn dripped her way through the front door. Feeling instantly guilty for dirtying up Carla's clean floors, she all but stripped right there in the foyer, grabbing an afghan off the back of the couch and wrapping it around her chest as a makeshift robe.

"Hi Carla!" she cried, not wanting to scare her in case she had her earbuds in. "Just letting you know I'm in here!"

"Okay Taryn!" Carla called back. "I'm in the kitchen! Watch your step!"

Taryn placed Miss Dixie on the coffee table and removed the memory card, ready to insert it into the laptop. At the last second, however, she realized she couldn't just walk around nearly naked with someone else in the house. Some people didn't appreciate that. She laid the memory card down in a garish leaf-shaped dish next to her camera and then went on into the bedroom where she shrugged into a pair of yoga pants and a ratty T-shirt. After running a towel through her hair and slipping on some fluffy socks for her perpetually cold feet, Taryn headed to the kitchen where Carla had stopped mopping and was now washing down the refrigerator.

Carla was cleaning in time to the music, Cyndi Lauper's "I Drove All Night," and Taryn admired the way she sang along with the words with gusto, not caring that her flat and off-key voice filled the room and could be heard by others.

"Hey," Taryn said, hating to interrupt her but really needing to pull out a drink.

"Oh, sorry," Carla apologized as she turned down the song. "You need something?"

"Yeah, just a drink. I can come back in a minute though if you're not finished."

"Nope, all done here. I'll move on to the living room."

"Really sorry about the living room floors," Taryn called out to the other room. She could hear Carla in there, moving furniture around and sweeping. "I tried to be careful."

"No problem! I hadn't cleaned them yet!"

When Taryn moved back to the living room Carla was dusting the coffee table, taking care around Taryn's laptop and Miss Dixie. "Did you get rained out?" she asked.

"Yep." Taryn flopped down in a chair and stretched her legs out over the arms. "Got a little bit done today, though, before the skies opened up. Hey!" Taryn leaned forward and studied Carla's bottom half with interest.

"Yeah?" Startled, Carla stopped moving, her dust rag and polish paused mid-air. "Everything okay?"

"Yeah, it's fine. It's just...are those Se7ven for All Mankind Jeans?" Taryn asked. Then consciously aware that she was staring at another woman's bottom, she blushed and averted her eyes.

"Yes, they're new," Carla replied with pride, doing a slow turn in the middle of the room. She didn't seem to mind showing them off a bit. "I just got them yesterday."

"Man, I love those jeans. I have one pair my boyfriend bought me for Christmas three years ago. I've about worn them out," Taryn sighed blissfully. "Those fit better than any jeans I've ever had."

"I love them too," Carla agreed. "I, um, had payday yesterday so I splurged."

Taryn nodded her head in approval. "I don't blame you. I mostly get mine at yard sales and thrift stores anymore. I haven't been on a real shopping spree in years."

Carla laughed. "Girlfriend, I know what you mean. It was a good payday for once. Some, um, overtime and stuff."

Must've been some overtime, Taryn thought in amusement. She knew from personal experience that those jeans could cost anywhere from $150 to nearly $300. Still, Taryn couldn't talk. Back in college when she got her first credit card the first thing she'd done was race to Burlington

Coat Factory and put $500 worth of clothing in layaway for herself. All the other college students at her university were wearing nothing but what she deemed "young professional CEO" (which basically meant straight black attire–not color) and she'd stood out like a sore thumb in her pink, frilly Betsey Johnson dresses and red cowboy boots with vintage skirts and rhinestones. She'd still rather buy clothes she couldn't afford than pay a bill.

"So have things gotten better since finding the snake?" Carla asked, breaking Taryn's thoughts. She'd left the room for a moment and was back with a laundry basket now, busying herself with the folding of the pillow cases and towels.

"Here, let me help with that," Taryn scolded her, leaping to her feet. She still wasn't comfortable with someone else doing her housework while she sat there and watched. Grabbing a fluffy towel, Taryn began folding under Carla's scrutiny. "Yeah, a lot better. Thanks."

"I think I'd a died if it would'a been me that grabbed hold of that snake," Carla swore. "Damn! I hate those things."

"Me too," Taryn agreed. "I don't do snakes. Or Bees." She'd started to add "or alligators" but then remembered that she hadn't talked to anyone about that besides David and Matt. David had called her twice that morning to check on her, but she hadn't returned his call yet. First it was because Matt was still there and then it was because she was trying to get stuff loaded up in the rain. The timing still didn't feel right.

"Well, all your time here hasn't been bad has it?" Carla asked, eyeing her carefully over a fitted sheet.

Taryn watched in fascination as the other woman quickly folded it like an expert and then put it aside.

"Huh," Taryn said in complete admiration. "I've never actually known anyone who could do that, other than my middle school Home Ec. teacher."

"I've been told it's a talent," Carla replied drily.

"To answer your question, most of my time here has been great."

"No other problems?"

Taryn, taken aback, tried to make her face impassive. "Nope. So far so good."

"Huh," she grunted in response.

The dishwasher stopped then, the timer making both women jump. "I'll get it," Taryn said.

As she unloaded it and listened to Carla put the linens away her mind raced with possibilities. Did her housekeeper know more than she was saying? Or was she just turning into a paranoid freak? She remembered what Matt said, about not trusting anyone but she didn't want to be *that* suspicious. She had to trust someone sometime, right?

By the time she had the last plate put away Carla was rolling the vacuum cleaner into the small hall closet.

"Alright," she chirped as Taryn re-entered the living room. "All done for the day. Thanks for helping!"

"I appreciate everything you do here," Taryn said warmly. It was on the tip of her tongue to invite her to stay and hang out or catch a movie with her later. She couldn't very well complain about not having friends or being lonely if she didn't make an effort, right? But the words just wouldn't form on her tongue.

Instead, when Carla said her goodbyes and sailed out the door, Taryn stood in the center of the room and allowed her shoulders to slump in defeat. "Damn it," she muttered. "Can't I at least even try to make a friend?"

Oh well. At least she could work.

Sighing in resignation, Taryn reached down to pick up her laptop and memory card and head out to the sunporch where she could see her lush backyard yet still be protected from the rain.

Her laptop was still on the glass-topped table, a thin line of dust under it where Carla had refused to move the device and had, instead, cleaned around it. Miss Dixie was nestled up against it, a little battered and beaten but still comforting–an old friend. However, the leaf-shaped dish where Taryn was certain she'd placed her 8 GB memory card was empty.

The memory card, holding at least six-hundred photographs she'd taken on the island so far, was gone.

SEVENTEEN

RPH 2015

"Are you absolutely sure you left it on the coffee table?"

"Oh for crying out loud Matt, I know where I put the blasted thing," Taryn complained as she rushed around the bedroom, digging under piles of clothes and throwing things aside. She was trying to find her favorite army fatigue capris. They were alluding her at the present time and she wasn't in the mood for their nonsense.

"It's just that sometimes your memory isn't as great as it used to be, not since the EDS has started to–"

"Well, we can't blame everything on the EDS," she snapped, cutting him off.

On all fours, she wiggled under the bed and reached out her hand towards a crumpled object just out of her reach.

Damn it, she muttered to herself.

Changing tactics, she turned around, slid her bottom half under the bed, and then felt for it with her toe. When the fabric touched her feet she clenched as hard as she could and then pulled herself back out.

"Ah ha!" she cried triumphantly, waving the capris in the air like a trophy. They were wrinkled but they would do.

"What are you doing?" Matt asked in amusement.

"Packing," she answered. "Amy's picking me up in half an hour."

"Well, I won't keep you," Matt said, all business-like again. "I just wanted to call and tell you to check your email when you have time. I found something during my sleuthing that you might be interested in."

"Oh yeah? What is it?"

Taryn put Matt on speaker while she quickly plaited her hair into two long braids and dashed on blush and lipstick before throwing them into her carry-on case. Since she'd only be gone for one night she was only taking one bag. He would've been proud of her if he could've seen her.

"Well, I've been thinking about that story that woman you met in the water told you. You know, the story about the secret meeting?"

Taryn nodded, even though he couldn't see through the phone. "Yep. I know the one."

"Well, it might not have jumpstarted the sinking of the Titanic or anything but apparently the rumor itself is true enough," Matt said. "I've done a lot of reading about it since I got home yesterday evening. Didn't even go to bed last night. I missed *you*."

He said this last part shyly and Taryn blushed. Their goodbye always felt so rushed, and so sad. She wasn't sure why, but each time they parted she always felt as though this time it was going to be the last, even when they made future plans as they were leaving.

"I missed you too," she agreed. "It was hard to sleep last night."

It had been, too. She'd tossed and turned until she'd finally just passed out rather than fallen asleep.

"So about this meeting..." he tried again.

"Yeah?"

"Well, I know you're in a hurry to get packed and out there. I sent you some links and highlights. Just check them out. I think you'll find them all interesting," he concluded.

"So are you now thinking that maybe there was some sort of conspiracy on the island? That maybe William wasn't guilty and he was just a red herring, sort of?"

A glance at the clock on the wall told her Amy would be there in ten minutes and Taryn wasn't even dressed yet. With the phone still resting on the bathroom sink, she tugged the capris up around her waist and was startled to find that not only did they fasten easily, she had some extra finger room in the waistband. Normally they were so tight on her that she had to lay on the bed and do a little dance to pull them on. She really needed to do something about her nausea and vomiting–not that she minded losing a few pounds. After all, she was still a woman.

"I don't know," Matt hedged. "It may not have anything to do with your story at all. Perhaps just a coincidence. It's worth looking into, though. You know who was in charge of hosting the big cloak and dagger scene?"

"No, who?"

"Georgiana's father," Matt answered smugly, pleased to supply her with information she hadn't yet uncovered.

"Oh," Taryn replied in a daze, leaning back against the tiles. "Well. That's very interesting."

"I thought you'd appreciate that."

The doorbell rang just then and Taryn slipped her cotton T-shirt down over her head. "Sorry Matty but I gotta go," she said. "I'll call you when I get there or before if there's a delay."

"Okey dokey," he sang. "Safe travels, sayonara, be well my queen, and I love you."

"You too," she threw in quickly and then stuck the phone in her pocket and grabbed her carry-on. It was going to be a long day.

*　　*　　*

"You have to pardon my driving," Amy warned her. "My boyfriend says I drive like a crazy woman."

Taryn, who white-knuckled her door handle, grimaced. "You're fine," she said through clenched teeth.

Oh dear God, she silently prayed, *please let us make it to the airport alive.* "I appreciate you giving me a ride up here," Taryn said aloud instead.

"I normally only work half a day on Tuesdays so this worked out well for me," Amy continued, her cap of blond hair blowing back from her face. She had the window of her Buick LeSabre all the way down, her tanned arm holding a cigarette and resting on the doorframe.

"My flight doesn't get back until tomorrow night at about 11:00 pm," she apologized. "If you want to I can stay at a hotel and then just ride back to the island with you the next morning."

"It's okay," Amy shrugged. "I'll pick you up and just stay with my boyfriend that night. He lives in Brunswick. I stay with him a lot anyway. We have some friends who rent out a warehouse space and we like to jam with them. You know punkgrass?"

Taryn nodded that she did but had very little to add. She didn't know any of the groups, except for The Tillers, and unlike most musical genres it wasn't something she was familiar with and felt comfortable discussing.

With Amy's vintage capris, man's western shirt, handmade necklace and earrings, and designer purse Taryn felt like she might be out of her league. In high school it had been the cheerleaders, rich girls, and football players who she'd had to compete with for popularity. As an adult, those seemed to be replaced by the hipsters. It was odd to her that these adults seemed to wear the same clothes she did, have similar musical tastes, were oftentimes artists such as herself, enjoyed old movies, and yet still seemed to live on an entirely different planet from her.

"So how did you wind up working at the hotel?" Taryn asked, hoping to take her mind off her nerves. Amy tailgated and then quickly passed the cars she rode on, paying no mind to whether she was passing them on the left or right as she erratically swerved all over her side of the interstate.

"I worked at a gift shop for awhile," Amy shrugged. "The pay sucked and I wanted something better so when the assistant job came open I applied. I had good references."

"Do you like it?"

Amy snorted. "I have a degree in Hospitality Management, which is more than I can say for my boss. I don't dislike it, but it's a pain in the ass working for her. And the pay is shitty."

Taryn heard that a lot, regardless of company or position. It didn't seem like anyone was getting paid enough anymore, whatever "enough" actually *was*.

"I'm sorry," Taryn offered sympathetically.

"So what do you think about our resident ghosts?" Amy asked and then followed the question with an immediate, "Fucking asshole!"

Taryn jumped, startled, and then realized Amy was screaming at the car in front of them who had slowed down to a turtle-like 85mph. When Amy laid on her horn for several seconds and continued to rage obscenities Taryn winced and fell farther down into her seat, embarrassed. She didn't mind a good curse word now and then (she, herself, was partial to "hell" and "damn it") but this was overkill.

Once Amy moved around the offending vehicle and was able to lay back on the gas she relaxed. "Sorry. So yeah, the ghosts?"

Taryn didn't exactly feel comfortable about opening up to the possibly insane woman beside her. Instead, she remained noncommittal. "Oh, they don't seem to bother me."

Amy managed to look disappointed. "Really? Because after I read about you online I thought you might be able to come down here and wipe them out."

"I, uh…" Taryn stammered. "I'm not a ghostbuster or exorcist or anything like that."

"I know," Amy laughed, a thin, brittle sound that didn't sound pleasant. "I just always figured that they wanted something. None of us have ever been able to figure out what that was."

Well, Taryn thought, *that was common enough ground for the both of them.*

While she was there Taryn figured she might as well ask her about the meeting that was supposedly once held on the island. "Hey, do you know anything about the meeting held there a long time ago? The one about the federal reserve?"

"Ha ha! Don't let Ellen catch you talking about that," Amy warned her. "Seriously. She is dead set on nobody bringing that shit up. But yeah, it totally happened. Everyone knows. Why? You think it has something to do with the ghosts?"

"I don't know," Taryn answered honestly. She recoiled as Amy barreled down on a rusty pickup and came within inches of rear-ending him before slipping over into the right lane and quickly exiting off. "It was a long time after the fire so it seems unlikely, although Adena Cottage *is* haunted. So I've heard," she added swiftly.

"Yeah, you never know, though," Amy mused. "They could've gotten the ball rolling sooner."

Taryn considered this. Amy was right, of course. Who knew *when* the men had started action– if the meeting was even real? What if the first meeting had been during that New Year's Eve?

Taryn could see a jet taking off less than a mile ahead of them and let out a huge sigh of relief. *Land, land!*

Amy, who seemed to assume Taryn had nothing interesting left to share, turned up her CD player. The rollicking song was part rockabilly, part traditional bluegrass and she knew every word. However, not only did she sing

256

along with the words–she added her own hand gestures and dance moves right there in her seat, frequently removing her hands from the wheel and turning sideways to serenade Taryn.

For the love of God woman, Taryn screamed inside her head, *look at the damn road!*

Just when she thought they were going to go the way of Dottie West and die in a car crash mere yards from their final destination, Amy pulled up to the unloading area and unlocked the doors. "Here you go my dear!" she shouted over the music. "Just text me when you leave! I'll drop you off and head on over to Steve's!"

As Amy was pulling away and Taryn was dragging her carry-on through the lobby Amy's boyfriend's name registered with her.

Steve? Was Amy dating the valet? Nothing surprised her anymore.

Well, most things didn't anyway.

*   *   *

BY THE TIME SHE LANDED, picked up her rental car, and was on the road it was already 4:00 pm. Since her hotel was out of the way, Taryn decided to head straight to her aunt's house. As it was, it would take her at least an hour to make the drive and she was running out of daylight. Because the house's electricity wasn't turned on, and it was kind of out in the middle of nowhere, should something happen Taryn didn't want to find herself stuck there after dark.

Along the way, Taryn stopped at a K-Mart and bought a cheap flashlight, some batteries, a few snacks and drinks, and bug spray. She had no idea what she'd find once she arrived, but she wanted to be as prepared as possible.

A good part of the drive to Sarah's house was on a busy highway. Although it was picturesque with the mountains off in the distance, there were lots of cars sharing the well-maintained road with her. She turned up her Patty Loveless "Classics" CD and loudly sang along with "Timber, I'm Falling in Love" and "You Can Feel Bad (If it Makes You Feel Better)" as she sped along the scenic highway. Unlike Amy, however, she refused to do any choreography while driving.

When she turned off the main road, however, and got on the county version things got bumpier and lonelier. Taryn lowered the volume and tried harder to concentrate as she dodged potholes and barking dogs and kept her eyes peeled for the bends that seemed to come out of nowhere.

She passed extraordinary covered bridges, mom 'n pop grocery stores, and gas stations that didn't have "pay here" options at the pumps. These were all mixed in with new Shell stations, showy Chinese restaurants with dazzling paintings of the Great Wall on the signs, and modern homes with RVs in the driveway that cost more than her college education. Like most places she visited, this part of rural New Hampshire was a land of contradictions.

Sarah's house was the only building on her road and, of course, was at the very end.

The driveway was unpaved and, thanks to an early afternoon rainstorm, black with mud. As Taryn turned off onto the ethereal lane she felt she was entering another dimension. The giant trees closed in around her, towering over her and her little Camry and managing to block out all the sunlight. As she inched along the narrow gloomy road she prayed she wouldn't get stuck. The woods enfolding her were dense and soundless; she rolled down her windows and couldn't even hear the songs of the birds, just the purr of her car's engine and the muted melody rising up from her radio.

Up ahead she thought she saw something big and black on the edge of the road. As she drew near she was almost certain it lumbered into the woods. A bear? It was possible. Sarah had talked about seeing them.

"Just don't feed them," she'd warned a young Taryn. "That's when you run into trouble."

The driveway wound on for more than two miles, an eternity when she couldn't drive faster than 10 mph. At last, however, she came to a small rise. With one final push on the gas, she heaved the car forward and the road suddenly opened into a generous meadow, wildflowers and thigh-high grass waving in every direction. The soaring mountains with their abundance of foliage and wildlife encircled the acreage, acting as a natural barrier to the outside world.

Sarah's farmhouse stood in the middle of the meadow, its familiar porch with the timeworn steps and splintering wood bringing tears to Taryn's eyes. She could almost see her aunt sitting in one of the rickety rocking chairs, a bowl of green beans in her lap, stringing them and tossing the bits into a strainer.

Taryn had spent some of her happiest childhood memories between this house and her grandmother's place. As Taryn grew older they'd stopped visiting Sarah for some reason, but she'd still kept in touch with her aunt over the years. Sarah's house was one of the first places she thought of when she needed solace or to remember where she came from.

She'd always loved her aunt and the house. Sarah had understood her like few others. Sarah's warm smile, youthful energy, and unorthodox ways had driven her mother (Sarah's sister) mad. Sarah with her talk of spirits, of "energy," of the beasts and fairy tales that might very much be real had been Taryn's bedtime stories when she'd stayed there at the house.

And now Aunt Sarah was gone. She'd died sick and alone.

The waves of guilt nearly brought Taryn to her knees as she stood in the middle of the unkempt yard and stared at the rundown beauty in front of her, remembering all the things she'd lost: her parents, her grandmother, her aunt, her fiancé...

And how could she, someone who loved the past and tried to preserve it the best way she knew how, let something like this happen to her own aunt's place?

Disgusted with herself, Taryn marched up to the porch, ready to do what she should've done a year earlier, and peered inside the windows. They were caked with dirt and cobwebs and these she brushed away with her hands. The interior still contained all of Sarah's furniture, just as she'd left it. It was now covered with sheets, giving it the appearance of bulky ghosts. Lying await in a sea of antiques and magazines.

A complicated locking system hung over the brass doorknob but when Taryn gave it a push it dropped into her hands. With her flashlight ready she entered the foyer and began her exploration.

The house, which had always been full of laughter and Motown when Sarah was alive, was as quiet as a tomb. As Taryn shuffled through the deserted rooms and took stock of the damage done by neglect and the most recent storm she cried noisily, appalled by the mistreatment and her own delay. Over and over again she lectured herself aloud.

"You should've been here," she snapped with bitterness. "How could you have let this happen?"

The worst of the damage was to the two guest bedrooms upstairs and the small nursery, which had always housed Sarah's doll collection. A tree had, in fact, fallen in on the nursery. Although plastic had been nailed down to the roof and the limbs had been removed, there was still much that needed to be cleaned up. Several of the dolls now lay scattered in the middle of the floor, their porcelain faces smashed and shards of glass littering the ancient Persian rug. Water was still managing to find its way in, in spite of the effort that had been made to keep it out. Taryn knew from experience that if the roof didn't get patched or replaced altogether, soon the entire house would suffer.

And those were just the things she could see. Who knew what kind of mold was growing in the walls and cellar?

Sarah's room was miraculously intact.

Taryn stood in the doorway of her late aunt's bedroom and smiled through her tears at the floral bedspread, Sarah's delicate fairy collection lined up across her chest of drawers, the old-fashioned loveseat in the corner with the multi-colored handmade quilt neatly folded on the back, the ruffled throw pillow in the old rocking chair that had been brought in from the front porch...

Taryn felt guilty touching anything at all in the house, much less in that room, but she couldn't help herself.

The heavy, antique vanity set that had once belonged to Taryn's grandmother Stella was still resting on Sarah's bureau. The silver was tarnished, but the glass was unspoiled. Taryn picked up the comb, brush, and mirror and gingerly placed them in her knapsack. Her aunt and grandmother wouldn't mind. After all, the house had been left to her and she needed a reminder of the ones she loved.

As she was placing the padlock back on the front door, this time ensuring it was secure, the antique ring on her finger began to burn.

"Shit!" Taryn cried, dropping the lock on the porch with a loud "clang" and crying out in pain. She looked down at her hand and saw that her finger was turning scarlet, as though she'd been holding her hand in a pot of boiling water. "What the hell?"

When she inquisitively touched the band the pain ripped through her other finger, the ache simultaneously icy and searing.

263

Unsettled, and for the first time consciously aware that she was physically alone and not just emotionally, Taryn bent down and grabbed the lock and secured it again–this time with haste.

Still nursing her painful fingers, Taryn leaped from the porch and began making her way to her rental, her shoes barely making a sound in the overgrown yard. The sun was beginning to set and Taryn was startled to realize that she'd been inside longer than she'd thought.

When she glanced at the clock on the dashboard and saw that it was after eight 'o clock she scoffed. "Oh, that's not possible."

She figured she'd been in there an hour, an hour and a half tops. Not more than the two hours her clock implied.

The ring on her hand continued to ache as she turned around in the patch of grass that served as a parking spot and began driving towards the gloom of the woods.

Even as a child, Taryn had always been painfully conscious of the feeling that someone or something at her aunt's house had watched her. She'd felt it with nothing more than slight curiosity while she played, slept, and moved about the property on her endless adventures. It had never frightened her; indeed, sometimes she'd found it comforting.

Now, however, as the unseen eyes bored into her back Taryn trembled from the iciness and tapped the gas harder than she needed.

She was no longer the trusting, innocent child she'd once been. Not everything that watched her was benevolent.

EIGHTEEN

*G*erald P. Evans was a short, stocky, and nervous-looking man with a facial tick and pants that stopped a few inches too short, revealing his burgundy socks.

Taryn could smell the lawyer on him as soon as he entered the cramped, cheesy hotel bar. She'd spent a lot of time with attorneys over the years. First there had been the ones who'd overseen her parents' estate and then the one who'd been in charge of her grandmother's and then, the last one, the woman with Andrew's estate. Since Taryn and Andrew were engaged but not married she hadn't been entitled to much, other than the house and property they'd owned together. His parents had allowed her to keep whatever she'd wanted of his, though, and she'd kept most of it. They lived in a small condo in St. Petersburg, Florida and simply didn't have the room.

"So you saw the house," he began in a voice that was more feminine than it should've been.

"Yes," she agreed, taking a sip of her whiskey and Coke. She thought the situation called for alcohol. "It's not as bad as I'd thought, but worse than I can afford to handle."

"Unfortunately these things tend to happen when a home goes empty for an extended period," he replied prissily.

Taryn bristled at the remark. "Well, I am unable to live here full time. I have a home in Nashville, and I've signed a lease."

Of course, that lease was up now and had been as of last month. But that wasn't any of his business.

"Of course, of course," he replied, his cheeks turning pink. "I didn't mean to imply that–"

"It doesn't matter," Taryn cut him off. "You're right. I'm just not sure what to do at this point. Can you lay out everything that needs to be done to it to make it livable?"

Taryn listened in earnestness. Heart continued to sink lower and lower as he went over the costs for the new roof, central heat and air (it only existed in part of the house), new wiring for the electrical system, plumbing updates, new insulation, and a better drainage system. "As it is, the cellar floods every time it rains, both from problems with the gutters that need replacing and orthostatic pressure from an underground water source," he explained.

"Good Lord," Taryn sighed. "How in the world did Aunt Sarah even *live* there?"

Gerald shrugged. "She was a stubborn woman. She used all three of her wood stoves in the winter and constantly had wood delivered up there. Didn't care for air conditioning from what I heard. And only one of the bathrooms is usable. She kept it in order and just let the others go."

Taryn shuddered. "And wood delivery? How were people even able to get up there in the winter to bring it to her? How did she get out?"

Taryn could only imagine trying to get down that driveway with three feet of snow on the ground.

"Well, she didn't get out much there in the end. She had a snowmobile, however, and used it when she needed to. Road department felt bad for her and cleaned the drive when they could. Like many folks around here, she started collecting her wood back in the summer to let it dry out properly. There are good folks around here. They helped her out," he added with pride.

"Listen, I'm going to have to think about this and figure out what I want to do," Taryn said, feeling like she'd been punched in the stomach. "I don't want to make any hasty decisions right away."

"If you want my advice," he leaned in towards her, his tiny little eyes shifting nervously behind his glasses, "I'd sell. You'd get a fair price for the land alone. Too much house and too much work to fix it yourself. You're looking at a money pit. Just take what mementos you want and leave the rest of the trouble for someone else. Start yourself a nice little nest egg."

With that, the attorney, who Taryn was disliking more and more by the minute, leaned back in his chair and crossed his arms with smugness. She wished she'd met the other attorney, the one who'd been keeping in touch with her up until now. She'd liked him. This guy was a tool.

"I don't know about that yet," she said politely, forcing a smile on her face through pursed lips.

"Well, it would be nearly impossible for you to secure a construction loan of that magnitude. You, a young woman like yourself who's not gainfully employed," he added, narrowing his eyes at her.

For the second time since he sat down, Taryn bristled at his words. "Well, thank you, but I am employed. I am just self-employed. I actually run a successful business." There was no reason for him to know that she'd bought the underwear she was wearing seven years ago. And that they had come from a package of five, on sale at Walmart. And that she'd been overdrawn so many times in the past year that her bank had simply stopped sending her the notices, probably figuring that they were wasting too much paper.

"I just meant that you would be in far over your head with this," he insisted. "It's too much!"

If there was one thing Taryn hated more than anything else, it was someone telling her what to do. Likewise, she couldn't stand it when someone told her what she couldn't do. Like it was any of their business. If she wanted to do something, then by God she'd find a way to get it done.

Rising to her feet, Taryn smiled sweetly down at the portly man, masking her irritation behind southern charm. "Thank you for your time. I appreciate it. I'll be in touch."

After paying at the bar, Taryn stalked to the elevator and muttered angrily to herself on the whole ride up to the tenth floor.

She'd be damned if she was going to let someone she didn't even know boss her around. If she wanted to live in Aunt Sarah's house and pay to fix it up, she'd do it. She *would* do it.

*   *   *

The air was thick, almost chewy. Gasping for breath, she felt the weight of a thousand pounds on her chest and wanted to scream for air. When she opened her mouth to gulp what she craved, she found her lungs filled with dense smoke that burned her throat and stomach as it slid down the narrow passage.

She couldn't see. The room was dark, and a thin film covered her eyes, distorting the world around her.

Taryn wasn't herself again. She could feel her bare legs under the long nightgown and felt it scrape the floor as she crawled on her hands and knees, coughing and sputtering.

When her head touched something hard, and a dull pain traveled down her neck and spine, she rose to her feet and flattened her breasts against a wall. Closing her eyes now, she inched along, arms outstretched, searching for a way out. She couldn't see the fire, but she could hear it. She never knew flames could be so loud. These were thunderous, though, and in their roaring drowned out everything else.

She didn't know where she was or how she got there; she just knew she needed to get out.

She knew she was dying, knew her lungs and heart couldn't take much more. When her left hand touched another wall and she realized she'd hit a corner she crumpled to the floor in defeat, her eyes stinging from tears *and smoke. Sobbing now, she raised her arms over her head and scratched weakly on the wall above her.*

"Help me," she whispered hoarsely, knowing the flames were growing closer and would surely drown her out. "Help me."

Her last thought, before fading into total darkness was,

Why didn't he...

*   *   *

"So how was your visit to the mountains?" Amy asked cheerfully.

Taryn closed her eyes, too chicken to watch the scene on the interstate unfold a second time. "Not as good as I'd hoped," she answered, praying the ride would be mercifully short, but not so short that Amy put anyone's life at risk.

"Shame," Amy replied with what sounded like genuine regret. "Well, you didn't miss much. Actually, I don't know. I didn't go back to work yesterday, so I don't know if anything happened or not."

Taryn smiled but kept her eyes closed.

"Hey, you okay?" Taryn could feel Amy turn and study her from the driver's seat. For a moment the car swerved dangerously to the right and Taryn grabbed ahold of the arm rest in fear.

"Just tired," she replied as Amy straightened the vehicle and almost overcorrected. "I didn't sleep well last night."

"Trouble sleeping in a new place?"

"Nightmares," Taryn answered shortly.

"Yeah. I get them a lot too. Steve says that they're a product of working around so many ghosts," Amy cackled.

"Your boyfriend, Steve? Is that the same guy who's a valet?" Taryn asked with interest.

"Yep, same dude. We've been dating for two years now. He's pretty cool. He's an artist you know," Amy declared with pride. "Kind of a starving artist if you know what I mean. He took the valet gig to pay the bills. His real love is art."

"I didn't know that," Taryn said. "That's pretty cool."

"Yeah, well, we don't plan on making the hotel our full-time gig forever," Amy swore. "We're starting a kind of artists' colony over in Brunswick. They've put some work in the downtown. I mean, it's still a little ghetto in some places, but the town's shaping up. I think one day it will be as awesome as Savannah. I'm kinda glad of being in on it from the ground floor if you know what I mean."

"Yeah, I think that's pretty awesome," Taryn replied truthfully. "So what do you guys do?"

"Well, Steve lives with five other guys in this big old Victorian house they're trying to renovate. His roommate bought it dirt cheap a year ago, and they're making the downstairs a studio and gallery. They all live upstairs."

Taryn could hear the pride in Amy's voice. She loved the fact that young people were getting together to make changes in their city. It was an exciting time to be young these days, and she'd started noticing a lot of kids trying to rehab, restore, and save their history and culture. She respected that.

"You should come chill with us some night. Hang out with us in Savannah," Amy suggested as she took the Brunswick exit at top speed. "There's some awesome clubs and cafes up there. Live music if you're into that."

"Yeah," Taryn agreed. "Sounds nice."

As they sailed over the soaring bridge at breakneck speed, Amy turned up Sturgill Simpson and sang along at the top of her lungs. In spite of Taryn's fear of plunging into the water below, with the windows down and the summer breeze pouring through the car she couldn't help but smile. She was starting to get used to, and *like*, the companionship.

She hadn't thought she'd be that happy to return to Jekyll Island, considering everything that had happened. As it turned out, she felt a little bit like she was going home.

NINETEEN

*T*ryn was stretched out on her couch, catching up on her DVR'd DIY shows when she suddenly remembered the email Matt had sent her the morning before.

"Shit!" she exclaimed. She jumped off the couch and began firing up her laptop.

With touring Sarah's house, meeting with the attorney, and then passing out fairly early at the hotel she'd totally forgotten to get online. She'd texted Matt when she landed both times but hadn't talked to him yet. She needed to read that email before she called him, or else it would hurt his feelings. After all, he had worked hard doing research on her behalf.

Sure enough, he'd written her a long message and included several links, attachments, and screen shots.

Dearest Love,

Hope your short trip goes well and that this finds you well. Know that I am always thinking of you and just a thought away if you need me.

Like I said before I left, I've continued to research our story and what may or may not have happened on our island. I did manage to uncover a few pertinent pieces of information that may be of value.

Although I still haven't been able to determine if the clandestine meeting regarding the formation of the Federal Reserve is nothing more than an urban legend, and we'll probably never know for sure, it appears to have more truth than not.

The Federal Reserve was created in 1913, but the meeting supposedly took place three years earlier in 1910. The meeting, cloaked as a "duck hunt," consisted of quite a few members of the Club and several names of well-known bankers and U.S. senators you'd recognize. These are: Senator Nelson Aldrich, Frank Vanderlip (from CitiBank), Henry Davison of Morgan Bank, George F. Baker (president of the First National Bank), JP Morgan and Paul Warburg of the Loeb Investment House.

Bertie Forbes (you know, from the magazine) wrote about the meeting. His words:

"Picture a party of the nation's greatest bankers stealing out of New York on a private railroad car under cover of darkness, stealthily riding hundreds of miles South, embarking on a mysterious launch, sneaking onto an island deserted by all but a few servants, living there a full week under such rigid secrecy that the names of not one of them was once mentioned, lest the servants learn the identity and disclose to the world this strangest, most secret expedition in the history of American finance. I am not romancing; I am giving to the world, for the first time, the real story of how the famous Aldrich currency report, the foundation of our new currency system, was written... The utmost secrecy was enjoined upon all."

So why were these men anxious to form the Federal Reserve in the first place? Well, that's a complicated matter, and you can read about that in the attachments. The Cliff Notes' version is that it was partly due to a stock market crash that occurred in, you guessed it, 1907. The crash was called the "Wall Street Panic" and until the Great Depression 20+ years later it was the worst economic depression the country had seen. As you can imagine, lots of bad things happened. It finally ended with JP Morgan handing out personal loans to banks himself. Of course, everyone knew there wouldn't always BE a JP Morgan to get them out of trouble so they needed to create an emergency fund of sorts.

I'm attaching two documents and several links that you might want to peruse in regards to this event. Fascinating reading, really, and I am not even that interested in economics and the history of banking.

I have no earthly idea how this fits into everything else that went on, but there you go, love.

Be well,
Matt

Taryn sighed and looked at the attachments. There were a lot. Still, the idea of a secret meeting on the island was kind of fun and she dug the whole secrecy of it. She'd sort through the research later. There was a second email from Matt, written an hour after the first, and she turned to it now.

Hello my dear!

I thought I'd separate these letters since they're technically different topics.

So…we know very little about Mr. Hawkins and his lovely wife, other than the fact that they'd been to the Club in the past and must have been wealthy. I did some more digging and found out more information, some of which I think will be pertinent.

It appears that our Mr. Hawkins was an attorney from Manhattan. His lovely wife, Rachel, was from a wealthy Boston family. She came from big money; he did not. They met through acquaintances while she was visiting New York with her family. It seems that Mr. Hawkins swept her off her feet. Although the law firm he was a junior partner at was a prominent one, he'd more or less worked his way up to it. I didn't uncover anything about his family or background.

I found some letters from her family on Ancestry.com. He was not pleased with the match, but her father finally allowed it to go through. Unusual for the time, her father remained in charge of her money and inheritance until his death. (I guess in those days it should've gone to the husband as soon as they married but you know more about these things than I do.) I imagine her father still didn't trust the man and was afraid he'd run off with her money. Anyway, that didn't last long–her father died in a hunting accident when she and William had only been married for two years. And guess who her father had been hunting with that afternoon? Yep. His son-in-law.

I believe a Club member had to sponsor a new member. I don't know who sponsored the Hawkins on the island. I couldn't find any other correspondence between Rachel and any of her family members after her father's death. Before his death there were letters from cousins, aunts, and uncles. Afterward, nothing. I've taken screenshots and attached what I was able to find.

So, my love, there you go. I hope that will perhaps shed a little bit of light on some of the story.

Alas, I fear that I could find no connection between the "secret" meeting and the sinking of the Titanic. I tried.

Stay well love,

Matt

*   *   *

TARYN HAD A LOT TO THINK ABOUT as she put the finishing touches on Ivy House. It was her last day to work on that cottage, and she spent her afternoon going over the smallest of details, ensuring that everything about it was perfect. She'd probably finish Adena Cottage the next day if all went well, and then wait a day or two to wrap things up. It was almost time to leave.

And she still wasn't sure what was going on.

"Help me, help me," she heard the voice cry out over and over again in her mind.

But it was too late to help anyone who had died on that island. Rachel, William, and everyone who'd been alive at the time of that fire were gone. She couldn't help any of them.

At any rate, how could she help Rachel? Rachel's death was a tragedy, of course, but it had also been avenged. Her husband had gone to the gallows for her. Justice was served. What else mattered?

"Unless he's not guilty," she said aloud, pausing with her paintbrush in the air.

A seagull flew overhead and cried in agreement, its high-pitched call ethereal.

Tourists milled around the grounds and talked in low voices, some with expensive point and shoot cameras in hand. She watched them absently as they knelt down and zoomed in on bees and flowers, taking their time while impatient spouses and children stood by and tried not to complain.

Taryn was having a hard time concentrating. There was something she was meant to be doing, but she didn't know what that was.

"I can finish this back at the house," she sighed at last, disappointed at her lack of concentration. "Sorry Ivy."

Ivy House had yet to come to care for her presence and was unimpressed by her departure.

She was on the golf cart, slowly driving down Stable Road when something flashed from the corner of her eye. Lost in a daydream she nearly ran into the man who was also not paying attention to her as he crossed the street. Slamming on the brakes, she came to a screeching halt just inches from his feet. Both jumped and let out startled cries.

"I am so sorry!" she cried to the figure in front of her.

He'd been doubled over at the waist, trying to catch his breath from the scare, but when he straightened up and looked at Taryn she thought her heart would stop. The eyes, the baseball cap, the smug smile—she was absolutely positive she was looking at the same young man she'd seen that night on the beach.

"Are y-y-you okay?" she stammered.

Straightening his ball cap he dusted off his pants and turned to face her. "Yeah. You just want to be careful what you're doing," he replied smoothly. "You're liable to get hurt around here."

"I wasn't the one crossing the street without looking both ways," she tried to joke but felt uneasy from his piercing gaze.

The man laughed, an ugly sound escaping from a face that wasn't altogether unattractive. "Yeah, but you never know what you're going to run into around here if you don't watch it."

With a sly smirk, he turned and sauntered on across the road then, leaving Taryn alone.

*   *   *

THE NIGHT AIR FELT GOOD AGAINST HER SKIN. In spite of the bugs that bit at her legs, leaving behind small welts, she was enjoying sitting on her patio, listening to the night sounds.

Feeling off centered, she'd treated herself to a seafood dinner at one of the local restaurants and then took a nap. Now, at almost midnight, she was wide awake. She liked this time of night on Jekyll, when most people were going to bed and the island came alive with its real inhabitants. Although she'd met a coral snake and an alligator, both of which had tried to kill her, she was falling in love with the wildness. It was a quiet wilderness that crept behind the modern façade of middle-class civilization and this fascinated her.

Yes, there were brick ranch houses, a Dairy Queen, and a water park where one could buy $4 colas.

There were also hills of fire ants that could literally kill a person and alligators in the golf course ponds.

A crackling of wood startled her, breaking the natural sounds of the night, and had Taryn jumping to her feet. It was the sound of footsteps, and they were close.

Remembering the man she'd nearly hit on the road, Taryn's pulse quickened and she realized, again, that she was without weapon or cell phone.

"Shit," she muttered and quickly looked around for something hard or sharp.

The big citronella candle she'd bought from Target was the best thing she had so she lifted it by the handle. She took a few cautious steps towards the corner of the house. Quietly walking on tiptoes the way she'd done at her grandmother's house when she wanted a midnight snack but didn't want to wake anyone up going down the stairs, she pretended she was as light as air.

"Hello!" she called, trying to keep the tremble from her shaking voice. "Who's there?"

The crackling came again, this time the unmistakable sound of someone walking on dry sticks. The heavy footsteps were getting closer and Taryn was about to turn and run into the house when David came into view, the flames from the candle throwing shadows upon his face.

"Oh my God," Taryn breathed, lowering the candle and taking a step back. "You scared the hell out of me."

For some reason, she wasn't entirely at ease with his presence, however, and her heart rate did not lower. It was late, after all. What was he doing there?

"Sorry," he apologized, walking towards her. His hair was disheveled, wild looking, and she could see that his hands were black from dirt. "I had to come and see you."

She considered asking him inside but then decided that if she needed to make a break she should be in a place that had more than two exits.

Oh stop it Taryn, she chastised herself as she pointed him to the other chair. *Matt has you totally paranoid. You like David.*

Yeah, you like David, came another smaller voice that she tried to ignore.

"What's the matter?" she finally asked when she found the right words.

"I found something," he said, his voice animated and his eyes lighting up. "I found something you won't believe."

"Yeah?" she asked, still not willing to trust him but wanting to. "What was it?"

"I–I don't know if I should tell you," he said at last, looking down at his feet.

"Um, you came sneaking around here at midnight to tell me something that you can't tell me? That doesn't make a whole lot of sense dude."

David brushed back a long strand of his hair and then got up. She watched him prowl around her backyard, as lean and graceful as a big cat. There was definitely something on his mind. His body was taut, and she recognized the way he kept smoothing his hair back and popping his knuckles. He was full of nervous energy.

"Okay," he finally said, stopping in his tracks and turning to stare at Taryn. She could barely make out anything more than the outline of his body in the darkness. "I was taking a walk on the beach tonight, up by where they're building the new hotel? And there were some men there. They didn't see me so I watched them for a few minutes. I thought, you know, that they might be trying to steal something."

Taryn nodded in encouragement for him to continue.

"They were digging, and one of them brought something up. It looked like tools, but it was pretty dark so it was hard to see. I hid in the dunes. After oh, about half an hour I guess, they all piled up into a truck and left. They had a big bag of things they'd found, all kind of clinking together."

Taryn sat back and listened, her face impassive. He watched her as he spoke and she got the feeling that he was fishing for a reaction. When she offered none, he went on.

"When they left I got up and went over to where they'd been digging. They'd thrown a tarp over the spot and I lifted it up. Taryn! It was full of artifacts. Just full," he nearly shouted in excitement.

Taryn hadn't noticed the small canvas bag slung over his shoulder until he took it off. Holding it out before him, he stomped over to her chair and knelt beside her on the ground. "Look, look what I found!" One by one he laid out a variety of weapons at her feet. With the amount of grime and dirt embedded in them it was impossible to tell how old they were, but they clearly weren't new.

"And this, too."

The last thing he placed at her feet was a skull. It was a small one, no bigger than a child's, and Taryn recoiled slightly, both enthralled and shocked by it.

"I know, I know. I shouldn't have taken anything but I need proof," he declared as he straightened and began pacing again. "I knew they'd find something. I wonder how long it's been going on."

Taryn kept mum about her own experience and gingerly ran her fingers along the handle of what looked like a knife. "I don't know. Are you going to tell anyone?"

"Well yes, of course," he answered. "In the morning. It's just...have you seen anything going on?"

His penetrating gaze cut through her to her soul and Taryn shifted away her gaze, pretending to study the tiny skull. A warning bell went off in her head. What if David was lying? What if he was in on it? What if he was behind the whole thing and, rather than trying to help preserve he was a grave robber, and they were doing this for him? He could be fishing for details from her, trying to ascertain how much she knew.

It *could* happen.

Or, then again, it was possible she'd just been watching too much television.

"No, nothing," she answered at last. "I haven't seen a thing."

TWENTY

*I*vy House was finished.

Taryn had the painting safely tucked away in its case back at the house. For good measure, she'd slid the case under the couch. She was paranoid and knew it, but there was something rotten in the state of Denmark. Until she could figure out what it was, she wasn't going to take any chances, especially where her paintings were concerned.

She was sad that this was her last day with Adena Cottage. She really felt like the two of them had bonded.

"I'm sorry," she whispered as she set up her easel. "I don't know what you want. I'm trying."

It made zero sense to her that it was the hotel that had burned, yet it was the cottage calling to her. She'd put the majority of her attention on the hotel and had received nothing in return. Why the cottage?

"You escaped the fire," she muttered aloud, dabbing at the sky above the slanted roof. "You didn't fall in until much later. What happened here?"

She'd gone through a dozen scenarios.

Rachel was actually murdered in the *house* (not the hotel) and her body was hidden in her room to cover it up.

William had been having an affair with Georgiana in the cottage and had killed his wife to get her money and be with his mistress (the most logical explanation).

Some kind of secret meeting was held in the house and they'd plotted Rachel's murder there. (That seemed unlikely. She'd found nothing that pointed to Rachel's involvement in anything.)

And, well, that was all she had. Basically nothing.

Taryn had never before been involved in such a convoluted mess. It was stressing her the hell out.

"Look," the house whispered, and Taryn stopped and looked up.

Adena Cottage was quiet, unassuming. A light breeze had the Spanish moss dangling above her swaying gently back and forth. A large European hornet attacked a blossoming bush a safe ten feet away. The trolley tour ambled down the road, the echo of the guide's voice reverberating through the speaker's static. The dank, thick smell of the nearby marsh mixed with the sweetness of the magnolias.

"Look." The honeyed feminine voice wafted through the gentle breeze and wrapped itself around Taryn, demanding something of her she couldn't give.

"Look at what?" she cried, throwing down her brush in anger. "What do you want me to look at?"

Miss Dixie rested on the ground beside her, her strap wrapped around Taryn's foot. She didn't like taking chances with her camera, either. The strap tightened now and squeezed her ankle, the pressure sending a shooting pain up her leg. Like a vine, the strip of fabric climbed higher and higher until it reached her thigh and the camera was dangling in the air, brushing her foot.

"Look." The voice was sharper now, demanding.

Taryn swallowed hard and with shaking hands reached down and tugged at the strap, loosening it from her leg and gently pulling it away. She held it in her hands now and studied the LCD screen. She'd already taken hundreds of pictures of the cottage. There was nothing left to look *at*.

Still...something was insisting that there was.

"This is it," Taryn said with more conviction than she felt. "This is your last chance. If you have something to show me, then you're going to have to do it now."

Taryn moved around the house one last time, taking pictures in a steady rhythm as she tried, once again, to go over every inch. She even aimed the camera at the lawn, figuring this time she'd cover all the bases. When she finished, she returned to the golf cart where the top offered a slight shield and allowed her to see her screen more plainly.

Nope, nothing. There wasn't a single thing that stood out in her pictures. They were all ordinary shots.

"I tried, okay?" she grumbled, strolling back to her canvas. "I did my best. There's nothing there."

*   *   *

"Did you finish your painting lovey?" Eldean smiled indulgently at Taryn as she poured her another glass of ice cold sweet tea. It had taken Taryn awhile to be able to drink tea again after what happened to her at Windwood Farm, but she loved it so much that she couldn't give it up forever.

"Yep," Taryn replied, patting the case beside her. "Finished it this afternoon."

"Wonderful! But I gather that means you'll be leaving us soon."

Taryn nodded. "I'm leaving in three days, Sunday. I hate to go. I'm starting to feel settled here."

"It happens," Eldean smiled, her eyes crinkling. "That's why so many people are building over on St. Simon's."

Taryn was surprised at just how settled she really was feeling. There was still a darkness that ate at her, still an undercurrent of something that nipped at her skin when she was out at night. A general feeling of uneasiness still frequently fell over her and threatened to unsettle her.

And yet...

She thought about sitting out on the back patio, watching the fireflies and smelling the marshes and the peace that came with having her own space.

Of walking along the sandy beach, the one that felt like it was all hers, and watching the waves roll in while she picked up sand dollars.

Of driving to Brunswick for groceries or visiting the farmer's market by the roundabout over on St. Simon's. Of how much fun it had been to cook in her own kitchen, the hot smell of supper drifting through the rooms of her tiny house.

Walking under the Spanish moss as she unloaded her art supplies from her golf cart and listening to the sounds of children's laughter and bicycle wheels speed by while she painted.

Going for the late afternoon bike rides of her own, feeling the wind in her hair and the invigorating pull of muscles in her calves.

She hadn't hurt nearly as much since she'd been down there. If she could just learn to live with the spirits, learn how to cast away the darkness better...could she learn to be happy there?

Taryn's phone dinged just then and she pulled it out and checked her messages.

"Hey doll! I found something else out about our Mr. Hawkins. Check your email. Matt."

Since her food hadn't made it yet, Taryn pulled her laptop out and fired it up. That was the third thing she wasn't taking any chances with that day, either. All of her photos were saved on it. If someone got ahold of it, why, it would feel like she'd lost half of her life. She still hadn't found her other memory card.

When her inbox popped up on the screen she opened Matt's latest message and read:

"Hello my queen! So, more digging on my end...I have something new for you. Remember how I said we knew next to nothing about William's family? As it turns out, there was a reason. He apparently had a daughter out of wedlock. She was four years old at the time of his death and lived in Boston, Massachusetts. His financial records

show that he sent money back to her mother each month. Of course, I have no idea if Rachel knew about this but it is obvious that this was an affair he had. I suppose at least we can say he tried to do the right thing. Write back soon! Love you. Matt."

"Well," Taryn said out loud as Eldean placed a Cobb salad in front of her.

"Everything okay dearie?" her server asked, glancing at her computer. "Bad news?"

"Weird news," Taryn corrected her absently. "Hey, you might know something about this. William Hawkins?"

"The jackass who burnt the hotel down?" Eldean nodded? "What about him?"

"Did you know he had a daughter? That he'd had an affair?"

Eldean's forehead creased while she considered this and then smoothed out again. "Nope, can't say that I did. Don't surprise me none, though."

"Yeah, nothing surprises me anymore," Taryn agreed. "Oh well."

As Eldean walked away and Taryn attacked her salad it made her laugh to think that Matt had been able to dig that up. How did he accomplish such things? Had Rachel found out about his child and threatened a divorce? Would that have been possible in that day and time? Taryn didn't know.

When Eldean came back to clear her plates, Taryn thanked her. Eldean waited longer than necessary, though, and watched as Taryn shut down her laptop. "Say, I was wondering," she began shyly.

"Yeah?"

"Could you show me your painting? I mean, if it isn't too much trouble?"

Taryn smiled. "Sure. You can tell me what you think."

She unzipped her portfolio bag and carefully removed it. Carrying it over to a nearby table, she moved back the salt and pepper shakers and smoothed it out, using the shakers to hold down the edges. "Okay," she said when she was ready. "Tell me what you think."

Eldean walked over and studied the painting. She looked at it long and hard and then finally let out a deep whistle. "Wowee! That is really something else. No wonder they hired you! Looks like you could walk right through the front door!"

It was the best kind of praise Taryn could receive. "Thank you!"

"I mean, look at that," Eldean continued in awe. "That tree right there looks so real you can feel the breeze blowing the moss. And the porch is three dimensional, like you could walk right on it. How'd you do that?"

Before Taryn could answer, Eldean was moving on to something else. "And the windows? You even made the clouds reflected in them. Very clever of you! And I especially like the touch of her standing there with the Bible in her hand!"

Taken aback by her last words, Taryn leaned forward and looked at where Eldean was pointing.

"B-but–" Taryn stammered.

"Everything looks so real," Eldean gushed. She gave Taryn a big thump on the back that nearly sent her into the table.

Taryn, unable to speak, couldn't tear her eyes away from her painting. Sure enough, in the top window stood a young woman. She was almost certain it was Georgiana. Although she had no memory of painting her and was certain that the figure hadn't been there that morning, Georgiana was plainly staring out the window right at the viewer, a thick book in her right hand.

*   *   *

CONSIDERING THAT SHE WAS ONLY meant to come out twice a month, when she got back to the house Taryn was surprised to find Carla stomping around her living room. As she muttered to herself she waved a dust rag in one hand a bottle of furniture polish in the other.

"Hey Carla," Taryn called, trying to balance her laptop, knapsack, and portfolio case. "What's up?"

"Nothing," Carla fumed, taking an angry swipe at the television stand before quickly moving on to the coffee table. "Sorry, just agitated."

"Okay. No problem. Been there."

Taryn put everything on the floor and then began taking her laptop from its case. "Are you not coming in next week or something?"

"No." Carla blew a stray strand of hair from out of her eyes and then slumped her shoulders. "I just had something on my mind and forgot that I'd already been here. Figured while I was here I'd just go ahead and clean."

"Gotcha." Taryn desperately wanted to ask her about her missing memory card but didn't want to offend her if she hadn't really bothered it. She hoped there would be a way to slide it into the conversation later.

"So your fellar seemed nice," Carla remarked, her voice softening some.

"Yeah, he's a keeper," Taryn replied absently as she opened her inbox. She had a million things to do, but first she wanted to write Matt and tell him about the figure in Adena's window. The hotel office was already closed so she'd wait and take the paintings there in the morning. She needed to frame them at any rate. Steve had delivered the ornate gilded monstrosities before she left for New Hampshire and they were currently propped up against her dining room wall.

"Are you okay?" Carla asked tentatively.

Taryn glanced up and saw that the other woman had stopped cleaning and was staring at her with interest.

"Yeah, yeah. I'm fine. Just a lot on my mind, you know?" Taryn replied with a wave of her hand.

"Uh huh." Carla did not appear convinced. "Hey, when I got here you had a visitor."

"Really? Who?"

"Tall, good-looking Indian guy. Indian as in tee-pees and tomahawks, not as in people from the subcontinent," she specified with a grin. "Kind of a hottie if you're into that sort of thing."

Taryn frowned. "That's David. He's here to keep an eye on the hotel builders. He works in preservation too, in another kind of way. Did he say what he wanted?"

"Nope, but it was weird," Carla relayed, her forehead creased as she remembered the incident. "He was in your backyard when I got here. Walked around from the back of the house and made me jump a mile. Spoke for a second then got on his bike and rode away. Seemed distracted."

Worried now, Taryn put her computer aside and settled back into her chair. "Did he say what he was doing in the back?"

"Nope. Just that he was looking for you. I don't know, maybe he knocked and when you didn't answer he thought you were out back. I mean, your golf cart was gone. He should've known better," Carla pointed out. "He was kind of short. Not rude, but like he was worried about something. His hands were real dirty, too. So was his shirt."

Taryn wondered if he'd been up all night and returned to the building site to poke around some more. She'd almost convinced herself that he was in on the crime she'd witnessed and had made up his own story about seeing the people just to see if she'd give anything away. Now, however, she worried that perhaps he'd been telling the truth and now he was in over his head.

"Carla, do you know anything about that new hotel going up?"

It might have been her imagination, but Carla seemed to avert her eyes for a minute and glance down at the floor, a slight blush rising up her neck. She quickly composed herself, however, and smiled lightly. "Not any more than anyone else. My brother works there. Says the general manager and project manager are real assholes, pardon my French. But that's all I know."

"What does your brother do?"

"He's construction. He does foundations, you know? Footers and stuff. The early work."

Taryn nodded. "I briefly dated a guy who did that after my husba–my finance," she corrected herself, "passed away. They make good money."

Carla shrugged again and looked uncomfortable. "He does okay. Could always do better I guess. It's hard for him to keep a job."

Taryn took a deep breath then and decided to go for it. "Has he said anything about maybe, oh I don't know, finding anything while they've been excavating and digging around?"

This time, she was certain Carla's discomfort was not in her imagination. Not only did she stare at her feet, but she also began wringing the cleaning rag through her hands until her fingers were coated with the amber polishing oil. Finally, she exhaled quietly and said, "No, not really. Just a bunch of old shells and stuff. You know. What you usually find when you dig around here."

Taryn was convinced now that Carla knew something she wasn't sharing. She also knew when to stop, though.

"So you guys have lived around here your whole life?" Taryn asked, changing the subject.

Carla looked visibly relieved, and Taryn watched as her face relaxed. "Yeah, yeah. There's six of us in my family.

Big family, you know? My two youngest sisters are in college. One's going to be a nurse," she said proudly. "She'll be the first one of us to graduate. The other one is going to be a teacher."

"Wow, that's really nice," Taryn said encouragingly, and she meant it. "I bet your mama is real proud."

Carla nodded eagerly and wiped her oil-stained hands on her work pants, leaving behind streaks of yellowish brown. She reached into her pocket then and pulled out her phone. After clicking on it a few times, she found what she was looking for.

"Look," she said proudly, walking towards Taryn and holding her phone out. "Here's my whole family."

Taryn leaned over and looked at the screen as Carla pointed. "That's my two sisters, my oldest brother Timmy and his kids and wife. My youngest brother Dewayne, he's in the army, and that's Johnny. He's the one working the construction. He's had a hard time, you know, in and out of rehab a few times and did a stint in jail for six months but he's clean now," she added in a rush. "He's really trying this time."

Taryn nodded absently, but she knew the color had drained from her face.

Carla's brother Johnny, the construction worker and former addict, was the same man she'd seen digging around in the dark. The same one she'd almost run over that very afternoon.

TWENTY-ONE

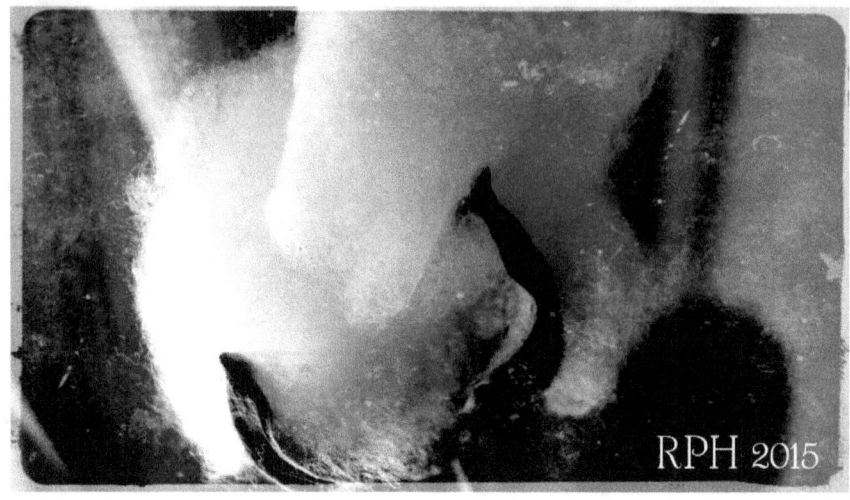

RPH 2015

"Stunning," Ellen gushed for the third time in as many minutes. "Absolutely stunning."

Taryn bristled with pride, feeling the tips of her ears grow warm as she watched her current boss nearly touch her nose to the canvas and then back away again, continuing to study Adena Cottage. Amy stood off to the side and sent Taryn a wide grin and comical wink.

"This truly is amazing. And I love the way you've included a figure in the painting as well. It's subtle and not even that noticeable from a distance, but it's just one of those wonderful details that bring it to life," Ellen declared. "I have to say, this most certainly exceeds any expectations I might have had."

"Well, there's another one so don't get your hopes up yet," Taryn warned her.

Taryn then removed the cloth she'd draped across the framed painting of Ivy House and stood back to let Ellen scrutinize it as well. It was always difficult to reveal her final product to her boss. In most jobs the person who hired her was somewhat involved with the process, often checking in on her and the work to see how it was going. Some even offered suggestions which Taryn always smiled politely at and tried to utilize when she could, if for no other reason than to stay on their good side and receive the recommendation she needed. However, Ellen had left her almost completely alone and hadn't even bothered to see how she was coming along, save for once when she was first getting started.

The reveal for Ellen was a complete surprise.

Taryn watched now as both Ellen and Amy moved in together and studied the historic cottage, now entirely intact and in all its glory, brought to life on her canvas.

"My God," Amy breathed, her eyes wide in appreciation. "It looks like the house is breathing. Like it's alive!"

"Well, it is a little," Ellen agreed. "And our artist here understood that."

Taryn brimmed with pride. It was one of the few times Ellen had referred to her as an "artist." She found herself reveling in a mixture of satisfaction and sadness. It was always hard to say goodbye to her paintings once they were finished. She'd lived with them for so long, after all. She almost felt like they were friends. She'd talked to them, taken care of them, pampered them, sang to them, carried them around, worried over them...and now they were leaving her.

"My dear," Ellen turned to Taryn again, her face aglow. "You have a true gift. We will be honored to show these to the architect, use them in our renovations, and display them proudly in our lobby for everyone to see."

Taryn felt the prickles of tears forming behind her eyes and told herself that it was probably from exhaustion. She stayed up all night worrying about the events that had unfolded on the island, trying to fit the canvases into the ornate frames, and piecing together the fragments of information she had that didn't make sense on their own.

"I imagine I need to go ahead and pay you now, although it seems a shame to just let you go," Ellen said worriedly as she walked back to her desk.

"We don't have to do it right now," Taryn said, always a bit uncomfortable when it came time for final payment.

"I'm not leaving for another two days. If that's okay, of course."

"Oh Taryn, we were planning on you staying for another week," Ellen laughed. "You finished early. Stay on if you'd like. Enjoy the island, do some sightseeing. You've earned it. In fact, I'd like for you to come to dinner tonight. We're having a lovely seafood dinner tonight with a celebrity chef. We had several cancelations. You're welcome to bring a guest if you'd like. Your young man perhaps?"

Taryn was surprised. She didn't know Ellen knew about Matt. Of course, Amy probably told her when she'd let them root around in the records.

"I'd like to come, yes," Taryn answered. "What time does it start?"

"It's rather late at 9:00 pm. That's the seating time our cancelations were for I'm afraid," she said with regret.

"No, that's fine," Taryn assured her. "I'll be there. And thank you."

In fact, nine o'clock would be perfect. It would give her plenty of time to do what she needed to do and get cleaned up first. She'd had an epiphany in the middle of the night. She just hoped her instincts were right this time.

"'Look'," she repeated to herself as she hopped in her golf cart and started back to her house. "'Look.' Okay, Georgiana. I'm certainly going to try."

"I don't like it, Taryn," Matt said worriedly as she filled him in on her plans. "I don't think it's a good idea at all."

"Oh, stop worrying," she scolded him. "I'll be fine."

"And what about your housekeeper and her brother? She has to know what you saw and she must have been the one to let him in with the snake."

"That's funny. Last week you thought it was David," she reminded him.

"Yeah, well, he's not off the hook yet either," Matt muttered.

"Look, I'm keeping my mouth shut about that. David has kind of taken over that nonsense, and I'll let him deal with it. It's his area anyway, not mine. Besides, I've got other things to worry about," she said.

"Have you talked to him?"

Taryn slipped on a pair of loose fitting pants and rummaged through her dresser drawer for socks. She needed to be as completely covered as possible for what she was about to do. "No, actually. I went over to his house earlier to see if I could find him, but I didn't see him. I was going to ask him something."

She left out the part where she was going to ask him to accompany her to dinner that night. She'd rather wait and tell Matt afterward, especially since he was still so paranoid about the other man. It was funny that he wasn't necessarily concerned that they were going to form a romantic connection–he was concerned David might try to kill her. What had her life turned into anyway? An Investigation Discovery show?

"Ah ha!" she cried triumphantly.

"What? Everything okay?"

"Oh yeah," she replied, tossing the socks on the bed. "I just finally found two socks that didn't have holes in them."

"Well, before you run off on this wild goose chase, I need to talk to you," Matt began in his most serious tone.

Taryn glanced at her watch. It was a little after six. She still had time. She'd need to hurry, though.

"I've told you, Matt, I'm going to go over there. It won't take long and–"

"No, it's not about that," he sighed with resignation. "I can't tell you what to do. Or what not to do. It's about something else."

Taryn stretched out across the foot of the bed, threw her legs up in the air, and began tugging on her socks. She let the phone, on speaker now, fall beside her head. "Yeah? Shoot!"

"It's about Sarah's house."

"Oh." Taryn stopped what she was doing and let the sock dangle from her toes. "What about it?"

"I want you to fix it."

Taryn laughed. "Well yeah, so do I. I don't want to sell it. But I don't have that kind of money and no bank is going to loan it to me, not with my employment status and credit report."

"I have the money."

"What?"

Matt took a big breath, and she was surprised to find he sounded nervous. "I want to fix it for you," he finally said in a rush.

"What?" He'd spoken so quickly she wasn't sure she'd understood him correctly.

"The money," he explained. "I want to invest the money and fix the house for you."

Taryn was speechless, not normally something that happened. A million thoughts rushed through her mind, but she couldn't grab onto a single one of them. Her head was suddenly a big jumbled mess.

"Oh," she finally said again. It was all she could manage.

"The thing is, I have the money, but not all of it. I'd need a loan as well. And I could get one. There's just one small catch to it," he explained, sounding logical and clear-headed again, like the Matt she knew.

Taryn knew what the catch was. "You can't get a construction or renovation loan on a house you don't own," she quietly finished for him.

"Right."

"I can't..."

"I know what you're thinking, Taryn, and I have a solution," Matt explained gently. "Sell me the house. Sell it at a fair price. I'll get the loans, I'll get it in working order for you, and then I'll sell it back. You'll win both ways. You'll make some money from the sale, and you'll get your aunt's house fixed."

"And then what?" she asked.

"I was thinking that perhaps it could be our home," he said shyly. "Or maybe just a summer home. A vacation home. Whatever you want."

Taryn suddenly found herself faced with a proposition she wasn't ready for. Their home? A home she'd share with Matt? It was a big step, even just as a "vacation home." Things did not always work out well for Taryn. She'd had a slew of bad luck. What if something happened between the two of them and she lost her house? Lost Sarah's house due to a fight or silly argument or–

"Everyone wins, Taryn," Matt interjected gently. "Nothing bad will happen. I can put the title in both of our names. I'll sell it back to you for $1 and you can own it outright if that's what you want, without my name attached at all."

"But you'd still be stuck with the loan payments," she pointed out. That didn't seem fair.

"I don't care. Let me do this."

"But you can't buy it from me," she insisted. "I didn't do anything to earn it. I could sell it to you for $1. Would that work?"

"I don't mind paying a fair price for it, Taryn. Why not get it appraised and let me pay what it's worth?"

"Because that's not right."

"It would give you some extra cash so that you're not so worried. You could take some time off..."

"It would be taking money from you, Matt, and I won't do that." The idea was mortifying. She didn't need him to take care of her financially. "And the down payment you'd use? The money you'd invest in the house? I know you've been saving that for years. You can't use that for a house that's mine."

"Ours," he corrected. "Or yours if that's the way you want it. I need to do this for you. I can't let you lose that house. At least think about it, okay?"

Taryn hung up the phone a few minutes later in stunned silence. What he was offering was an unreal proposition. It would solve one of the biggest problems in her life at the moment. Sarah's house would be fixed and Taryn would have a place in which she could live. She'd have a *real* place to raise a family in if she wanted. She could get out of her cramped, soulless apartment in Nashville. She could start the next phase of her life...the next phase with Matt.

"I can't lose that house," she whispered to herself. "I can't."

*   *   *

SHE DIDN'T HAVE MUCH TIME and had to move quickly. The car or golf cart would've been faster, but Taryn chose her bike since it was less conspicuous, and she could tie it to the bike rack with all the others nearby.

The good thing was that at 7:30 pm most people were safely tucked away at home or in restaurants, enjoying supper. There wasn't anyone milling around Adena Cottage when she walked up to it. Not a soul in sight.

Her tennis shoes were a change from her regular sandals, but a necessity. They felt tight on her feet as she walked around the back and studied the windows on the lower floor. She didn't know what she'd find inside and didn't want something biting her or, worse in her mind, to step in the middle of a pile of something icky. Her pants and long-sleeved shirt were hot and she was already dripping sweat from the ride over on the bike. She'd have to work at breakneck speed if she was going to do what she needed to do and get back to her house, shower and change, and make it to the hotel in time.

The back of Adena backed up to a grove of trees. There wasn't a road, building, or bike path that someone could be using and, therefore, watching her. She was shielded there, unlike the front of the house which faced the road.

Luckily for her, one of the windows on the first floor had all the glass knocked out of it. Taryn placed her hands on the frame and shook it slightly, testing its strength. It didn't move. Taryn took a quick look around to make sure nobody had walked up to the house, grabbed hold of the ledge, and hoisted herself up with a grunt.

She barely moved.

"Well shit," she grumbled.

She'd never had a lot of upper body strength.

This time she spread her hands farther apart, pulled, and used her legs to push against the side of the house. She could feel herself moving upwards at last but when her upper body reached the windowsill she was unable to control it and suddenly found herself flying through the opening, arms flailing and feet kicking behind her.

With a mighty "thump" she landed inside the house, her face slamming onto the wood.

"Oooh," she moaned, curling up in the fetal position and rubbing her shoulder. She'd landed on it hard, but it didn't feel broken or even dislocated. That was something at least.

When the stars behind her eyes disappeared and she felt steady on her feet again, Taryn stood up, dusted her pants off, and looked around. She'd landed in what appeared to be a dining room. It still boasted a heavy sideboard and mahogany table with seating for ten guests.

She wasn't worried about the floor on the first floor caving in. In spite of its outward appearance, the foundation was still good. Adena had a solid base of nineteen brick piers in the basement, along with a steel support system. Trusses distributed the weight. She hoped they'd continue to work.

She'd tucked her flashlight into the back of her pants and brought it out now, just in case. Shadows bathed the house, but since it was still daylight outside it wasn't yet dark. She could still see to move around.

A light scratching sound came from the room next door, followed by the scurry of tiny feet. Mice. Well, she'd seen worse.

Taryn knew where she had to go, but she wasn't looking forward to it. The cottage was in dire condition, even by her perilous standards. As a teenager and young adult, she hadn't thought a thing about climbing through windows and stalking around abandoned houses with rotting floors and questionable roofs. Now she knew it was just plain dumb luck that had kept her from getting hurt or worse.

Taryn cautiously slipped through the rooms on the first floor, mildly disappointed that she didn't have time to stop and take pictures. She walked carefully through the dining room, gun room, parlor, and what appeared to be a servant's dining room.

She loved the peeling wallpaper, original wainscoting, cracked crown molding, and antique furniture that had been left to rot in some cases. It looked like someone had just gotten up and left one day and never returned, leaving the house mostly intact. She hoped that when they began renovating it they were able to go in first and salvage many of the pieces that were still there.

There were eight rooms on the first level. At least, there were eight rooms she had to walk through to get to the staircase. There were some on the other side of the house that she couldn't enter at all and she skirted around these, crossing her fingers that what she was looking for wasn't in any of them.

The giant winding staircase was a thing of beauty. Mice and rats had made nests in the corners of the steps over the years and bits and pieces of their former homes were scattered across the stairs. Sand had blown in as well, leaving a dusty film to coat the beautiful wood. Still, the banister was ornately carved and shone through the years of neglect, giving her a glimpse of what it might have once looked like.

Taryn tested the first stair with her weight and gave a little bounce. It didn't even creak. She moved up to the second and did the same. The bottom of the stairs felt sold enough. From her current position she could look up and see the second-floor landing. There wasn't any noticeable water damage or other issues with the floor, not any she could see at least, so she was going to give it a try. She only needed to go in one room up there and it was on the other side of the landing. She knew its placement from studying her own painting.

"Oh please don't fall in on me, please don't fall in on me," she chanted as she tiptoed up the stairs, focusing on treading lightly and making herself as weightless as possible.

Near the top, she looked back down behind her and became acutely aware of how high the staircase actually was.

It was a long way to fall if the floor decided to give out on her. She trembled then, the flashlight in her hand shaking.

"You can do this," she said encouragingly. In two more steps she'd be at the top. "You can do it!"

The landing was a different kind of beast. As soon as she put her foot down on it the floor gave a disgruntled moan under her weight. The wood felt spongy here, bouncy. Taryn took a step forward and there was a faint but clear "crack" underneath her.

"This is the hardest part," she reminded herself. "Get past this where there isn't much support and get to the bedroom."

Closing her eyes and biting her lip, Taryn gathered her courage and quickly moved the ten feet to the other side, taking care not to run and to keep her weight distributed evenly on the sides. Waddling in such a way was awkward but when she reached the bedroom door she let out a huge sigh of relief.

"Oh man," she laughed. "Well, that was fun."

It was starting to grow dark now. The sun had set and the last rays of sunlight filtered in through the upstairs windows, tossing long shadows that seemed to reach out to her. She needed to hurry before she freaked herself out.

The heavy bedroom door was open a few inches, the brass knob tarnished and dull. Taryn gave it a push and stepped inside.

This room, Georgiana's bedroom, was pitch black. The windows had been boarded up in here, keeping out any pale remnants of light that might have existed. Taryn flipped the flashlight on and kept the beam low to the ground.

Like the other rooms in the house, there was still furniture left behind. A four-poster bed took up most of the floor, but the mattress and bedding were gone, leaving behind nothing but an empty shell. A wardrobe was up against the wall; both doors flung open revealing nothing but a hatbox on a shelf at the top. A winged-back chair in the corner of the room had claw marks on it. The stuffing was pouring from it and littering the floor. It was difficult to tell what color it had originally been. Aside from what looked like a music box on the ornate fireplace mantle, there was nothing else left in the room.

"Well, now what?" Taryn muttered. She was agitated and disappointed. When she'd seen the image of Georgiana standing in her window Taryn had been so sure that she was trying to tell her something. With the book in her hand, the Bible Eldean had claimed, Taryn had convinced herself that she was meant to explore the bedroom and find it.

"It's supposed to be here," she wailed. "Damn it!"

Taryn stomped her foot on the floor in frustration, forgetting to be careful. The wardrobe doors shook and then slammed shut, the wood cracking under the force.

Startled, Taryn trained her flashlight on the wardrobe and began walking slowly towards it. As she drew nearer, the doors began slowly opening again, the creak of their movements sounding like the opening to a portal in another world. When Taryn arrived at her destination both doors stood wide open again, the hollow blackness inside reminding her of a giant mouth, open and ready to swallow her whole.

Hand shaking, she shone her flashlight around the interior, the pale beam seeking the dark corners and crevices. There was nothing there. Taryn pushed against the back, hoping for a secret compartment or small door to pop open, but nothing moved.

Again sighing in disappointment, Taryn turned to leave.

She'd barely taken a step forward when the bedroom door slammed shut, the strength of it powerful enough that even the boards on the windows rattled. Nails flew through the air and rained down around her, scattering on the floor. She watched as some rolled under the bed and disappeared.

A low earthy voice filled the room then, its authoritative tone belying the smooth femininity. "Look," it commanded, seemingly coming from all directions, and yet nowhere, at once. "Look."

Swallowing hard, Taryn turned back to the wardrobe. She tried hard to keep the flashlight steady as she did another swoop. She couldn't see a single thing other than the hat box. But surely, if there had been something inside of it, the box wouldn't have been left behind? Still, it was the only thing she had to go on.

Stuffing the flashlight down the front of her pants so that the light pointed upwards and illuminated her face and ceiling, Taryn stretched up on her tiptoes and brought down the octagonal hatbox.

She knew before she even removed the lid that it was empty. Still, she balanced it on her knee and removed the top. Sure enough, there was nothing inside, not even a hat.

"There's nothing here," Taryn complained. "Honestly, there's nothing here!"

"Look! " The voice shouted again. More nails flew from the boards and one sailed across the room and scraped Taryn's arm.

"Oh my God, I'm looking, I'm looking," she grumbled, returning to the hat box.

After turning the box over and over again in her hands, and seeing nothing, she put it on the floor. Now, with the lid in her hands, she turned to it. There obviously wasn't going to be a book hidden in the lid. She flipped it over three times and was about to set it down as well when she noticed something odd. On the underside of the lid was an advertisement for the hat company. The faded ad contained a picture of a hat, along with the address of a shop in New York City. The paper had yellowed with age. There wasn't anything unusual about it at all. If the flashlight hadn't been at such an odd angle, causing a shadow to fall across the lid, she might not have even noticed the other thing.

The advertisement wasn't flat. There was something under it.

Using her fingernail, Taryn peeled up part of the paper and to her surprise found that the edges had been sewed down with white thread. A few good tugs had the paper ripping in her hands and a small, silver object landed on the floor by her feet. Taryn knelt down and moved the flashlight around. When it landed on the tiny key, Taryn picked it up and studied it in the faint glow. It was a tiny key, not big enough for a door. A box perhaps?

She spent the next few minutes searching the room, looking for something the key might fit in. She couldn't find anything that would work.

Realizing that she only had about forty-five minutes to get home, get dressed, and get to the hotel Taryn slipped the key in her pocket. "Okay," she said to the room in general as she placed her hand on the knob and gently re-opened it. "I 'looked.' I'll keep trying. But I am running out of time. You're going to have to help me."

The house didn't answer.

TWENTY–TWO

"My my," Steve drawled as Taryn stepped out of her car. "Someone done beat you with a purty stick!"

"Oh please," Taryn laughed but still smoothed down her dress with pleasure.

It wasn't often she got the chance to dress up and go someplace nice. She hadn't had much time to shower and change after her adventure at Adena Cottage. Still, she'd managed to smudge on some makeup, braid her long red hair (still damp from the shower) so that it hung neatly down her back, and throw on a forest green dress that swept the floor but was still anything but conservative with its deep plunge and jersey knit that clung to her curves.

She thought she looked nice.

Steve was also looking dashing in his pressed uniform, slicked back hair, and sparkling eyes. When he leaned in to take her car keys from her she sniffed at him appreciatively. "You smell nice," she flirted companionably.

"Yeah, well. I try," he winked. "You here alone? Where's your man?"

"He had to go back to Florida," she replied. She'd tried to find David again to extend an invitation, but he still wasn't answering his door or phone. His voicemail was full. She was getting worried.

"Well, Amy's in there alone and I'm sure she'll be glad to have someone to sit with," he informed her. "She's got that table to herself. I would've gone with her but they offered me over time and I couldn't turn that down. Bills to pay and all that."

"Yeah, I hear that," Taryn agreed. When she got to the top of the stairs, picking up her dress as she walked so as not to trip over the ends, she stopped and turned. "Thanks for parking my car. Don't mind the mess!"

"Sure thing sugar," he called and threw a kiss up at her.

Taryn pretended to catch it and laughed.

She was looking forward to the evening.

*　　*　　*

"If I eat one more thing I'm gonna die," Taryn moaned.

Amy nodded in agreement. "I'm getting fat," she complained, patting her flat stomach as she leaned back in her chair.

"Oh please," Taryn scoffed. "Look at you."

The other woman looked fetching in her deep blue miniskirt that matched her eyes, peasant blouse, and stiletto heels. Taryn wished she could wear stilettos. They made the legs look so much better. Taryn knew she'd trip over them and break her neck.

They'd eaten their fill of shrimp and grits, scampi, catfish, tilapia, buttered rolls, baked potatoes, and a summer salad with strawberries and walnuts. Now both women were miserable but happy.

"Hey, is that key lime pie they're bringing around?" Taryn asked, straightening in her seat and craning her neck as a server passed.

"You can't be serious," Amy said, raising her eyebrows.

"I am always serious when it comes to dessert," Taryn said.

When the pie was placed in front of them, Amy slid hers over to Taryn. "There you go. Knock yourself out."

Taryn did a little happy dance in her chair and dug in. There was always room for pie.

"So you haven't heard from this guy at all in a few days? Not since he showed up at your house?" Amy asked.

Taryn, with a mouth full of pie, nodded. She hadn't given Amy the whole story but had shared enough. "Yeah. He came over with some things he'd found on the beach. All excited, you know? Left about an hour later and I haven't seen him since."

Amy frowned. "Where did he find it?"

Taryn had never been much a liar. She tried to keep as close to the truth as possible. "Near the place where that hotel is going up."

"I've heard that project manager is a real jackass," Amy confessed. She picked up her fork and speared an edge off of the slice of pie Taryn was nibbling on.

"You want?" Taryn asked, starting to slide it back over.

"No, just a taste." But Taryn noticed that while Amy talked she continued to eat. "Steve's mentioned him a time or two."

"How does Steve know him?"

"I don't know," Amy shrugged. "I think they met in a bar one night. Sometimes Steve goes out for drinks after work. I don't go unless I'm staying with him for the night. I don't like to be out on the road, even after one drink. That interstate's dangerous you know. Crazy-assed drivers."

Taryn nearly choked on her pie.

A Celtic group had been hired to sing and play for the evening, and they were coming back on again after taking a break. The female singer was a young woman with a deep powerful voice that reminded Taryn of Allison Moorer's. She began drifting into a slow rendition of "Carrickfergus" that had the diners lowering their voices and turning to face the stage, mesmerized.

Although Taryn was generally someone who would've dropped everything to hone in on good music, she was antsy, ready to take the next step with what she'd unearthed that evening. "Hey," she whispered to Amy. It seemed rude to talk at a normal level now, what with everyone entranced in the song. "I want to tell you something."

Amy moved her chair in closer and leaned her head down to Taryn. "Yeah? What's up?"

"Please don't tell Ellen but I went inside Adena Cottage today."

Amy's eyes grew wide. "No kidding? And you're still alive? Damn! What happened?"

Taryn quickly gave her the abridged version of what had been happening since she'd been on the island. She told her about the bad dreams, the voice telling her to "look," her camera revealing the deaths at the hotel and the reconstruction of Adena Cottage, and the image appearing in the window.

"And you didn't paint that?" Amy asked, shivering dramatically in the warm room.

"No, I didn't. It appeared there all by itself. Listen," Taryn added, "I'm only telling you these things because Ellen said that it was you who found me and that you already knew about my...stuff."

Amy nodded. "It's okay. I think it's cool. So how can I help? What can we do from here?"

"I don't know," Taryn replied, her face burning in frustration. "I've done everything I possibly could. I thought for sure that since Georgiana appeared in the window there was a clue for me in the bedroom and that since she was holding the book I was meant to–"

"You mean the Bible?" Amy interjected.

"You think it's a Bible too?" Taryn asked. "I looked all over the room and inside the wardrobe. I couldn't find a book of any kind. It's possible that it's someplace else in the house, but I didn't have time to look anywhere else."

Amy pursed her lips and tapped her fingers on the table. Taryn noticed that they were perfectly manicured with little designs on them—butterflies. She felt the urge to hide her own broken nails, nails that were stained with paint and Linseed oil.

At last Amy stopped her tapping and exhaled slowly. "Okay, I don't think we have anything of Georgiana's here," she said. "Not a book anyway, or a box or any secret treasure. We do have something else, though, that might be useful."

"What's that?"

Amy stood, removed the napkin from her lap, and motioned for Taryn to follow her. "Come on, I'll show you."

The music had changed by the time the women left the dining room. All five musicians were engaged in an upbeat jig, a song about war. The Irish sure were happy enough to engage in battle, Taryn thought as they waved goodbye to Ellen and the hostess and started down the hallway.

Taryn followed Amy past the beautiful bar and down a flight of stairs. It was quieter there, almost still. Everyone

330

else was either in the dining room, in their rooms, or out at one of the other restaurants. The only thing Taryn saw at first were restrooms, but then she noticed a long glass case against one of the walls, directly below a picture taken of the original hotel. Amy was standing by it.

"A few years ago we bought these cases and started trying to put up displays of our history," she explained. "You can find these all throughout the historic district. There's only two left in the hotel. This is one of them. Let's see if this helps."

Taryn glanced down and studied the objects enclosed in the case. There were skeleton keys that fit rooms from the original hotel, a lantern, brass doorknobs, and crystals from the chandelier that once hung in the ballroom. Lastly was a black book, charred and in bad shape. The letters were difficult to make out on the cover, but by using her imagination Taryn could just about make out the words "Holy."

"It's a Bible," Amy offered. "Some people thought it was in poor taste. I think it's kind of cool. I mean, why not? It is a part of our history."

"Is this Georgiana's?" Taryn asked hopefully, tracing her finger around the book through the glass.

"Nope, afraid not. But it's close. It's Rachel's."

"Rachel?"

"Yeah. The only thing that survived their room."

Taryn suddenly remembered the newspaper article and how William had only asked for two things–his family Bible and to visit his wife's grave. "Is this the Bible he had in jail?"

"This is the one," she nodded.

"How did it get back here?" Taryn wondered aloud.

"I guess someone brought it back after he died," Amy shrugged. "You want to take a look?"

Taryn nodded with excitement. "Hell yeah!"

Amy dug around in her tiny purse until she produced a key and then gently unlocked the case. Taryn reached in and carefully removed the fragile book, taking care not to damage it. She started to open the stiff cover, but it wouldn't budge.

"Huh," Taryn said, puzzled. Was it too old? Had the fire fused the pages together?

"It's locked," Amy supplied helpfully, pointing at the side.

Taryn turned it over and looked. Sure enough, there was a small lock keeping it bound. "Well that's weird," Taryn said. "Why would you lock a Bible?"

The light that flashed through her took a second to hit her but when she did she laughed.

"Don't know," Amy replied. "We tried opening it once before but didn't want to break it out–"

"Allow me," Taryn said. With her fingers mentally crossed for luck she opened the small purse she carried for the evening and searched for the tiny key she'd found at the cottage. Amy's eyes widened when Taryn brought it out. "Ready?"

Amy nodded and both women leaned in to watch as Taryn put it in the lock and turned. It stuck at first and she thought it wasn't going to work. She was afraid to force it and was just about to give up when the small clasp finally gave and the pages popped open in her hand.

As Taryn and Amy stared at the thin pages, spidery handwriting, and ink blots Amy shook her head and swore. "Well, I'll be damned."

"It's not a Bible after all," Taryn mused. "It's a diary."

The scent of smoke surrounded them then, so light it was almost imperceptible. Neither one could be absolutely certain whether it was real or not.

TWENTY-THREE

*T*ryn locked the doors and drew the curtains. Then she double-checked all the rooms, going so far as to look under the bed and in the closets.

There was no good reason for her to feel as unsettled as she did, but she'd been uneasy on the whole drive home.

"It's because you've snuck a historical artifact out of a majorly important hotel and could get arrested," she told herself, trying to lighten the mood.

She'd promised Amy that she would get the diary back in the morning, or maybe even later that night, before anyone noticed it was missing. Amy had left the case unlocked for her. That might have been the other reason

Taryn was paranoid. If anyone stole anything from the case, it would be on her head.

She could've waited until the next day, gone to Ellen and explained what she'd found and how she needed to look at the diary, but she couldn't wait. Her attempts at locating Ellen in the dining room failed.

"I'll read it, put it in a safe place, and take it back first thing in the morning," she said to the room.

Turning the lamp on in her bedroom, Taryn fluffed her pillows, grabbed her a drink, and settled into the bed with the book in her hands. She was finally going to get to the bottom of things...

THE DIARY

December 15, 1903

William and I are to marry in ten days. Tonight, as he called on me, he had grave news to share. William informed us tonight that he has a child, a daughter, not more than an infant. My father was astounded and angry. After many attempts to quiet him, my father was finally subdued enough to let William explain. The child's mother, Kivalina, was an immigrant. Her father had been his client. Upon falling in love with one another, they married not four months after meeting. Kivalina perished in childbirth and her father passed not three days later from heart sickness. William firmly believes it was brought on by his daughter's sudden departure. William's daughter, Lydia, was not even one week old. Distraught, William himself went into a deep melancholia. He feared for his new child and felt unable to provide for her as a father should. He shed tears in front of us as he told us of how he sent his baby Lydia to live with distant cousins and how he's been providing for her financially for the past three years.

336

Naturally, upon hearing this news, we were shocked and saddened. Even Father, however, couldn't deny that William had behaved in a most honorable way. He is allowing our marriage to continue since it is perfectly respectable to marry a widower. William assured me that it was his meeting me that helped bring him out of his melancholia. I do hope that one day I can provide him with another family.

January 24, 1904

Tonight William learned the horrible truth about me. Though we haven't been married for even a month yet, and only just arrived home to New York from our trip abroad, I fear that he may have regrets.

My terrible fear of the dark is unbearable. When William darkened our bedroom before I was ready I screamed in terror, crying into my pillow and thrashing about until he was forced to pick me up and carry me from the room like a child. He sent for the doctor immediately and I was administered a tonic that mercifully sent me into a deep sleep.

I am ashamed to face my beloved husband this morning, ashamed to tell him the awful truth–that I am nothing more than a frightened child when it's dark and I am unable to see.

January 27, 1904

I am quite weary, having been unable to sleep for three nights. I've complained of headaches and other ailments when darkness falls and William has allowed me to stay up in our parlor, reading quietly with the fire going. He claims he is lonely for me at night and I miss him. I just cannot possibly return to that horrible room with all its darkness. The fire is not enough in there. I must have every corner illuminated. I don't know how to tell him this. He has been simply wonderful, ensuring that Cook brings me broths and pillows for my back and head. I must sleep eventually, however. I cannot stay awake forever.

January 28, 1904

I slept for some time this mid-afternoon. It is not so terrible in our bedroom when it is daylight outside. As the sun pours in and lights up my bed and the floors I find myself sinking into a wonderful sleep, free from dreams.

Then the sky darkens and I am frightened again and wake up. I hurry down the stairs to the parlor where I am able to sit in a cheerful setting, free from shadows.

I am so very weary. I will have to face our bed again soon. William is afraid he has done something wrong. If only I had someone to talk to, but I haven't yet made any social acquaintances here in the city.

February 18, 1904

At last I broke down in tears and told William about my horrible secret. He was aghast at my story, of how as a child my nanny would lock me in my tiny wardrobe for hours, hardened to my cries and pleas. He held me in his arms and rocked me back and forth as a child as I admitted with shame the water that had passed from me in fear and I'd soiled myself. How I'd had to clean it up myself with the hem of my nightgown.

"Did your father not move to save you from this travesty of injustice?" he bellowed, his face red with anger.

I told him of how I'd try to talk to Father, but he'd been busy. My mother had passed away when I was a young child. There was nobody to save me, nobody to unlock the door and let me out. I'd often spend entire nights locked in

339

the tiny room, with the shadows and monsters clawing at me and whispering in my ears. I'd once fainted from the fear and had woken up to Nanny throwing water in my face, screaming at me.

He now understands why I fear the darkness.

"Good God woman," he cried. "I swear on my life I will never let you see another dark room as long as I live."

That night he brought dozens of candles and oil lamps to our room. He placed them in all the corners and lit them, one by one. He left instructions with my maid to ensure they never went out, not until daylight broke, and the room was once again lit by the sun.

I slept soundly then, safer than I've ever felt.

April 10, 1906

William and I have been invited to a beautiful club and hotel on the sea. We leave soon and I couldn't be more excited. My maid is a flurry with activity, packing our trunks and suitcases and running around like a mad woman, gathering the things we will need.

William ensured that I would have all my candles and lanterns and that he, himself, would see to their activity.

I'd hoped that I would be able to share the happy news of a child by now, but it seems that the news is not mine to give. Last night I spoke to William about Lydia, about inviting her into our home. He thought it was a grand idea and said he'd speak to her caregivers soon. Oh! To hear little feet in our rooms. I have been incredibly lonely, although William does his best to entertain me. We went on a picnic in the park on the first warm day and then on a ride through the woods on our horses. I miss my father with dreadful sadness, but his death was not a shock. He'd been careless for years and I'd often warned him about his expeditions. William feels terrible about the accident. He and Father had become like father and son, especially since William's own family has perished.

September 18, 1906

Our journey to the seaside was magical. William had a wonderful time hunting with the other men and socializing in the evenings. Everything about the Jekyll Island Club was magnificent, from the parties and glorious displays of food to the beautiful beaches and charming ladies. I made several friends, including Georgiana Lewis whose father owns a stately cottage there. Georgiana is the only other person in the entire world who knows my secret and she even brought me over one of her own lanterns, an elegant piece that let out copious amounts of light. Georgiana's father welcomed William as well and he spent many evenings there, socializing with the men while the other ladies and I played games and gossiped.

I so want to return.

June 6, 1907

We had hoped to return to Jekyll Island this season but I've had a struggle, and it has delayed our journey. I did conceive a child in the springtime but carried him for only three months. We've suffered a terrible loss and I've been overcome with melancholia and have taken to my bed for more than a month. In sickness, my dreadful fear has worsened. The nightmares are even more awful than normal and I find that I am in need of more lights. It is difficult for William to sleep in the bed with me, with the room so bright. He has taken to lying with me until I drift off to sleep and then he leaves for the guest bedroom. I feel as though my fears and troubles have driven my own husband away and for this I am ashamed.

I do hope to get better soon. We had planned on Lydia coming to visit us in the autumn and the idea of her sunshine and light is what keeps me hopeful.

December 1, 1907

I am glad to see a new year approaching. My ailments have worsened, and we were not able to host little Lydia in the fall. Although I am able to move out of bed, it is difficult for me to dress and see to my toilet. My maid must do far more than she should and, of course, William helps as well. The melancholia will not lift and I fear it will pull me under. The horrible, horrible dreams will not leave me. I often wake up, even with the room illuminated, clawing at the air and crying out to be saved.

We did receive an invitation to Jekyll Island. Georgiana has invited us to a New Year's Eve ball there. I do not feel well enough to travel so far by train but am aching to see her and I know William wants to go. I have decided to make the journey at whatever cost. My husband deserves it and it will be nice to be around friendly faces again. Perhaps the sea air and scenery is just what I need.

December 25, 1907

We've been on the island for five days. Today is Christmas Day and it's been a wonderful day, full of joy and friends and music. My spirits are lifted, and I can feel myself starting to feel normal again. I think this island is saving me.

We did have a moment of trouble when we first arrived because even with Georgiana's lantern and my candles the room was terribly dark. The lantern went out in the darkness before dawn and we couldn't ascertain why. I woke up in fear again, screaming, and the doctor had to be summoned. William ensured that we were moved to a brighter room, however, and there hasn't been any trouble since.

I am determined to be happy and content on this trip and to ensure that my husband is as well. Perhaps this is the time we shall conceive again, God willing.

December 27, 1907

In only two weeks we will be home again. I do so wish we could remain here. I am ever so much happier here on the island than I am in New York. I do believe I have even put on some extra weight, although I can't get my hopes up and think it might be due to a child. I couldn't bear to face that disappointment again.

The only thing that has mired this visit has been Georgiana. I'd hoped to spend more time with her and visit like we did on our last trip. She'd been ill or busy, however, and has had little time for me. I imagine I am not the most interesting of guests here at the Club but she was so lovely to us on our last visit. I am trying not to take it personally and let it hurt my feelings.

She was so gracious when she brought the lantern to me, although it hasn't worked as well as I'd hoped. William had to visit the mainland and purchase more candles for the room. I know it must have frustrated him since he spend almost an entire day getting there, finding them, and returning but he didn't once complain.

Still, the New Years's ball is in just a few nights and I am near giddy with the excitement. The Clubhouse is all aflutter with activity and everything looks so festive. This has, by far, been the best Christmas I have ever seen.

Rachel hadn't written any other entries. Taryn looked up and closed her eyes, feeling like she'd been punched in the stomach. As someone with a fear of the dark herself, she felt

345

Rachel's pain. What a terrible thing to suffer through as a child. These days Rachel might have benefited from a good counselor, or at least some good sleeping or anxiety pills. Who knew what they were giving her back then, what "tonic", to knock her out?

Of course, Rachel had no idea that her last entry would, in fact, be the last. She'd died just a few days later.

Although Rachel's handwriting stopped, the diary itself did not. There was more.

Taryn read on with curiosity.

May 26, 1908

William was hanged today. I did not go, although many others did. I couldn't bear to see his body be carried away. It is difficult to believe he's gone. A light has gone out in this world, and it will never be the same again. There will never be another man such as he.

I am writing this now before I forget everything that happened. I swore to William on my soul that I wouldn't let anyone see Rachel's diary. She'd been dreadfully ashamed of her illness and phobias and he'd sworn to protect her. He was also protecting his daughter, little Lydia. Last night when I made my last visit to the jail he gave the diary to me

346

and I promised to protect it and keep it a secret, along with the other events that have transpired.

It was the very least I could do, considering it is my fault that Rachel died.

There is more that I want to share. William has suffered a great injustice and has done it silently, to protect those he loves.

He was *not* in the hotel when the fire began. I know this because he was with me.

It is no secret that I was very fond of him. I grew to be quite fond of Rachel, but William is the one I loved and will always love. I've carried the feeling for more than a year, feeling the fire inside grow stronger and stronger with each passing day. To simply see him on the lawn, to brush against him in a room, to hear his laughter echoing through the walls...my body burned at the very thought of him. It was almost more than I could take.

In another life I would've been his wife. I should have been his wife. The injustice of it makes me want to sob.

Rachel, though a sweeter soul never lived, was my rival in every sense. Her pliancy and vulnerability angered me at times. I often found myself wanting to lash out at her. I envisioned myself pulling her hair, ripping her dresses to shreds, even throwing her into the icy waters. The thought of her with my beloved was more than I could bear.

347

And yet...she never did a moment of harm to me. I am a terrible, dreadful person.

I feigned illness at the ball and retired early, much like his wife. I then sent for William under the pretense of sending Rachel another lantern. After all, the one I'd intentionally given her was not working well. I knew this when I sent it to her, thinking that its failure would bring him back to me, if only for one more visit. I did not know he'd find other means of bringing lightness to her.

We were alone in the house when he entered my rooms. I know it was improper, but I'd waited so long to tell him how I felt. I hoped he would return the feelings. I thought he would. I thought I'd seen signs from him, signs that he felt the same way. Surely the way he smiled at mem, touched me in passing, called my name–surely those were indications that he harbored desire for me as well?

I was wrong.

William, though ever loving and considerate, did not return my advances.

"I'm sorry Georgie," he said sadly. "I love you dearly, but my wife is my world. I won't betray her trust. I lost one love and I won't do it again."

I was ashamed. Not only had I acted in a most appalling and indecent manner, I was deeply embarrassed at being rejected. I handed him my lantern then, hiding my tears, and asked him to take it to her. My hand slipped, however, and it broke, sending oil all over his pants. Horrified, the two of us went downstairs together to find something in which to clean them.

We hadn't heard Papa and his friends enter the house. They were in the parlor then, he and his bankers, and talking. I knew that our country was facing a crisis but to hear them speak of it petrified me. Their voices were raised and they were shaking in anger.

"Something has to be done!" Papa shouted. "We must protect ourselves."

As William and I remained hidden in the doorway, we listened to them plot and plan, ideas that would be detrimental to many and beneficial to only a few. I was saddened by the selfishness and could see that William was as well.

The oil on William's trousers must have been thick because someone noticed the scent then. They discovered us and were horribly angry. They accused William of spying and threatened him repeatedly. He swore he would talk of nothing and made to leave.

That was when we saw the fire at the hotel.

William *did* try to get inside and save his wife, but it was too late. The hotel was a towering inferno. By the time we arrived the grass was littered with bodies, our very friends whom we had just seen hours earlier.

I fear that it was the very lantern I gave her that started the fire in Rachel's room. I will forever feel responsible for her tragic death, and for what transpired to William, although for a brief moment I felt a small spark of elation–if she were to die that would leave him to me at last!

I had only to look at William's face to know that he would never truly love again, not even me.

Another meeting was held, this time with William in attendance. He had heard too much, he knew too much. "If you speak of this then we will find your daughter and she will pay, not you."

"I'm innocent of the fire," William exclaimed. "I didn't kill my wife! If I don't defend myself I'll hang. At least let me say I was here. I don't have to talk about what was said."

"Too risky," another gentleman, whose name I don't wish to speak of, interjected. "We can't take that chance."

"Keep quiet about our meeting and we shall see that your daughter and her family are forever taken care of," Papa promised.

I was sickened.

William went to the gallows protecting his family.

I will never, *ever* forgive my father.

I will never, *ever* forgive myself.

*　　*　　*

TARYN'S EYES WIDENED as she sat back against her pillow, the diary clutched to her chest. He hadn't started the fire. He hadn't cheated on his wife. William Hawkins had done nothing wrong, *nothing*.

The injustice of it made Taryn want to scream.

And the secret meeting that came later? They must have ironed out some of the details because the Federal Reserve wasn't a bad thing. Had Georgiana talked them into making changes for the good of the whole? Or had their guilt about what happened to William had an effect on them?

One thing was for sure: William and Rachel Hawkins were innocent in the whole mess.

They'd both paid with their lives for things that other people had done to them.

TWENTY-FOUR

*T*e *smoke filled the room and squeezed Taryn's throat.*

She coughed into her pillow and then turned over in her sleep, trying to get away from the putrid stench. It followed her, however, and slid into her lungs and up her nose, sending her into another coughing fit that had her almost waking up. In her sleep, she could feel the heat and kicked off her blankets when her feet grew uncomfortably warm. The dark room in her dream was closing in on her again, the walls slowly crushing her as she reached out and tried to push them back.

Taryn moaned and cried out in fear of the tiny dark space but then the smoke came again and her cries were drowned out by another coughing fit.

Her feet and legs were burning and now the heat was rising to her face. In a twilight daze, Taryn swiped at her shoulders and forehead and tried to push the rest of the covers off. What's wrong with the air, she thought groggily, still lost in her dream and unable to focus. When did it start getting so hot in here?

Something crashed then, the sound of glass breaking into tiny little pieces. Taryn shot up fully alert now, her ears peeled for the sounds of an intruder.

She was met by a wall of dirty gray, with just the faint hint of orange behind it.

As the smoke pressed into her, finding its way inside, Taryn gagged. "Oh my God," she cried, her eyes filling with water, blinding her. "Oh my God!"

This was no dream.

With her bedroom door open she could see the flames in the living room, engulfing the chairs and leaving a burning trail into the dining room. The flames licked the ceiling in there, the black smoke rising and spreading into her bedroom.

Taryn jumped from her bed and ran to the door, the thick smoke blinding her. The front door was ablaze, and as she looked towards the kitchen she saw in horror that the back exit was blocked as well. "Shit, *shit!*"

Trying to remember everything she'd learned in her fire safety class in elementary school Taryn dropped to her knees and crawled back to her bed. She tried putting as much distance between herself and the smoke that would surely kill her before the flames. Quickly pulling a pillowcase from her pillow, Taryn tied it around her head, covering her nose and mouth. She found her sandals by the bed and slipped them on. Somewhere along the way she'd read that one should wear closed-toed shoes when they were flying so that, if there were a crash, they wouldn't get cut on the debris. That felt relevant now, somehow.

The nearest window was just a few feet away and Taryn crawled to it now. When she tried raising it, however, she found it wouldn't budge.

The first real waves of panic sank in and she was nearly blinded by fear as she dropped back to the ground and cried. The flames from the other room were getting closer now and she heard the sound of more glass breaking. She had to get out of there. Through the murkiness her grandmother's ring sparkled, and Taryn suddenly felt a new burst of energy.

She could do this.

With new determination she crawled to the second window and tried it. It was also stuck. The lamp on her nightstand was heavy, so she pulled on the cord and yanked it from the wall. Using all her strength, she slammed it into the glass, yelling like a mad woman.

Nothing happened.

Something happened in the air just then, a shimmering that wasn't caused by the fire. The air around her seemed to part for just a second and in the clearing the figure of a woman appeared. It was so brief that Taryn couldn't be sure it was even real, but when the ethereal arm pointed towards the bathroom Taryn understood. As she stood to run from her bedroom the diary, still on the bed where she'd left it upon falling asleep, caught her eye. She grabbed it, stuffed it into the back of her pajama pants, and ran into the bathroom just as a cloud of flames burst into the bedroom behind her.

The tiny window over the toilet was only about fourteen inches tall and twenty inches wide, but it was all she had. Balancing on the back of the toilet, Taryn pushed at the glass and screamed with relief when it opened, the cool night air rushing to her face. She thought she could hear someone calling her name from the outside, but she ignored it and focused on pulling herself up by her arms. Her bedroom was engulfed in flames now, the heat licking at her feet and legs. She kicked at it by instinct as she wiggled through the small opening, straining against the tight sides. When half of her body was out in the open, strong arms came from out of nowhere and grabbed hers. For a horrible instant she thought she'd be stuck but then the other arms pulled again and she was free.

David caught her in his arms and began to run with her, his long hair wrapping around her shoulders. She continued to cough and cry as he hurried to the road. There were others there with him, faces she didn't recognize. In Taryn's confusion, she wouldn't understand until much later that they were firefighters and that the second sound of shattering glass had been them breaking through the front door to get to her.

"It's okay," David murmured, gently removing the pillowcase from her face. It was covered in black. "It's okay."

In a wild panic, Taryn struck at him and pushed him away. "What are you doing here? Did you do this!? Did you try to kill me!?"

David looked at her, hurt in his eyes. "No. No! I thought, I knew. I–"

"Did you set the fire?!" Taryn screamed again.

A man in a cumbersome hat and uniform walked up to her then. His face was streaked with black, his eyes red and watery. "Ma'am," he spoke softly, tapping her on the shoulder. "Ma'am, your friend here saved you. He's the one who called us. The police have the one who did this. He's in the car over there."

356

Taryn turned and looked at the police cruiser parked in the middle of the road. Other people had filed out of the houses, watching her house go up in flames while the firefighter attacked it with the force of water, unlike anything she'd ever seen. Some were gathered around the cruiser, not hiding their curiosity as they looked inside.

Taryn stepped away from David then and walked towards it, the diary still stuffed in her pajama bottoms. The people around her stepped aside as she neared them, some reaching out to touch her as she passed, offering their sympathy in quiet tones. When she reached the window she bent down and looked in.

It wasn't anger, but sheer disappointment and sadness that filled her when the familiar eyes gazed back at her.

"Oh," she said sadly, backing away.

David strolled over to her and herded her back to where the detective and fire marshal were standing.

"He works at the hotel, right?" the detective asked.

When Taryn couldn't answer, David nodded. "Yes," he replied. "He's the head valet. Steve Parkinson is his name."

Taryn burst into tears then, grief swelling inside of her.

"Taryn? It's okay," David said, giving her a squeeze. "You got out. It's okay."

"Not it's not," she sobbed, crying as if her heart would break. It would never be okay again.

"Is it Steve?" he asked.

"NO," Taryn wailed. Lifting a shaking finger, she pointed at the smoldering inferno. "It's my camera. Miss Dixie's still in there. She's gone. I've lost my best friend, David. I've just lost my best friend."

*   *   *

"It's *my* fault," Amy cried again. Taryn sat up in the hotel's comfortable bed and hugged a pillow to her stomach. Amy had been with her for almost an hour and had, so far, done nothing but apologize. "I am so sorry. I didn't know; I *swear* I didn't know."

"It's not your fault," Taryn replied.

Amy looked miserable. Her bloodshot eyes were glassy from crying and her pixie hair was disheveled, sticking up every which way. The day before, when Carla had visited her, she'd informed Taryn that Amy had apparently made a scene at the police station. She'd screamed at Steve and went so far as to picking up a stapler from a nearby desk and hurling it at him.

They'd restrained her for his safety.

358

"He knew where the spare key was to your house. He got in through the front door," she spat in disgust.

"Was it him—"

"With the snake?" Amy finished.

"And the alligator?" Taryn asked.

Amy looked down at her feet, ashamed. "Yes," she whispered.

But it hadn't been him who stole the memory card. That had been Carla's brother. He'd been in the house with them when it went missing. Carla hadn't expected Taryn back so soon and had made him hide, afraid she'd lose her job since he had a criminal record. When Taryn left the room he'd slipped out, but not without grabbing the card first.

"I'm sorry Taryn," Carla said the day before when she'd visited Taryn and returned it. "He saw the card on his way out. He thought you might have taken pictures that night on the beach when you found the sea turtle."

Like Amy, she'd been ashamed of her loved one's part in it. Like Amy, she had also thrown a fit at the police station.

"And for what?" Taryn asked bitterly. "For what? For a hotel?"

"I know," Amy nodded. "It's ridiculous. When they found those pirates' graves, though, and all of those artifacts the project manager knew they'd be held up for weeks, maybe months. He'd lose his bonus, the general manager was upset. You know how people get over money."

"So they paid their own crew to go in at night and remove what they could?" Taryn pressed.

"Yes. And Steve had been promised a good position there. Head of Guest Services. It was going to pay real well," Amy dabbed at her eyes with her fingertips. "When they saw you there on the beach they thought you'd talk. He just meant to scare you. He wanted to impress his new boss."

"Um Amy, that's more than just fetching coffee. That's psychotic." Taryn tried to be diplomatic in the way she pointed this out but failed.

"He's always been obsessed with money," Amy agreed. "And sometimes he could be hateful. He, he was arrested for assault on his ex. But I just thought she was crazy. I guess she wasn't. I guess this is him."

"I'm sorry," Taryn said and did feel sorry for her. Amy had certainly dodged a bullet there. "But why did he come back last night? I was getting ready to leave."

"It wasn't you; it was your friend."

"David?"

"Yeah. That was my fault, too. I told him about the stuff David found. He went to his house to look for it and couldn't. He thought maybe David had taken it to your house and might still be there. He was just going to scare you, he said. Get you to tell him where those things were. But he used too much gasoline and the fire got out of hand. He just ran."

Taryn shook her head in disgust. She thought she could come up with at *least* a dozen ways of getting someone to talk that were better than trying to smoke them out. It didn't seem like the appropriate time to bring them up, though.

"I'm real sorry about your camera, too," Amy said, her eyes filling with tears again.

Taryn hung her head and stared at her pillow. She couldn't think about Miss Dixie. Every time she tried she broke out into sobs. It was crazy to think about an inanimate object that way, but they'd been through so much together. The thought of her beloved camera, charred and broken, unloved. The firemen hadn't been able to find her yet. When they did, she wanted to give her a proper burial.

Sometimes life was too hard.

*   *   *

ELLEN'S FACE FLOODED WITH RELIEF when Taryn walked into her office.

"Oh my dear, I was going to come to you. You didn't have to come all the way over here," she said as she ran out from behind her desk.

Taryn shrugged, embarrassed. "I needed to give this back to you," she said and handed Ellen the diary.

Ellen took it in her hands and smiled. "All these years. The answers were right in front of our noses. Who knew? You've provided a valuable service to us, Miss Magill. And poor Mr. Hawkins."

"Poor Mr. Hawkins," indeed. He hadn't murdered his wife at all. It had all been a terrible accident, and he'd been a willing victim to the gallows, fearing for his child's life and protecting the ones he loved.

"It's a sad love story really," Taryn mused thoughtfully.

Ellen nodded her agreement. "It truly is. We might never know who threatened him, and why. But what a fine man he was to do what he did. How brave."

Taryn concurred. "And the ghost story about the candle on the grave..."

"To protect his poor little wife from the dark she was so very much afraid of," Ellen murmured. "Our island is a place of beauty and mystery. But also of sadness. You can't have a place full of this much history without getting the bad along with the good."

Taryn knew that to be true.

A knock on the door came then and Amy stuck her head in the office. "The gentlemen are here to see you Mrs. Russo," she said nervously. Amy still acted nervous around Taryn, as though she wasn't sure how to behave. Taryn hoped in time she'd come to realize that she was just as much of a pawn as everyone else.

"Show them in, Amy," Ellen ordered. She then turned to Taryn. "I was going to bring them to you but now that you're here...I am sure you'll want to hear what they have to say."

The men who entered the office were dressed in business suits and impeccably groomed. Taryn recognized expensive clothes and quality leather Italian shoes when she saw them. They shook Ellen's hand first and then Taryn's. Once they were all seated, the older of the two began to speak.

"Miss Magill," he began in an authoritative tone, "we're from the Richfield Group and own the hotel and condo property going up on the other side of the island."

Taryn nodded, confused. She had no idea where this was going.

"We're aware of your situation and have spoken to Mrs. Russo here. Between us, we've all tried to come up with something that can repay you for your suffering."

The younger man, a pale gentleman with a thick head of light blond hair spoke up quickly, "Although we know nothing we can do would ever repay you for everything you went through..."

"Yes, well," the other man continued. "We think we've reached a conclusion that might help. Mrs. Russo here would like to extend you the opportunity to stay in the hotel until Labor Day if you'd wish, free of charge of course."

"All your meals, access to the water park, carriage rides, whatever you'd like would be covered," Ellen smiled warmly.

Taryn's heart nearly stopped beating as she looked back and forth at the other adults in the room.

"If that is not to your liking, we would also like to offer you accommodations at one of our properties," the older man resumed his speech. "We have hotels and rentals all over the world. Or, you could choose to remain here on the Golden Isles. We have fourteen rental homes over on Saint Simon's and I am positive we could find something that would suit you."

Taryn's heart began to beat furiously. Stay there until Labor Day?

"Of course, we would also like to provide all your meals and entertainment, wherever you go," the younger man added.

Taryn tried not to show any excitement. After all, they were offering this because, between the two companies, their employees had tried to kill her.

While they let the proposition sink in, the older man reached into his briefcase and pulled out an envelope. "And this, of course, is for your trouble," he said, handing it over to her. Taryn accepted it in trembling hands. "Of course, this is not to replace the previous offer. This is in addition to it."

Not to be outdone, Ellen fumbled around on her desk and produced an envelope of her own. "And this is from us," she declared, handing it to Taryn.

Taryn, dumfounded, sat in her leather chair holding both envelopes in her hand. She had no idea what to do. Was she meant to open them then and there? "So do I need an attorney or something?"

The three of them laughed then, quick nervous sounds that amused Taryn. Yes, she probably did need an attorney. But Taryn wasn't that kind of person.

Rather than opening the envelopes there in the room, she stuck them in her knapsack. "I appreciate your offers, but I'd like some time to think about them if that's okay."

"Perfectly fine," Ellen replied.

Taryn stood then and, in a daze, said goodbye to everyone. She was still in a daze as she walked across the grounds towards San Souci, the annex that held her hotel room.

David was waiting for her on the porch.

"Hey there," he said shyly as Taryn neared the steps.

"Hey," she replied, feeling awkward. She still felt terrible about accusing him of setting fire to the house.

"Everything okay?" he asked.

Taryn nodded and then grinned. "I think I just got paid off for everyone's workers trying to kill me."

"How'd you make out?" he teased.

"I don't know yet," she replied. "I'm still too surprised to look."

"Listen, about what happened…"

"Don't worry about it," Taryn said. "I owe you an apology. I'm sorry. Are we good?"

"We're good," he said.

"In that case, there's someplace I want to go. You up for a ride?"

TWENTY-FIVE

RPH 2015

"You've still got your wheels, I see," David laughed as they turned out onto Riverview Road."

"Yep. They gave them to me," Taryn grinned.

"Dang. What do I have to do to get one of these babies?"

"Well, you apparently have to wake up with a snake in your bed, get chased by an alligator, and have someone try to burn you alive."

David shrugged, his long hair streaming behind them as Taryn picked up speed. "Eh, I've done worse for money."

"That's what this was all about, wasn't it?" Taryn mused. "Money."

"That's what most everything is about these days it seems. So hey," David said lightly, changing the mood. "I'm staying on a few more months. I'm going to head the excavation here."

"What?" Taryn asked in surprise, glancing over at him in delight. "Well, that's awesome! So were the remains they found native?"

"Depends on your definition of 'native'," he joked. "It looks like they were pirates. Either way, they've been here longer than us."

"I thought you worked with Native American history though."

"I'm an archeologist. I work with all of it. It's just that Creek Indians are my specialty. This is a major job. It wouldn't normally go to someone low down on the totem pole, no pun intended, like me. So I guess helping you out of the fire had advantages to me as well." David reached over and patted her on the leg. "Not that I wouldn't have tried to save you anyway, of course."

"So why were you at the house that night? It was two in the morning. I hope you weren't trying for a booty call," she teased him.

He might have blushed, but his face was so dark it was hard to tell. "If I tell you, you might not believe me."

"Try me," she challenged.

"Someone had broken in on me that evening. I'd spent most of the night at the police station. They really ransacked the place. I'm guessing they were looking for the artifacts, but I'd already taken care of that. I spent the afternoon over in Brunswick, renting one of those climate-controlled storage units and putting them someplace safe."

So that's why I couldn't find him all day, Taryn thought to herself.

"I came back home wiped out and fell asleep. I was just getting into the middle of the most excellent of dreams when a sound woke me up. I thought someone was coming back in on me again so I jumped up and grabbed my knife. It wasn't the intruder, though. It was a woman. She had long dark hair and was wearing a white dress. She just stood there at the foot of my bed and pointed out the window. 'Look,' she commanded. Just 'look.' That was all. She disappeared. I felt like a fool, let me tell you, standing there in the middle of the floor in my underwear, brandishing a knife. But that's when I smelled the smoke. I ran to the window and saw the flames. I don't know what made me think it was your house. The thought just popped into my head."

Taryn shouldn't have been shocked, not after everything she'd seen and been through, but she was. "Damn."

"Yeah, you're telling me," he muttered. "Do you think it was that Mary-the-Wanderer?"

Taryn shook her head as she pulled into the parking spot in front of the Horton House. "I don't think so," she replied. "There are many spirits here. I think it might have been Georgiana. She's also told me to 'look' a few times. It seems to be the only word she knows."

"Well, you're lucky to have a spirit watching out for you," he said. "She was adamant that I help."

"Thank you for what you did." Taryn hopped from the vehicle and then reached behind her, feeling for Miss Dixie. It took her a moment to remember that she was no longer there. Taryn's face fell and for the second time that day she felt her eyes welling up with tears.

"It's your camera isn't it," David said sympathetically. He walked around the golf cart to where she stood and rubbed her lightly on the back. "I'm so sorry. If I could've gotten inside…"

"I don't know what to do without her," Taryn cried. "She's always with me. I know it's stupid to be so attached to an inanimate object, but it's like–"

"She's not just your camera; she's also your eyes," David finished. "It's okay to grieve something you love."

Taryn nodded miserably and wiped at her eyes. "I want to show you something," she said, trying to compose herself. "It's over here."

She led David through the trees on the other side of the road, towards the tiny cemetery. "See that wall up there?" she pointed.

David nodded.

"It's where Rachel is buried. There's a legend on this island that says each night a candle appears on her grave. That her husband placed one on it while he was in jail and now he continues to do it in death. I thought he did it out of guilt."

"But he didn't?"

"No, Matt was right. It was out of love."

They'd almost reached the enclosure when Taryn stopped walking and turned to face David. "She was afraid of the dark. Deathly afraid. Her nanny used to lock her in a small closet when she was a child. Her fear was so strong that each night she lit dozens of candles at home. Her husband and maid would ensure they kept burning until morning. He brought her the candle so that she wouldn't be alone here in the dark."

"So the fire at the hotel was an accident?" David prodded.

"Just an accident. She must have knocked one over and it caught her gown. Maybe she did it in her sleep," Taryn added. "Her husband took the blame for her death. There were lots of reasons he did that, but the important thing to remember is that he loved her. He wouldn't have hurt her."

They began walking again.

"And you found all this out?" There was a touch of amazement in David's voice as they reached the gate.

"With a little help," Taryn smiled. "I hope his name will be cleared now and that, wherever they are, they're happy."

"So it wasn't her ghost trying to give you a message this whole time?"

Taryn shook her head and undid the latch. "No, I think her spirit has passed on. It was Georgiana's. I think in some ways she loved William. She kept the diary safe for him until she died. She kept his secrets. But now that time has passed she knew it was time to talk. Hopefully, her spirit will be at peace now as well."

Rachel's grave was on the other side of the small enclosure. Someone had placed fresh flowers on it. It wasn't the flowers, however, that caught Taryn's eye. It was the glint of sunlight, reflecting off of something shiny.

"What the hell?" David exclaimed as she rushed forward.

Taryn, who thought she'd never be surprised by anything ever again, felt her mouth drop open. The gate closed behind her with a loud "bang" as her hand dropped limply to her side. She was unable to move.

"Taryn," David's voice quavered as he dropped to the ground by her headstone. "Taryn, you'd better come here."

Taryn moved slowly across the patchy grass, unable to take her eyes off the object in front of her. She was a little beaten, a little black from the smoke, but resting right under the inscription on the stone was Miss Dixie.

Taryn fell to her knees and grabbed her camera, clutching it to her chest. She wasn't even warm from the sun. She hadn't been there long.

"Well," David said in a strangled voice as he smoothed back his hair and shook his head in disbelief. "It seems as though Georgiana wasn't the only one looking out for you."

Taryn's bags were packed and in her car. Her laptop, which had been safely tucked away in her trunk the night of the fire, was untouched. Her newly recovered memory card was where it belonged, in her camera, and Miss Dixie was buckled into the seat next to her.

"I'll come visit in a few days," Amy promised.

Taryn shut her door and rolled down her window. "I'm planning on it," she smiled.

"When's your boyfriend coming back?"

"He's on his way right now. He should be here in a few hours."

Amy nodded and smiled. "It will be good to have someone there with you for awhile. But enjoy yourself! No work!"

"No work," Taryn agreed but thought that maybe she'd do some painting for herself. It had been a very long time since she'd done it for the simple pleasure of creating something.

"I can't believe you gave up Paris and London for Saint Simon's," Amy teased her. "You sure you know what you're doing?"

Taryn laughed. "I like it here. I'm looking forward to settling in over there and resting. I'm feeling more like myself than I have in a very long time."

As Taryn pulled out she saw Amy behind her, standing in the road, waving. She raised her hand and sped off, feeling good about everything that had happened.

David would work with the hotel group and ensure that no graves were disturbed and what artifacts they did discover would be properly labeled and given to the right places. Amy and Carla both still had their jobs, Johnny and Steve were in jail–along with the project manager and general manager of the new hotel.

Taryn had enough now to get her aunt's house fixed and then some. Matt had acted happy for her, but there was something in his tone that made her feel like a part of him was hurt as well. She thought maybe he'd been looking forward to taking care of that for her. She'd need to work on that, on letting him get closer and not just act like her research assistant when she was on the job.

As Taryn sailed over the Sydney Lanier Bridge, she rolled her windows down and slipped on her cheap sunglasses. With Dwight Yoakam's "Secondhand Heart" cranked up, the sun in her eyes, and her hair whipping across her face she laughed with happiness.

There was a new chapter starting in her life; she could feel it. And it felt wonderful.

The End

Author's Notes

And here is where I try to set some records straight about how much of the book is true, sort of true, and not true at all.

For starters, the Jekyll Island Club Hotel on Jekyll Island is very much a real place. It is beautiful, charming, and haunted. It truly was created as a playground for the rich and famous. The porch, bar, ballroom, croquet lawn, dining room with tea, and valet stand are all real.

The fire, however, exists only in my imagination. The hotel never burned down like it does in my book. Still, the fire is not entirely fictional. I actually based that particular storyline on a real fire that occurred in northern Kentucky at the Beverly Hills Supper Club. A popular nightclub, it caught fire during a busy night and killed many, many people. It's considered one of our country's worst entertainment disasters. If you do a little searching you can find interviews with the survivors, as well as lots of news stories and videos. It's a chilling story and, unfortunately, real.

There are cottages that belong to the hotel. And yes, some of them do look like little mansions, containing as many as 15 rooms. Ivy House and Adena Cottage are fictional. Ivy House, however, is loosely based on Hollybourne, which is the only standing cottage that hasn't been completely renovated. It is reportedly haunted and some of the tales Ellen mentions about the house are real stories I heard while on the ghost tour of the property.

The Horton House is a real place and is also reportedly haunted, much in the same manner that I describe in the book. There *is* a tiny cemetery across the road from the Horton House and the description of it is accurate. Rachel Hawkins (a fictional character) is not really buried there, though. However, the part about Taryn visiting the cemetery and feeling someone close to her sighing is a true story. It happened to me while I was there by myself.

Mary the Wanderer is a real ghost that haunts both Jekyll and St. Simon's. I haven't seen her.

Rachel and William Hawkins are fictional characters. The story about Rachel's grave is a true ghost story, but takes place on St. Simon's Island, not Jekyll Island. The story was told to us by our guide during the ghost tour of St. Simon's. Apparently, a young woman was buried in Christ Church cemetery. Like Rachel, she was deathly afraid of the dark because her nanny used to lock her in the closet as a child. Supposedly, the woman had to light candles every night. One night wax burnt her and she developed an infection, an infection that eventually took her life. Each night visitors are meant to be able to see a candle light appear on her grave, a practice her husband started and apparently continues in death. Our guide told us that the cemetery became so popular with late-night visitors that they had to remove the headstone. I have no idea if this story is true or not, but I liked it anyway.

All of the beaches are real.

Yes, there are alligators on Jekyll Island, but they're mostly on the golf course and what they call "alligator pond." They don't normally attack people.

Sea Turtles are protected on the island. If you're there in the summer you'll find markers for their eggs. Please don't disturb them. The Sea Turtle Center is fun to visit and I recommend it, regardless of age.

The wildlife and vegetation of the island are much as I described. And there really are a ton of golf carts and bicycles. I borrowed a bike from a friend while I was there and rode all over St. Simon's Island with my son.

The story about the airport having remains under it is true. There is also a park on St. Simon's where native remains were discovered as well.

Lastly, all the characters in the story are fictional. None of them are based on any real people.

I truly did visit all the locations in the book. My family and I went to Jekyll and St. Simon's twice over the course of a year for me to conduct research and spent an entire month renting a house there so that I could get a feel for it. It is magical, ghosts or not.

VISIT AMAZON!

Did you like what you read? Reviews are very important to authors–leaving a review is like leaving an author a tip!

Visit the book's Amazon page at:

http://www.amazon.com/Jekyll-Island-Paranormal-Mystery-Taryns-ebook/dp/B014ZMXJI8/

Want MORE?

Want to learn about Taryn's beloved grandmother and get a glimpse of Taryn when she was a child? The companion novella to the Taryn's Camera series entitled *Stella* is 100+ pages and available in the *Ghost Children* anthology.

For more information visit:

http://www.amazon.com/Haunted-Children-Collection-Stories-Beyond-ebook/dp/B0149ES7J8/

Reviews of the *Taryn's Camera Series*

WINDWOOD FARM

"This is an absolutely wonderful book and I didn't want to put it down. It was exciting and sad but it was uplifting too." (Kim @ **The Open Book Society**openbooksociety.com/)

"I won't spoil anything but this book has great characterization, loads of atmosphere and is never dull. The first book in the Taryn's Camera series so roll on number two!" (**A Drunken Druid's Reviews** the-drunken-druid.blogspot.com/)

"The author does a great job painting just what life in a small town in Kentucky is like. She also writes a great mystery." (Lisa Binion @ **The News in Books** thenewsinbooks.com/)

"while I do not believe in ghosts and such, this book was written in a way that I was able to enjoy it and go along for the ride and "believe" the story."- online reviewer

"a great chiller that was perfect summertime reading!"- online reviewer

GRIFFITH TAVERN

"I actually love Rebecca's descriptive style of writing which kept feeding my imagination and continuously created images and pictures in my mind"- online reviewer

"If you like old houses, historic preservation, AND creepy ghost stories, it's right up your (darkened, cobwebby) alley"- online reviewer

"This was a book that was an absolute pleasure to read. A book that I couldn't wait to get back to"- online reviewer

DARK HOLLOW ROAD

"Her characters are rich, her story lines are enticing and as a reader these combine to make for a lovely journey through a small southern town"- online reviewer

"I've enjoyed all of the Taryn's Camera books. They have so many things I love - old houses, ghosts, a likable main character I can relate to, and realistic descriptions of small town Southern life. But this one goes a step further, addressing real life issues with a depth of emotion that can only come from someone who knows this region and its issues firsthand. Highly recommended."- online reviewer

SHAKER TOWN

"a paranormal whodunit with lots of surprises"- online reviewer

"As always wonderful thorough research was done. Great presentation. I did not want to stop reading until I finished"- online reviewer

"Wonderful story, history, background and my favorite characters! You won't be disappointed with this newest adventure of Taryn and her camera!"- online reviewer

ABOUT REBECCA

Rebecca Patrick-Howard is the author of several books including the paranormal mystery trilogy *Taryn's Camera*. She lives in eastern Kentucky with her husband and two children.

Visit her website at www.rebeccaphoward.net and sign up for her newsletter to receive free books, special offers, and news.

REBECCA'S BOOKS

TARYN'S CAMERA SERIES

Windwood Farm (Book 1)

The locals call it the "devil's house" and Taryn's about to find out why!

Griffith Tavern (Book 2)

The old tavern has a dark secret and Taryn's camera's going to learn it soon.

Dark Hollow Road (Book 3)

Beautiful Cheyenne Willoughby has disappeared. Someone knows the truth.

Shaker Town (Book 4)

Taryn's camera is finally revealing a past to her that she's always longed to see-the mysterious Shakers as they were 100 years ago. But is she seeing a past she hadn't bargained for?

Jekyll Island (Book 5)

Jekyll Island is known for its ghosts, as well as its fascinating history, but now the two are about to take Taryn on a wild ride she'll never forget!

Black Raven Inn (Book 6)

The 1960's music scene...vibrant, electrifying, and sometimes even deadly...

Muddy Creek (Book 7)

Lucy did a bad, bad thing when she burned down the old school. Now it's up to Taryn to find out why.

Bloody Moor (Book 8)

The call it "the cursed" and the townspeople still fear the witch that reigned there a century ago. But this haunted Welsh mansion has more than meets the eye!

Sarah's House (Book 9)

When Taryn inherited the old, rambling house from her beloved aunt Sarah, she never knew that she'd find herself in the middle of a mystery-and friends with a ghost!

Taryn's Pictures: Photos from Taryn's Camera

Taryn's Haunting

Taryn's been hired to paint a historic Appalachian boarding school, but even this beloved abandoned campus hides a darkness-and some ghosts!

Matt's Haunting

When Matt starts renovating the old cottage on the remote Irish island, he finds himself right in the middle of a murder mystery-and a haunting!

Andrew's Haunting (Coming Soon)

Historical architect Andrew Terry didn't expect to find love in the decrepit southern mansion; he didn't expect to find ghosts, either.

KENTUCKY WITCHES' SERIES

A Broom with a View

She's your average witch next door, he's a Christmas tree farmer with sisters named after horses. Kudzu Valley will never be the same when Liza Jane comes to town!

Broommates

When Bryar Rose makes a fool of herself on national television, it's time for her to return to Kudzu Valley. But now that she's accused of murdering half the town, will anyone truly accept her?

A Broom of One's Own

What does a witch do when she can't get rid of the restless spirit that haunts the old cinema? Call for backup! (A Taryn's Camera/Kentucky Witches crossover)

MOUNTAIN MYSTERY SERIES

Superstition Mountain, Book 1
Wren has just taken a job in Superstition Mountain, Kentucky where the locals are friendly, the scenery gorgeous, and all the urban legends and folk stories come to life!

GENERAL FICTION

Furnace Mountain: Or The Day President Roosevelt Came to Town
When Sam Walters invited the president to visit his Depression-era town, he never dreamed of what would happen next!

Things She Sees in the Dark
Eight-year-old Ricky disappeared on an evening bike ride; his young cousin was the only witness. Unfortunately, the traumatic event left her with no memory of the evening-or even of her cousin Ricky and the years leading up to it! Now, 30 years later, her memories are starting to return. Can she solve the case that no detective has been able to crack? And will she live through it, if she does?

Consumed

Claire's idyllic, small town life is about to come crashing down around her. As she becomes more and more obsessed with a local missing person's case, a sinister presence settles into her house.

TRUE HAUNTINGS

Haunted Estill County

More Tales from Haunted Estill County

Haunted Estill County: The Children's Edition

Haunted Madison County

A Summer of Fear

Rebecca thought the summer job at the beautiful place in the White Mountains of New Hampshire was a dream come true. It was about to become her nightmare. Nobody had told her about the ghosts...

The Maple House: A True Haunting

The beautiful house on top of the mountain was one of the most coveted places in the county. This family, however, wasn't living the dream life there. Under constant attack by the paranormal, some of them wouldn't even make it out alive.

Four Months of Terror

The single mother was excited to move her small family into the old house that was once a part of the Underground Railroad. The ghosts that haunted the house, however, were not as thrilled with their new tenants.

Two Weeks: A True Haunting

The old house in the country held some terrible secrets. Laura's family wasn't going to know what hit them.

Three True Tales of Terror

A bundle of true hauntings including *A Summer of Fear, The Maple House, and Four Months of Terror.*

NONFICTION BOOKS

Coping with Grief: The Anti-Guide to Infant Loss

Three Minus Zero

Finding Henry: One Woman's Solo Quest to Find Love, Life, & Crepes in Eastern Europe

Estill County in Photos

Working the Case: The Role of Social Media in the Murders of Shanann Watts, the Delphi Daughters, and the Hart Children

Jekyll Island

Resources

http://www.jekyllislandhistory.com/federalreserve.sh
tml © Tyler E. Bagwell 2008 The Jekyll Island duck hunt
that created the Federal Reserve.

Griffin, G. Edward (1998). *The Creature from Jekyll
Island : A Second Look at the Federal Reserve.* American
Media. ISBN 0-912986-21-2.

Bagwell, Tyler E. (2001). *Images of America: Jekyll
Island - A State Park.* Arcadia Publishing. pp. 6–8. ISBN 0-
7385-0572-2.

Bagwell, Tyler E.; The Jekyll Island Museum
(1998). *Images of America: The Jekyll Island Club.* Arcadia
Publishing. ISBN 978-0-7385-1796-4.